MAHMOUD DARWISH

Concerning a Human Being

Over his mouth they bound the chain.
His wrists to the rock they tied.
The rock in which the dead have lain.
  'You're a murderer!' they cried.

They stole his food, clothes, livelihood.
They flung him into the cell of the dead.
They seized his symbols of nationhood.
  'You're a common thief!' they said.

They hunted him out from every harbour.
They took his sweetheart away,
His land, so small, yet his dear treasure.
  'So now you're a refugee!' they say.

O bleeding eyes! The night is ending!
O bleeding palms! O bleeding wrists!
Nero died. But Rome is standing.
By her witness, she resists!

The detention cells will soon be gone.
No more links will be left for the chain.
The seeds must die in an ear of corn
For the valley to be filled with grain.

A seed may die in an ear of corn.
Yet the valley shall be filled with grain!

TRANSLATED BY WILLIAM JAMES DONALDSON

'An Insan (Concerning a Human Being) from the poet's second collection
Awraq al-Zaytoun (Leaves of Olives), 1964

Banipal Books

First time in English translation

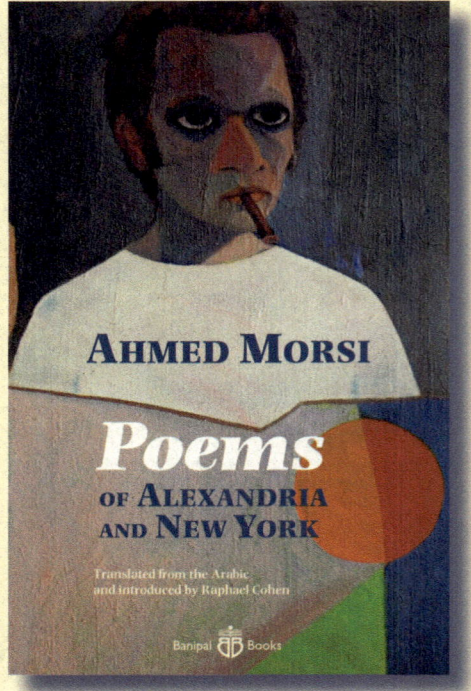

Ahmed Morsi is a renowned painter as well as art critic, journalist, and poet. *Poems of Alexandria and New York*, his first volume in English, translated and introduced by Raphael Cohen, captures the modernity at the heart of all his works and his Surrealist humour.

ISBN 978-1-913043-15-5 Paperback, Ebook

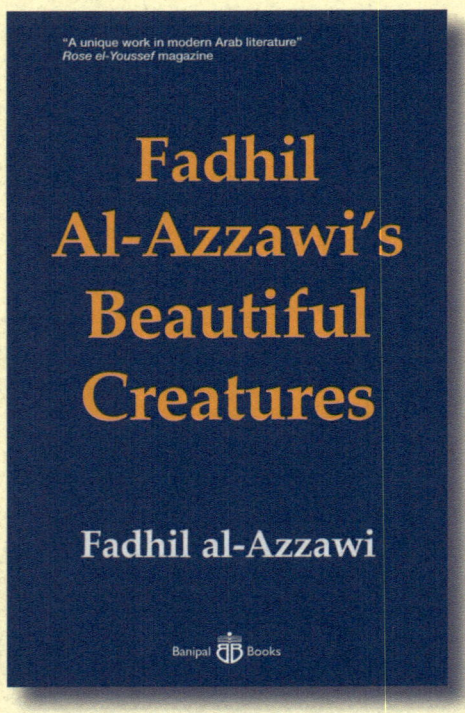

"A unique work in modern Arab literature"
Rose el-Youssef magazine

First English translation, by the author himself, Iraqi poet and novelist Fadhil al-Azzawi, of his acclaimed 1969 open work, written in defiance of the "sanctity of genre" and to raise the question of freedom of expression in writing. *Fadhil al-Azzawi's Beautiful Creatures* was the core of a new vision of life after his and the country's tough political experiences, especially the bloody coup of February 1963.

ISBN 978-1-913043-10-0 Paperback
Also Ebook and Hardback

Available now

www.banipal.co.uk

ABU DHABI
INTERNATIONAL BOOK FAIR

معرض أبوظبي الدولي للكتاب

وحدها الأحلام تحرك القلوب
DREAM NO SMALL DREAMS TO MOVE HEARTS

23-29.05.2021

مركز أبوظبي للغة العربية
Abu Dhabi Arabic Language Centre

adbookfair.com

 ADBookFair   ADIBF   adbookfair   abudhabibookfair

Sheikh Hamad Award for Translation and International Understanding (SHATIU) is accepting nominations for the year 2021 in the following categories:

1. **Translation from Arabic into English**   (200,000 USD)
2. **Translation from English into Arabic**   (200,000 USD)
3. **Translation from Arabic into Chinese**   (200,000 USD)
4. **Translation from Chinese into Arabic**   (200,000 USD)
5. **Achievement Award**   (200,000 USD)

SHATIU is also accepting nominations for achievement awards in translation from and into the following languages:

- Translation from Arabic into Amharic
- Translation from Amharic into Arabic
- Translation from Arabic into Dutch
- Translation from Dutch into Arabic
- Translation from Arabic into Modern Greek
- Translation from Modern Greek into Arabic
- Translation from Arabic into Urdu
- Translation from Urdu into Arabic

Deadline for submissions is 15/8/2021

Please visit our website

www.hta.qa/en

for information about the Award, rules of submission and nomination forms.

    HamadTAward   Phone: (+974) 66570349   Email: info@hta.qa

DIGITAL BANIPAL
Complete archive of issues for institutions and individuals

Banipal's digital edition offers readers all over the world the chance to flip open the magazine on their computers, iPads, iPhones or Android smartphones, wherever they are, check out the current issue, search through back issues and sync as desired. Now a very necessary online tool for these pandemic days of working from home.

A year's digital subscription comes with full access to the full digital archive, back to Banipal No 1, February 1998 – for individuals and for institutions (based on FTE). Print and digital subscriptions are still separate for the moment.

With lockdowns and restrictions on travel in many countries, we are offering a special 20% discount on individual subscriptions until 30 June 2021.

Preview the digital archive, preview the current issue, check out the Free Trial issue: *Banipal 53 – The Short Stories of Zakaria Tamer* and then subscribe.

To get the discount code and subscribe, go to:
www.banipal.co.uk/subscribe/digital/

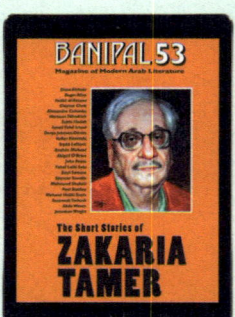

Free trial issue

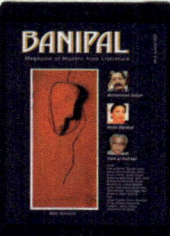
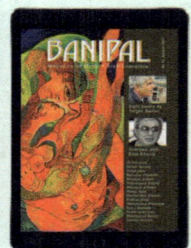

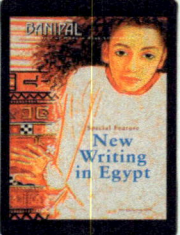

Subscribe Directly to Digital Banipal

Individual: exacteditions.com/banipal   Libraries: institutions.exacteditions.com/banipal

BANIPAL
Magazine of Modern Arab Literature

Banipal magazine, founded in 1998, takes its name from Ashurbanipal (668–627 BC), the last great king of Assyria and patron of the arts, whose outstanding achievement was to assemble in his capital Nineveh, Mesopotamia, from all over his empire, the first systematically organised library in the ancient Middle East. The thousands of clay tablets of Sumerian, Babylonian and Assyrian writings included the famous Mesopotamian epics of the Creation, the Flood, and Gilgamesh, many folk tales, fables, proverbs, prayers and omen texts.

Source: Encyclopaedia Britannica

PUBLISHER: Margaret Obank

EDITOR: Samuel Shimon

CONTRIBUTING EDITORS
Fadhil al-Azzawi, Peter Clark, Raphael Cohen, Bassam Frangieh, Camilo Gómez-Rivas, William M Hutchins, Adil Babikir, Imad Khachan, Khaled Mattawa, Clare Roberts, Mariam al-Saedi, Anton Shammas, Paul Starkey

CONSULTING EDITORS
Etel Adnan, Roger Allen, Isabella Camera d'Afflitto, Humphrey Davies, Hartmut Fähndrich, Ibrahim Farghali, Naomi Shihab Nye, Nancy Roberts, Susannah Tarbush

EDITORIAL ASSISTANTS: Rosie Maxton, Becki Maddock, Joselyn Michelle Almeida, Annamaria Basile, Stephanie Petit

COVER PAINTING: Mahmoud Shukair © Kawoosh

LAYOUT: Banipal Publishing

WEBSITE: www.banipal.co.uk

EDITOR: editor@banipal.co.uk

PUBLISHER: margaret@banipal.co.uk

INQUIRIES: info@banipal.co.uk

SUBSCRIPTIONS: subscribe@banipal.co.uk

ADDRESS: 1 Gough Square, London EC4A 3DE

PRINTED BY Printforce, Biggleswade SG18 8TQ, UK

Photographs not accredited have been donated, photographers unknown.

This issue: *BANIPAL 70 – Mahmoud Shukair, Writing Jerusalem*

This selection © Banipal Publishing. All rights reserved.

This issue is ISBN 978-1-913043-20-9.

RRP £10, €12, US$15

No reproduction or copy, in whole or in part, in the print or the digital edition, may be made without the written permission of the publisher.

BANIPAL, ISSN 1461-5363. Published three times a year by Banipal Publishing, 1 Gough Square, London EC4A 3DE

Supported using public funding by
ARTS COUNCIL ENGLAND

www.banipal.co.uk

INTERNATIONAL PRIZE FOR ARABIC FICTION

The Eye of Hammurabi by Abdulatif Ould Abdullah

The novel opens with the interrogation of a man in a military encampment after has fled from the angry inhabitants of Douar Sidi Majdoub. This village is named after a Muslim saint, whose tomb he and a German archaeologist have dug up in search of a manuscript leading to ancient artefacts.. He now faces serious charges, from conspiracy with foreign organisations against his country to murder. His accusers offer him a deal to protect him from the anger of the mob in exchange for a full confession. Throughout the course of the cross examination, he revisits his past to explore the roots of his present dilemma and tells stories which blend imagination and reality, illusion and the truth.

Notebooks of the Bookshop Keeper by Jalal Bargas

Set between 1947 and 2019, this novel is based on several notebooks of stories about people facing different hardships, such as losing their homes or not knowing who their family are. Their interwoven destinies reveal the value of the house, as a symbol of one's homeland, as opposed to the surrounding ruination. The central character is Ibrahim, a bookshop keeper, a cultured man and voracious reader of novels. In fact, he even takes on the identity of the protagonists in novels which appeal to him. However, due to his isolation, loneliness and maltreatment by a cruel world, he suffers mental illness and descends into full schizophrenia. He attempts suicide, before meeting the woman who will change his life.

The Calamity of the Nobility by Amira Ghenim

The Calamity of the Nobility relates an important, untold story from Tunisia's contemporary history. Its hero is the historical figure, the reformer El-Taher El-Haddad. Although historical references do not mention anything about his relationship with women, except for his desperate defence of them, the author adds an imaginary love affair with a woman called Lella Zubaida to her fictional retelling of his life. The novel gives prominence to the voices of female narrators, as custodians of memory who contradict a distorted, patriarchal version of history.

– THE 2021 SHORTLIST – SIX NOVELS AND SIX AUTHORS

The Bird Tattoo by Dunya Mikhail

The Bird Tattoo is a painful novel about the sale of Yazidi women in Iraq by ISIS. It focuses on Helen and Elias, who fall in love and marry, and their experiences with the organisation. Alongside this tragedy, the novel sheds light on aspects of Yazidi folklore, rich in astonishing customs and legends.

File 42 by Abdelmeguid Sabata

File 42 follows two parallel storylines. In the first, Christine Macmillan, a successful American novelist, and Rasheed Benaser, a young Moroccan researcher and doctoral student, embark on an investigation to find the unknown author of a forgotten Moroccan novel from 1989, in which Christine's father, Steve, appears as one of the characters. Steve worked as a soldier at an American military base in Morocco during and after the Second World War. Their search leads them to a 1959 event – the tragedy of the poisoned cooking oil, one of the worst disasters to occur in the years after Moroccan independence. The second plot line is narrated by Zuheir Belqasem, a rich and delinquent Moroccan teenager who rapes Al-Ghalia, an underaged maid. His mother uses her influence as a prominent lawyer to close the case and send him to Russia to pursue his university studies. However, horrors await him there which no-one had foreseen. Written in the style of a "crime thriller" full of suspense, *File 42* explores themes of reading and writing, as well as the issue of human worth and the Moroccan's search for dignity, as a fundamental human right.

Longing for the Woman Next Door by Habib Selmi

On the face of it, they have nothing in common, apart from both being Tunisian and living in the same apartment building. He is in his sixties, educated and married to a Frenchwoman. She is several years younger and from a lower social stratum, and married to an eccentric man. At first, he is cautious and patronizing. But later, the rules of the game change. The novel explores a rich, turbulent and extraordinary relationship, which celebrates life in its simplest and most beautiful manifestations but is also tinged with darkness and tragedy.

THE SHORTLISTED AUTHORS

Abdulatif Ould Abdullah

Abdulatif Ould Abdullah is an Algerian writer, born in Mostaganem, Algeria, in 1988. He graduated with a Diploma in Architecture from the University of Algiers and he writes on cultural subjects for newspapers and online. He is the author of three novels: *Out of Control* (2016), *Flaunting Finery* (2018) and *The Eye of Hammurabi* (2020), for which he is shortlisted.

Jalal Bargas

Jalal Bargas is a Jordanian poet and novelist, born in 1970. He works in the field of aeronautical engineering. For many years, he wrote articles for Jordanian newspapers and headed several cultural organisations. He is currently head of the Jordanian Narrative Laboratory and presents a radio programme called "House of the Novel". His published work includes two poetry collections, short stories, travel literature and novels. His short story *The Earthquakes* (2012) was winner of the Jordanian Rukus ibn Zaid Uzayzi Prize. His novel *Guillotine of the Dreamer* (2013) won the Jordanian Rifqa Doudin Prize for Narrative Creativity in 2014, and *Snakes of Hell* won the 2015 Katara Prize for the Arabic Novel, in the unpublished novel category, and was published by Katara in 2016. His third novel *Women of the Five Senses* (2017) was IPAF-longlisted in 2019.

Amira Ghenim

Amira Ghenim is a Tunisian writer and academic, born in 1978. Having graduated with a Higher Teaching Certificate (agrégation) in Arabic Language and Literature and a PhD in Linguistics, she teaches Linguistics and Translation at Tunis University. She has published books on translation and linguistics and the novel *The Yellow Dossier* (2019), which won the Sheikh Rashid Bin Hamad Prize in 2020. Her second novel *The Calamity of the Nobility* was published in 2020.

Winner Announcement online 25 May 2021
www.arabicfiction.org

THE SHORTLISTED AUTHORS

Dunya Mikhail

Dunya Mikhail is an Iraqi poet, born in 1965 and living in America. She obtained a B.A. in English Literature from Baghdad University and a Masters in Eastern Literatures from Wayne State University in the U.S. She currently teaches Arabic Language and Literature at Oakland University, Michigan. She has published nine books in Arabic, several of which have been translated into English, Chinese, French, Hindi, Italian and Polish. Her first book in English, *The War Works Hard* (2005, translated by Elizabeth Winslow), was shortlisted for the Griffin Poetry Prize. *Diary of a Wave Outside the Sea* (2009), which Mikhail co-translated with Elizabeth Winslow, won the 2010 Arab American Book Award and *The Beekeeper of Sinjar: Rescuing the Kidnapped Women of Iraq* (co-translated with Max Weiss) was longlisted for the National Book Award for Translated Literature 2018. Mikhail's poetry collection *The Iraqi Nights* (2014) was translated into English by Kareem James Abu-Zeid.

Abdelmeguid Sabata

Abdelmeguid Sabata is a Moroccan author, born in Rabat in 1989. He obtained a Masters in Civil Engineering from Abdelmalek Essaadi University, Tangiers. He has written articles and translations on literary, cultural and historical subjects which have been published in print and online in Morocco and other Arab countries. He is the author of three novels: *Behind the Wall of Passion* (2015), *The Zero Hour 00:00* (2017), which won the Moroccan Book Award in 2018, and *File 42* (2020). He has also translated two novels by the French thriller writer Michel Bussi.

Habib Selmi

Habib Selmi was born in Al-Ala, Tunisia, in 1951. He obtained a Higher Teaching Certificate (agrégation) in Arabic Language before immigrating to Paris in 1985, where he now lives and teaches Arabic in a prestigious secondary school. His published novels include *Goat Mountain* (1988, English translation Banipal Books, 2020), *Portrait of a Dead Bedouin* (1990), *Sand Labyrinth* (1994), *Warm Pits* (1999), *Bayya's Lovers* (2002) and *Abdallah's Secrets* (2004). His novel *The Scents of Marie-Claire* (2008) was IPAF-shortlisted in 2009 and published in English translation by Arabia Books in 2010. *The Women of al-Basatin* (2010) was IPAF-shortlisted in 2012 and translated into French and German.

Alawiya Sobh

Azher Jirjees

Aida Fahmawi Watad

Fakhri Saleh

Ibrahim Nasrallah

10	Editorial
16	Ammar Almamoun reviews *al-Nawm fi Haql al-Karaz*, a novel by Azher Jirjees
20	Azher Jirjees: Three excerpts from the novel *al-Nawm fi Haql al-Karaz* (At Rest in the Cherry Orchard, translated by Jonathan Wright
38	Hassan Abdel Mawgoud: *A Bicycle Brings an Old Comrade*, a short story, translated by Raphael Cohen
50	Katia al-Tawil reviews *Lam yusalli 'alaihum ahad* (No One Prayed Over Their Graves) by Khaled Khalifa
55	Khaled Khalifa: Excerpt from his novel *Lam yusalli 'alaihum ahad* (No One Prayed Over Their Graves), translated by Leri Price
68	Interview with Lebanese writer Alawiya Sobh by Katia al-Tawil
78	Alawiya Sobh: Three chapters from her latest novel *An Ta'ashaq al-Hayat* (To Love Life), translated by Nancy Roberts

SPECIAL FEATURE

100	**MAHMOUD SHUKAIR, WRITING JERUSALEM**
103	Mahmoud Shukair: *Three short stories*, translated by Samira Kawar
121	Fakhri Saleh: *On the Literary achievement of Mahmoud Shukair*
128	Aida Fahmawi Watad: *Palestinian Writing, Inside a Closed-Open Cage*

133	Fayez Ghazi reviews the novel *Dhilal al-'A'ilah* (Shadows of the Family) by Mahmoud Shukair
136	Mahmoud Shukair: Excerpt from *Shadows of the Family*, translated by Karen McNeil and Miled Faiza
154	Hannah Somerville reviews *Mordechai's Moustache and his Wife's Cats and other stories* by Mahmoud Shukair, translated by Issa J Boullata, Elizabeth Whitehouse, Elizabeth Winslow and Christina Phillips
158	Susannah Tarbush reviews *Jerusalem Stands Alone* by Mahmoud Shukair, translated by Nicole Fares
162	Mahmoud Shukair: 26 *Micro Stories*, translated by Mayada Ibrahim
172	Ibrahim Nasrallah reviews *Faras al-'A'ilah* (The Family Mare) by Mahmoud Shukair
176	Mahmoud Shukair: *The Phantom*, a short story, translated by Paul Starkey
182	**GUEST WRITER** Trino Cruz *The Fertile Shore*, selected poems
	INTERVIEW
198	Interview with the editors of Maktoob, the project for translation of Arabic literature into Hebrew
	BOOK REVIEWS
203	Joselyn Michelle Almeida reviews *Fugitive Atlas: Poems* by Khaled Mattawa
208	Stephanie Petit reviews *De Weekendmiljonair* (The Weekend Millionaire) by Abdelkader Benali
212	Becki Maddock reviews *Agadir* by Mohammed Khaïr-Eddine, translated by Pierre Joris and Jake Syersak
	LITERARY AWARD
218	American translator Kay Heikkinen wins the Saif Ghobash Banipal Prize for Arabic Literary Translation
222	**CONTRIBUTORS**

Khaled Khalifa

Hassan Abdel Mawgoud

Trino Cruz

Kay Heikkinen

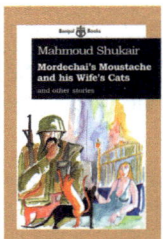

Book reviews

Maktoob Project: Arabic Hebrew Translations

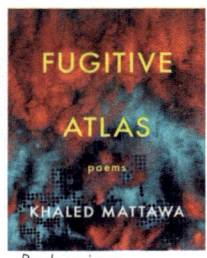

Book reviews

EDITORIAL

A LITTLE LATER THAN EXPECTED, we present a rich issue of diverse authors and literary news to keep you well occupied and inspired in this continuing time of Covid-19.

This major feature on **Mahmoud Shukair** was originally planned for earlier than this issue but it was decided to postpone it until now as a gift to this great Jerusalemite on his 80th birthday – which took place in March this year. *Banipal*'s relation with Mahmoud Shukair goes back to the early issues of the magazine; since No 7 in Spring 2000 we have consistently commissioned translations of his short stories and other writings – in that issue he described how he came to be a short story writer, publishing his first in 1962 and not stopping until, maybe, in 2013 when he published the first of three novels, a trilogy about Jerusalem family life. The feature *Writing Jerusalem* marks the sixty years that Shukair, born in the East Jerusalem village of Jabel Mukaber, writes the complex stories and tales of Jerusalem's people and places.

Literary critic Fakhri Saleh, in the article about his fellow countryman, describes him as "a founder of Palestinian fiction". He notes Shukair's "ability to portray village life in all its paradoxical diversity" and his "venture into the mysterious experience of living, in the face of which humans stand impotent, their hands tied as they confront the prospect of death and maybe annihilation". We feature four stories from Shukair's 2004 collection *My Cousin Condoleezza* – "The Way Naomi Campbell Walks", "Pablo Abdallah's Seat" and "Rumsfeld's Banquet", translated by Samira Kawar, and a long one, "The Phantom", translated by Paul Starkey. Also, 26 micro stories from the 1986 collection *Rituals of a Wretched Woman*, translated by Mayada Ibrahim. We look forward to assembling a future bumper collection of these fascinating, satirical stories, all of which enjoy Shukair's deadpan surrealist wit and humour, underscored by the trauma of occupation, and in which, as Aida Fahmawi Watad writes in her article, "he is capable of condensing the narrative of an entire people into a few lines".

Hannah Somerville finds the first collection of Shukair's stories in English translation, *Mordechai's Moustache and His Wife's Cats and other stories*, which Banipal Books published in 2007, a "riotous and winsome collection . . . fleeting, ethereal, often sad but never moribund, and infused with humanist sensibility". In 2018, a welcome second collection *Jerusalem Stands Alone* was published, thanks to Syracuse University Press, and is reviewed here by Susannah Tarbush.

Only the second part of Mahmoud Shukair's trilogy is available in English translation: *Praise for the Women of the Family*, (trans. Paul Starkey, Interlink, 2018) following its shortlisting for the 2016 International Prize for Arabic

Fiction. A review of it by Susannah Tarbush in *Banipal 65* can be read online. Reviewing the first volume *The Family Mare*, partly set in a remote region of the country, well-known Palestinian author Ibrahim Nasrallah writes that "Shukair wonderfully surprises us with his subtle meditation on the spiritual history of the Bedouins in that part of Palestine". The last volume, *Shadows of the Family*, is reviewed by Lebanese critic and author Fayez Ghazi, who relates how the novel's shadows "sprawl out from the confines of a small family across the entire Jerusalemite community", and is excerpted by translators Karin McNeil and Miled Faiza.

The issue opens with one of two excellent Arabic novels, coincidentally both longlisted for the 2020 IPAF, with reviews and excerpts of both. *At Rest in the Cherry Orchard* is by Iraqi author **Azher Jirjees**, now settled in Norway after being forced to flee Baghdad following an assassination attempt when he published *Terrorism . . . Earthly Hell*, a satirical book about terrorist militias. Reviewer Ammar Almamoun writes: "In this novel we discover a country where people's heads are cut off for sectarian reasons and bodies are buried in mass graves, and so the dreams of the inhabitants have to move through blood" as the author creates a multi-layered story of Iraq and his adopted country Norway, with excerpts translated by Jonathan Wright. Syrian author **Khaled Khalifa**'s novel *No One Prayed over Their Graves* is a profound epic of Aleppo, set before and after the city's 1907 floods, with reviewer Katia al-Tawil describing it as "a novel of the human inability to escape a deadly place", and the excerpt translated by Leri Price.

Along with the novels, we present a memorable short story "A Bicycle Brings an Old Comrade" by Egyptian author **Hassan Abdel Mawgoud**, translated by Raphael Cohen.

Lebanese author **Alawiya Sobh**, interviewed by Katia al-Tawil about her new novel *To Love Life*, explains that her "anger in the novel is directed against all systems, especially those that hinder the woman's freedom, contribute to her enslavement, or disregard the violence and tyranny she endures". It was shortlisted for the 2021 Sheikh Zayed Book Award, and we are pleased to include three chapters, translated by Nancy Roberts.

We welcome our Guest Writer, Gibraltarian poet and translator **Trino Cruz**, working in both Spanish and English, who is a long-time friend of *Banipal*.

Last but not least, we present an interview with the editors of **Maktoob**, the most recent and important project for translating and publishing Arabic literature in Hebrew.

Margaret Obank

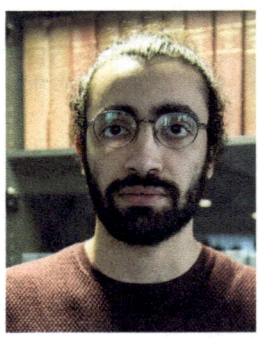

Ammar Almamoun reviews
Al-Nawm fi Haql al-Karaz (At Rest in the Cherry Orchard) by Azher Jirjees
published by Dar al-Rafidayn, Baghdad 2019.
ISBN: 978-9-9226077-4-0.
pbk, 223 pages

A Delirious Journey led by a Faceless Ghost

The notion that a book goes missing and is then found or that a lost manuscript is discovered after the author's death appears in some of the earliest novels, such as Cervantes's *Don Quixote*, which presents itself as the translation of a manuscript written by an Arab historian called Cide Hamete Benengeli and then is discovered and conveyed to us by Cervantes. This conceit – a chance event, a lost manuscript, multiple authorship – encourages us to think about the act of reading on several levels. There is the story of the book, the story in the book, the story of the author, the author inside the work and other poetics that overlap and through which the novel addresses itself as an art that reflects on the narrative and on the fictional devices that novels employ.

The Iraqi writer Azher Jirjees adopts this format in his novel *At Rest in the Cherry Orchard*, which was published by Dar al-Rafidayn in 2019. The novel, which reached the long list for the International Prize for Arabic Fiction (IPAF) in 2020, starts off with a mistake by a postman, which an Iraqi translator in Norway discovers through a chance encounter: the last work of Said Jensen, an Iraqi writer with Norwegian nationality, whose work had already appeared in several Norwegian newspapers. This latest work had not yet seen the light of day, and what we read is a translation of the Norwegian manuscript. We later discover that Jensen had been found dead at home in his library in Oslo, after taking an overdose of Ketamine.

The novel offers us three narrators: Jirjees, whose name appears

Azher Jirjees and the cover of the novel

on the cover; the translator, who renders the text from Norwegian to Arabic – and Said Jensen himself, supposedly a relatively well-known writer, who writes a kind of memoir through a mixture of autobiographical details, fantasies and historical events. Faced with this multiplicity of authors, we see their ghosts floating in front of us as we read, along with the ghost of Jensen's father, who died before Jensen was old enough to remember him, and who haunts him in his dreams. "Where's my grave?" asks the father's ghost – a question that troubles both Jensen's waking life and his dream life. Interestingly, this ghost differs from the ghost of Hamlet's father, who appears only a few times. It is also a ghost without a face, which worries Jensen; he then resolves to take a picture of his father, even if it is only of his remaining bones.

This impossible endeavour and the interplay between dreaming and waking life unfold in the form of the novel itself. The sections of varying length that make up the manuscript, and the incidents in which sanity and delirium overlap, are like a terrifying trip into a hellish forest littered with death and tortured bodies, like flashes of consciousness that linger a while before fading away. The ambiguity between reality and illusion forces us to question what we read, especially as the manuscript contains things that at first appear to be realistic, but that are then followed immediately by things that are clearly fantasy or science fiction set only in Jensen's mind. This ambiguity is accentuated by the splitting headache that often afflicts the writer, especially after the death of his Norwegian wife. This forces him to visit the doctor, who prescribes Ketamine, a drug that can cause dreams, hallucinations and emergence delirium. This raises two alternative possibilities. Did Jensen really go back to Iraq to look for his father's remains? Or are the stories that he writes just the fantasies caused by the Ketamine and the loss of his wife?

Viscous Dreams

If we suppose that we are part of a dream in which Jensen travels through time and imagines a flourishing Iraq, or sometimes imagines his own death, or even the ghost of his father, then in this novel Jirjees is tampering with one of the central elements of dreaming, which is that water is the liquid of time, imagination, and the elixir of dreams. But in this novel we discover a country where people's heads are cut off for sectarian reasons and bodies are buried in mass graves, and so the dreams of the inhabitants have to move through blood. Instead of swimming gently in water as in *La Loi du Rêveur* (The Dreamer's Law), the novel by Daniel Pennac, Jensen's voice delights in travelling through a viscous liquid, full of memories and pain. It may not be a river or a sea, but rather stains and various patches on concrete, inhabited by the ghosts of those who have passed away, among whom Jensen wanders without recognising their faces. In fact, he experiences the death and pain of each and all, one by one.

In this novel there's no escaping a journey full of blood and body parts, whether in real life or in the imagination: we read how Jensen manages to leave Iraq with great difficulty, bloodying his feet in the process, and then settles in Norway, where his feet freeze. But he falls in love and writes, which he loves. Yet the gore remains, appears in front of him and calls him back, rather like an obsession that inevitably consumes its victim, even if he's hallucinating at home without seeing anyone. This means there may be no end to the process of plunging into mocking, nightmarish memories and the paradoxes they contain. Jensen can be seen as an epitome of a grotesque, tormented body that has been subjected to unforgivable and unforgettable violence. This violence does irreparable damage; the only solution is to tame the body's memory since the alternative threatens what remains of the person's life.

The novel includes an ironic paradox about migration and the relationship between "guests" and "indigenes": Jensen writes about his travails satirically in an obscure Norwegian newspaper, produces short stories that are mentioned in the introduction, and that we read about in the body of the text as real-imaginary events that Jensen has witnessed, but these stories are addressed to a Norwegian audience. Jensen thinks he is amusing them at the expense of his personal tragedies and the tragedy of his people.

The title, *At Rest in the Cherry Orchard*, is an expression that recurs in the novel as part of the will of Jensen's neighbour, Jakob Jondal, who wants to be buried in a cherry orchard he has bought because he believes that the souls of the dead come to resemble the places where the bodies are buried. This is the eternal rest that Jensen strives for, although it is incompatible with the wishes of his ghostly father, who is thought to be lying in a mass grave in Iraq, and who entices Jensen to make an imaginary journey to find his remains, or to be more precise, to find any remains, because any of them are good enough to stand in for Jensen's father. But often death offers no repose, and here lies the depth of the crime inflicted on Iraq and the violence it has lived through. People's humanity is at stake because someone who has no grave is tormented, and those around him are tormented too. And so the question that the old man poses, "Where's my grave?", in fact casts doubt on his identity: one might say that Jensen sees the ghosts of all the victims, as someone without a face could be anyone. All those who have been gone missing, who have been detained and disappeared, have no graves. There is always someone who looking in his imagination and in the ground for the remains of a loved one or a relative, and therefore "does not sleep". They remain wandering forever, alive in the memories of those closest to them. And the only way to console those people is to tame the ghosts and question their sense of justice. But a poetic question remains: Jensen is buried in the cherry orchard in accordance with his testament, so will the ghosts haunt the orchard and infect it, in other words, make it their home? Or will the opposite happen — will the legend turn out to be true and the ghosts become part of the orchard?

AZHER JIRJEES

At Rest in the Cherry Orchard

THREE EXCERPTS FROM THE NOVEL
AL-NAWM FI HAQL AL-KARAZ
TRANSLATED BY JONATHAN WRIGHT

Introduction

If the postman hadn't made a mistake, none of this would have happened. It was bitterly cold outside at the time and it was snowing heavily, blanketing the roads and the pavements. Snowflakes also covered the mailboxes and hid the names written on top of them. As usual, I put on a long woollen coat and a hat with two furry ear flaps. Then I pulled on my fur-lined boots and went out to check the mail. I put my hand in the mailbox and found a newspaper with an invitation card tucked between the pages. This was puzzling, since I didn't have a subscription to any daily newspapers. I'd stopped my subscriptions when the translation agency where I work started providing the morning papers for free on the tables in the cafeteria. "So where did the invitation come from?", I wondered as I turned it over. The invitation, from the mass-circulation newspaper *Dagposten* wasn't addressed to anyone in particular. It was for a party celebrating the newspaper's golden jubilee. I suspected it was meant for my neighbour, retired doctor Morten Solheim, since he was a long-standing subscriber to the newspaper. I knocked on his door but there was no answer. I phoned him in case something bad had happened to him, since he wasn't in the habit of sleeping so late. A voicemail message told me he had gone to Antalya and wouldn't be back for three months. He does that every winter

– travels to sunny climes in search of warmth. I contacted the newspaper that had sent the invitation and confirmed that my suspicions had been well-placed: the invitation was indeed intended for my neighbour, and it had come to me only because of the postman's error. Very graciously, the editor apologised on the postman's behalf and suggested compensating me with a piece of cake if I accepted the invitation and attended the reception. I accepted willingly of course – who turns down an invitation from a gracious woman? And the following night I was there, dressed to the nines.

It was a lavish event attended by dozens of journalists, writers, newspaper staff, and readers. At the door stood an attractive woman in her forties in a long dress, wearing some beguiling perfume. She introduced herself as the editor in chief, Helena Jorstad. I returned her greeting and reminded her of her promise, and she laughed. After the speeches and the formal parts of the party, we met again at the buffet. She was carrying two plates, each with a piece of cake covered in chocolate. I took one and thanked her, and then we started chatting. I told her I'd liked this kind of cake since I was in Iraq, where my mother used to make it for holidays and parties. Helena stopped eating the cake as soon as she heard that. Her eyes opened wide and she rubbed her cheek with the tip of her finger. "In Iraq?" she asked. "That means you must know Said Jensen, the Norwegian writer of Iraqi origin!" "How could I not know him?" I replied. "I regularly read the things he has published in your paper and I've translated some of his short stories for the Arabic magazine *al-Shira'a*." Then I started listing the stories, expounding on Jensen and the bitter irony in his work. I told her about the story of the bird that lost its voice, the first one of his that I had translated, and "The Sheep's Lord", "Three on the Road" and other stories scattered here and there. Helena listened with great interest as she tried to polish off the cake on her plate. After that she told me there was something I had to see immediately. She invited me to her office on the second floor of the newspaper building, and I went without asking any questions. We went into the office and she took a brown envelope out of a drawer and put it on the table. She said it contained a hand-written manuscript in Norwegian and she had been planning to publish it, but was waiting till she could find someone to translate it into Arabic. She pulled it out of the envelope and waved it in the air. "This story by Said Jensen should first be read by those who speak his language, because of what it contains." Then she handed it to me and suggested I translate it into Arabic. I took the manuscript from her and immediately began to read the first page. Two years later, and all because of that postman's mistake, the translation is complete. This is the story.

The translator
Oslo 2010

1

He was standing on one leg like a statue hit by a stray piece of shrapnel. His face wasn't wholly visible because the straw hat he was wearing shaded his eyes, and his chin was covered with a white piece of cloth with faint traces of blood. He was tall and thin, with a long nose that almost reached his mouth and a ragged beard that projected from under the piece of cloth. I tried to approach him but he waved me away with his myrtle walking stick. We stood facing each other on an abandoned railway line with weeds growing up between the rusty tracks. Thick clouds were closing in, blocking out the sky and creating a dreary, stifling grey umbrella above us. The wind carried the sound of a crow and of trees rustling, though none were visible around us. There was just that forgotten railway track and the armies of ants carrying their winter supplies and disappearing into deep black holes in the ground. Finally he cleared his throat and, in a voice tinged with sorrow, said, "Where's my grave?" I went up to him to get a look at his face but he backed away, leaving a pool of blood behind him. A large hole stretched from under his neck to his navel. His torn, tattered and bloodied clothes showed serious damage in the lower part of his body. His only leg was connected directly to his stomach rather than to a pelvis, like a tower that has been blown over in a storm and then reassembled by a drunken ape, or like a wall that has been destroyed by a random shell and rebuilt by an elderly cripple. I felt dizzy and I collapsed to the ground. I tried to stand up again but I couldn't, while my father stepped back and moved away after giving up hope of hearing an answer. I stretched my arm out towards him, as if begging him to take me with him, but he disappeared on the horizon like smoke. Then a crow came up, flapping its wings and grabbing the dry myrtle stick in its beak. It threw the stick towards me and then moved off too. I took hold of the stick, leant on it and stood up. It was strong enough to help me up. I set off in the direction my father had taken along the railway track. I wanted to catch up with him and take the piece of cloth off his face, but an express train came from behind and ran me over.

I came to my senses. The coffee had boiled over so I turned off the stove. I poured what was left of it down the sink and started making another cup. It wasn't the first time I had seen my father: he would visit me from time to time, appear in front of me when my mind wandered. But despite his repeated visits, he would never show his face. His features always seemed to have disappeared and his appearance was incomplete. He visited me once on the balcony of the flat, with his head cut off and his voice coming out of a black hole in his neck. When I went up to him, he disappeared into thin air. Later he appeared in front of me at the metro station, split into two halves that looked quite different. One evening I saw him sleeping near me in the form of human dough without any covering of skin. I often saw my father, without seeing him. I often begged him to show me his face but he never did so.

In fact, I wouldn't know what my father looks like anyway. I've never seen him in my life and I don't have a single picture of him. He disappeared into the realms of oblivion before I came into the world and, on the day he was arrested, my mother burned all his books, papers, diaries and photo albums. That's what she told me. One night, in a low voice, she told me that in a moment of fear and panic she opened up the clay oven and threw in everything that belonged to my father or that pointed to him, and everything that made her anxious for his sake. My mother fed to the stove the memories of a whole life, and the damned fire turned them into worthless ashes, as the last trace of my father disappeared along with any future he might have had. He was a leftist opponent of the government and a wanted man. He had been imprisoned several times, and then released. Every time he came out he was missing another tooth, which meant that despite his young age, he had dental fixtures on both his upper and lower jaws. But he didn't come home the last time. They said he had died under torture, they said he had been fed alive to dogs, they said he had been thrown into the taciturn River Tigris, and they said he had been secretly buried in some graveyard. But they never gave us a body or any bones, or even a certificate to say he had departed this world. When I was five years old, my mother said, "Your father's in good hands." And when I asked her whose good hands he was in, she scolded me without explanation.

I went to bed after two thirds of the night had already passed. I turned out the light and put the sheet over my face in the hope of stealing a short nap, but it was no use. I couldn't get the image of my father with his broken body out of my mind's eye and that made sleep unattainable. I threw off the cover and went to the library. I was met by the empty frame hanging on the wall. I felt it was slightly tilted, so I put my index finger under the right-hand corner and pushed it up gently until it was level. Then I sat at the computer trying to get my father's ghost out of my head. I browsed the byways of the Internet far and wide. In the end I came across a poem by Badr Shakir al-Sayyab on a literary forum: "They stick out their necks from the thousands of graves, shouting at me / To come – a blood-curdling, bone-shaking call that scatters ashes on my heart. / The late afternoon here is like a torch in the shadows / Come and burn in it until sunset / My grandfathers and forefathers are a mirage that hovered on my cheek." I let out a sigh, and al-Sayyab moves on, thundering in his sad voice. "My mother calls from the grave, 'Embrace me, my son, for I have the coldness of destruction in my veins; warm my bones with the clothes on your arms and chest, and dress the wounds.'"

"My God! How come I can't escape the sound of graves tonight?" I said to myself as I was about to turn off the computer, but then I remembered that I hadn't opened my email since the previous Saturday. It had been such an exhausting week that I hadn't had a chance to sit down and look through my mail. I opened my inbox and found some emails that were not really very important. They were warnings to pay late bills, an invitation to take part in a workers' protest to demand a small salary increase, and advertisements from new companies. But finally I found an unexpected message from Baghdad, dated the previous Saturday.

Hi Said,
There's something important that can't be postponed.
You must come back to Baghdad immediately.
All the best,
Abir

2

For fourteen years I've been forgotten, living here in exile like a bear that's lost his partner. In this country the winter is long and dark and the snowfalls are heavy, while the summer is shorter than a tea-break on a journey. After the alarm clock rang, and before going into the bathroom, I was in the habit of opening the window to see how much snow had fallen overnight. Every time I would see the same scene: a white cloak covering the surface of the city and workers leaving the warmth of their beds, weighed down by thick coats and furry hats. I would dismiss it grumpily with a wave of my hand and close the window. My work in the postal service made going to work especially arduous because I had to sort hundreds of letters and parcels in the snow in the cold hours of dawn. I learned that being a postman in a country such as Norway meant familiarity with angry skies and the taste of hell, especially in winter, what with the cold, the ice and the constant danger of slipping. But in my case it wasn't just the sky that was angry with me: my boss was too. Kari Solberg, a thin woman in her sixties with a wrinkled crimson face, hated me instinctively. When she saw me, she felt like a scorpion had stung her between her thighs. She couldn't bear the sound of my voice and she looked away whenever I spoke to her, as if I were a frog covered in disgusting warts. If I said, "Please look at me, Mrs Solberg," she didn't respond. She pretended not to have heard, even when we were talking about work. When I got an address wrong, she used vitriolic, disgusting and hair-raising language against me.

Once, speaking to my colleague Daniel, she said, "Listen, Daniel, I can't bear that monkey called Said. You should keep away from him as much as you can during work hours." I'm much more handsome than a monkey, of course, but whenever I see her angry, there's a question that nags at me: why does this woman hate monkeys so much? And why can't she bear to look at their cute faces? I, for example, have never done anything to anger her, although I would like to do so, and I've never been negligent in my work with her. So what, I wonder, lies behind all this hatred? At first I thought she must have a grievance that she wanted to pursue against me, but over time I discovered that she didn't like foreigners in general and couldn't bear to look at them. In fact I was certain that she considered them all to be monkeys, even if they happened to have blue eyes. I was also certain that, however hard I worked, I would remain suspect in her eyes, which in the end forced me into social isolation. At seven in the morning I would arrive to pick up the mail, put it in the van and go around delivering until four in the afternoon, without speaking to anyone or even meeting anyone. In this way Kari Solberg made me as lonely as a leper.

3

The darkness finally dissipated and dawn started to etch its lines on the face of creation. I hadn't slept a single hour. Anxiety was burrowing away at my skull, like termites in wood. I tossed and turned in bed as I pondered Abir's last message: "You must come back to Baghdad immediately." What could I do there? She must have been joking. I had written to her, asking for an explanation, but she hadn't replied. Her Internet access was through local top-up cards and it ran at the speed of an obese tortoise. I went to the kitchen, drank a glass of water and went back to bed.

In all the time I had known her, Abir had never written such an obscure message. I came across her by accident when I was sitting at the computer one day, reading the news on a website. I caught sight of an interesting article on tombs in Iraq. That was exactly two years ago. When I read the article, I imagined my father's body lying on its back in a hole lit by the moon. I called out to him but a cloud of black bats blocked out the light and he disappeared. I looked up the name of the journalist who had written the article and ended up on her personal website. With one click, her personal details leaped up in front of me like salmon from a river: Abir Kazim, journalist and photographer, born in Baghdad, BA in journalism, participant in several local and international projects, works as a news correspondent for the BBC. "Great!" I shouted, clicked on the link to photographs of her, and gasped like a teenager when a beautiful woman walks past. She won my heart from the first gasp and held her place there, unchallenged – a woman of medium height, as slim as an orchid and meek as a dove. Abir had eyes the colour of honey and short hair the colour of dates. In the middle of her left cheek she had a beauty spot that the birds might think was a mustard seed.

In all the photos she was wearing a blouse and grey skirt that ended a fraction of an inch above the knee. She looked like a well-dressed student in university uniform. I copied her email address and sent her an instant message: "Good evening. I am Said, an Iraqi in the land of ice. If you wish, I can most solemnly swear that if you reply to this message, I will not only be happy, as my name Said implies, but Asaad, very happy indeed." Her answer came back the next day: "Welcome, Asaad," it said. Since then we have been exchanging emails and transcontinental e-kisses.

4

I silenced the alarm clock when it screeched at me at six in the morning. I should have turned it off the night before, because I didn't need it. My long vacation had started and I wouldn't have to see Kari Solberg's face for three whole weeks. I tried to get back to sleep, but it was no use: some messages keep you awake and shatter the peace of mind that protects you. Why did Abir want me to come back immediately, I wondered. Why now in particular? Going back to Baghdad became fashionable back in April 2003. At the time, thousands of Iraqis left their places of exile and returned voluntarily, some of them hungry for power like ravenous dogs, some of them to invest their assets in projects that would yield pure gold without taxes, and others in the belief that Iraq was now open enough to tolerate them. I had seen them packing their bags, leaving arduous years of exile behind them, but I never thought of doing likewise, and I never said to myself, even hypothetically, "Why not go back home?" For me the answer to the question was a foregone conclusion. I'm well aware that Abir loves Baghdad, even in its latest state of ruin, and she isn't thinking of leaving, but we have never spoken about the question of returning before. Over two years she has never once asked me about it. What's happened now, for God's sake? I pushed the bed cover off and went to the bathroom. It was raining heavily outside, although it was summer. I took the electric razor out of the drawer and started trimming my beard. It was long and shaggy and ugly. Unusually for me, I had a close look at myself in the mirror, and saw that an army of whiteness had made inroads on my scalp. My sideburns were tinged with grey and there were plenty of white hairs at the roots near my parting. Why hadn't I seen them before? Or rather, why was it today in particular that I was interested in counting the white hairs on my head? Did Abir's message have anything to do with it? I don't know.

I finished shaving and showering and went off to the kitchen naked. Being naked is the only good thing about living alone. Being alone means you can take your clothes off whenever you want and let the air brush your skin. I washed the dishes that had been gathering in the sink for days, then took some bread out of the freezer and put it in the oven. I rinsed out the teapot, filled it with water and put it on the stove. I threw in two cardamom seeds and waited till it started to boil. Then I put in three teaspoonfuls of the Sri Lankan tea sold by Kaka Sirvan, the owner of the oriental grocery on the edge of the neighbourhood. I took the tea off the stove and left it to brew gently, and went back to the bedroom. I got dressed and sprinkled a little aftershave behind my ears. I put the bottle back in its place and looked in the mirror. The black rings under my eyes were growing larger and the grey hairs made me uneasy. I opened the drawer and took out a small pair of scissors. I cut off a thin streak of grey that was hanging over my forehead, and another one that was buried in my moustache. I cut off three that were hiding in my sideburns, then moved the scissors closer to my parting to stop the creeping of the damned greyness towards it. But I felt it was futile, because such a small pair of scissors couldn't erase the effects of time and exile on my face. "It's quite clear. You've grown old, Said. A day in exile has the same aging effect as three normal days," the mirror said. I didn't care. I left it to its nonsense and left the room.

The smell of bread from the kitchen filled the sitting room. The tea was ready too. I took two eggs out of the fridge, boiled them and cut them into round slices. Next to them I put a piece of salty cheese and five olives. I didn't intend them to be five of course, but they were the ones left in the jar. I finished breakfast before seven o'clock and sat in front of the television screen in all my elegance. I picked up the remote and started switching between channels. I hadn't been inclined to sit immobile in front of the television screen before, but I'd become addicted to it as soon as the drums of war started beating two years earlier, and the name Baghdad was always in the headlines. At the time the world was interested in us and I spent the whole night switching channels and following the breaking news that appeared at the bottom of the screen. Sitting on the same sofa in the sitting room, I watched the UN inspectors leaving Baghdad, I heard the speech in which the US president gave his Iraqi counterpart forty-eight hours to leave the country or face war. After the deadline passed, I read on the same screen the urgent news that Zero Hour had come and that allied missiles had been launched against strategic targets in Baghdad. My friend Jamal Saadoun called me that day to tell me the good news, as if they had announced the sighting of the new moon and the start of the feast after Ramadan. He was overjoyed to see the night sky over Baghdad light up like day through the explosion of multiple smart bombs. "Have you seen what's happening, Said?" he said. "Didn't I tell you this day was bound to come? It's all over, all over. Hurrah hurray."

"What's all over, Jamal? And what's to celebrate? The country's on fire, man, and people are dying."

"No one will die, believe me. They know what they're doing. We'll finally get rid of the tyrant, and Iraq will become a paradise like Las Vegas in America."

I don't know who told him that. He swore that serious multinational corporations were waiting on the borders for the signal to go in, and they would transform the country.

"You're right. We'll get rid of the tyrant, but Iraq becoming a paradise like Las Vegas? Is that the joke of the season?" I commented, once my friend had done with his flood of solemn oaths to what he had said. He didn't like what I said and hung up without saying goodbye. Then I suddenly had a terrible headache, concentrated as usual in the back of my head, and it forced me to visit the doctor.

5

The city was decorated for Christmas and snowflakes were falling slowly, combining with the lights to create an otherworldly mood I had never seen before. I stood at the bus stop in my long woollen coat, planning to go to the library. I wanted to borrow a book about photography, a medium that I love, although I rarely use my camera and I'm lazy about changing the batteries, which went flat long ago. The bus finally arrived. I greeted the driver, then reached into my coat pocket for some money for the bus fare. But I couldn't find my wallet. I remembered that I'd left it on the bedside table. I slapped myself on the forehead and shouted: "*Khara bil-kaa'inat!*" The driver laughed at me swearing in Arabic and said, "Never mind, get on." He paid the fare from his own pocket and gave me a ticket. He was a young man with a distinctly Arab face, in his thirties, of medium height, with dark, deep-set eyes in a thin face and a small, trimmed beard. I thanked him and sat down in the seat immediately behind him He laughed away as he repeated the expletive I had used. "You reminded me of what our people say, man," he explained. Now I knew he was Iraqi, though I had thought him Palestinian. Then we started chatting and exchanged telephone numbers. Jamal Saadoun, the immigrant bus driver, thus became the only Iraqi in Scandinavia who knew my telephone number.

Since I had met him, Jamal had been tirelessly counting the days till the fall of the regime and a change of government in Iraq. He never harboured any doubts, never gave up hope that the moment would come. When it did come, as one of the countless victims of that repressive regime, he danced till dawn from joy. He had graduated from the engineering faculty at Mustansiriyah University and worked as an engineer for the Baghdad municipality. Once he had settled into his job, he asked to marry the neighbour's daughter and he was about to move on from bachelorhood. But because he had a beard and frequented mosques, informers, who were thick on the ground at the time, decided to keep a close eye on him and provide their masters with secret reports full of fabricated intrigues. In the end he was arrested on a charge of treason and news of him was as hard to find as the remains of a cat that had strayed into a cave full of hungry dogs.

6

The librarian pointed to a rectangular brass plaque that said Photography in black enamel. The plaque was on a large shelf of books and rare magazines on photography. I went over, picked out one of the books and sat down at a table to have a quick browse. On page 27 I saw a black-and-white photograph of a glider that took part in the Vietnam war, according to the caption underneath. The commander of the glider was giving a V-for-victory sign after unloading a pile of bombs onto the heads of the inhabitants. I remembered the sound of the first warplane I ever heard. I was nine years old at the time, playing ball in the alleyway with my friends when an air raid siren sounded and we ran home in panic. I went and hid under my mother's long dress, and awaited disaster. Some warplanes flew over at low altitude and the sound was deafening. My mother put her hands over my ears and recited from the Quran: "*Bardan wasalaaman. Bardan wasalaaman.* Cool and safe. Cool and safe", until the sound of the planes receded into the distance. I looked into my mother's eyes and saw a fear that would last a long time. In the meantime someone pulled out a chair and sat at the table. I came to my senses: I had my hands clasped around my head and I was chanting "*Bardan wasalaaman*" repeatedly.

7

Treason is well-known as an accusation made by bastards more often than drunks sing Atlal, the song by Umm Kulthoum. "You're a traitor" is an easy, readily made charge, like pot noodles. But these characteristically Arab noodles can easily lead you to the gallows to be hanged and bring shame on those you leave behind alive. Oddly, this vile charge is often thrown in your face without explanation or justification. You may not know what form your treason took or when or where or on whose behalf you committed the crime. Someone has simply called you a traitor and that is the end of the matter. Then there is nothing you can do, other than admit total surrender, sign a confession to treason, and then prepare to walk fearlessly to the gallows and put up with eternal shame.

The news that Jamal Saadoun was a traitor didn't reach his family: he languished in the dungeons of the feared military intelligence department for two whole years. He saw the sun only twice during that period, firstly in the annual delousing season and secondly when he had a burst appendix and was taken to hospital to have it removed. He was lucky nonetheless: he was released under a general amnesty decreed by the president and went back to his family. He says that when he came out of prison his father, al-Hajj Saadoun, who was waiting for him at the main gate, didn't recognise him. Because of hunger, fear and maltreatment, Jamal had lost two thirds of his weight and he was as pale as a lemon. He was shocked by the looks of uncertainty in his father's eyes. He went right up to him and said, "Don't you recognise me, dad? I'm Jamal." His father fainted in shock and the band of his headscarf fell off. His mother, who was standing behind the door at home, watching the street, bewailed the state of the remaining third of her returning son. The woman wept and screamed, beat her chest and rolled on the floor when she saw him coming towards her like a ghost from the vaults of hunger. Every time she beat her chest or forehead she cursed, fearlessly and without inhibition, those who had done this to her son. In the end his father had to silence her by force for fear the security men might come back and arrest Jamal again. "Enough shouting and cursing, woman," he said. "The walls have ears."

The times indeed dictated that such curses could only be whispered and were best left unspoken. The walls did have ears, as many fathers believed. But the returning son didn't tell his parents the whole story. He confirmed that to me. If he had done so, the screaming would have brought the roof down. He told me the most horrific part of it, however. He said the interrogating officer amused himself by stripping him naked and attached an electric wire to his penis. This had made him permanently impotent, he said.

"That's impossible! You must be joking," I said.

"Really, Said? Would I joke about such a thing?"

It wasn't a joke, as I had stupidly thought. Who would joke about his manhood? Jamal realised he had been sexually impotent since he was in jail. The interrogator had routinely attached the wire to his penis, saying, "You won't get out of here until I've killed it for you", and the bastard had carried out his threat. The tons of Viagra that Jamal had consumed after coming out of jail had not given him a single moment of sexual happiness with a woman.

8

On April 9, 2003, an American tank recovery vehicle drove into Firdos Square, surrounded by dozens of civilians, and brought down the statue of the dictator – a symbol that Baghdad had fallen and that the city and Iraq as a whole were completely under control. Soon after that the satellite channels started carrying pictures of people looting and setting fires. Bands of thugs, thieves and Baathist goons attacked government offices to loot them and destroy what was left of them, as tough US marines looked on. It looked as if they were working together to destroy the country, not just the regime. Jamal Saadoun phoned me at the time and told me he had decided to go back to Baghdad and wouldn't wait another day. He was going back to help rebuild the country, to use his expression. In order to preserve our close friendship, I didn't object to his decision or make any direct comment, but I joked with him, since a joke is a safe way to convey an idea without doing any harm.

"Okay, boss," I said. "So you've decided to go to Las Vegas!"

"Is Your Highness making fun of me?" he replied, with an affected chuckle that didn't disguise his irritation.

"Don't get upset, I'm just kidding. Anyway, please be careful and give my regards to Baghdad," I said in farewell.

"Okay, I will. So long," he said, and then hung up.

9

The only relatives I have left in Baghdad are my mother and my uncle Ibrahim, whom I couldn't stand. He was a vacuous Baathist with a bushy moustache. He wore an olive-green suit and from his belt hung a 9 mm pistol engraved with a portrait of Tariq ibn Ziad, the commander of the Muslim army that invaded Spain. Like other Baathists at the time, he had a large belly that hung out in front like a balloon full of water, and he carried under his arm a newspaper that he didn't usually read.

"Papa Aflaq has arrived, get ready for the bullshit," I would say, to tease my mother whenever Uncle Ibrahim was coming to visit us, and she would laugh. I nicknamed him Papa Aflaq because he was obsessed with collecting pamphlets written by Michel Aflaq, one of the founders of the Baath Party, though he never read a single line in any of them. He was obsessed with these booklets in the same way as he was obsessed with hanging up pictures of the president and carrying the loathsome party newspapers under his arm. I couldn't stand this arrogant, odious man who ate with his mouth open. If it hadn't been for his son Jalal, who was about my age and loved my mother as much as I did, I would never have stepped foot in their house. One day Jalal invited me to lunch. Uncle Ibrahim had hung up a giant picture of the president across the wall in the guest room. I remember it was a colour photograph in a gilt wooden frame and it showed the dictator standing and praying close to the lattice screen around the tomb of some holy man. "There is no power or strength other than in God. That man's so pious he's going to weep," I joked when I saw it.

"Please, Said, I beg you," Jalal replied. "Stop making sarcastic comments in case my father hears you."

But his father had heard me, I don't know how, and he started telling me off. We got into an argument and I left their house before lunch was served. He was rude and disrespectful to those around him, and for years he broke my mother's heart by describing my father and his political colleagues as traitors. In fact, the only sin my mother ever committed was deciding to be a mother in Iraq. She had bad luck and her few moments of happiness would amount to a story of very few pages. That story of happiness would begin when my father chose her as his partner in life; it ended three months after they were married. One night heavily armed men broke into the house, beat him up in front of her and dragged him off to a vehicle, whereupon he disappeared, leaving a wound in her heart that never healed. He loved her, my mother says, despite the short time they lived together under the same roof, and he was at a loss as to how he might make her happy. Despite his ideological position, he respected what she believed in and prayed to. Once she told me he loved maqam music and especially the singer Nazim al-Ghazali. He would sit in the courtyard of the house in the evening to smoke cigarettes and sway to the poems al-Ghazali sang:

> A dove came and cooed beside me,
> Neighbour, I said, do you realise the state I'm in?
> Love forbid, you have never tasted the pain of parting,
> And nothing has ever troubled your mind.
> Do feathers carry someone whose heart is saddened
> To a high branch in the far distance?
> Neighbour, fate has not been fair to either of us,
> Come and I'll share your worries with you, come.

But when he saw her slip into the room to pray, he stopped the record playing until she had finished. Nothing is better than love at making beliefs acceptable. My mother burned even those Ghazali records when she set about destroying almost everything that might remind her of my father. All that remained of him was an Indian-made bicycle and an Orient wristwatch. In the end, my mother had to sell them, along with some of the furniture, to buy a Singer sewing machine, which was a feature in almost every Iraqi house at the time. I would see her sitting at the Singer tirelessly night and day in order to provide for me. She was in the same position as hundreds of other widows whose husbands had been swallowed up in the prisons and who remained loyal to their memory. Umm Said, my mother, showed the door to all those who came seeking her hand. She took up sewing so that she could feed me without us having to humiliate ourselves. Our life was bitter in Baghdad. No one there offered us any help, not even Uncle Ibrahim, who treated us as if we carried a disease and he was worried we might infect him. My mother would constantly remind me of her relationship with her husband, Nasir Mardan, the teacher who lost his life because he wasn't content just to dream of freedom, but went further and spoke out about his dream. She wanted to fix the story in my memory and impress on my mind's eye an image of him being dragged off to his demise, so that I would learn by heart the principle that speaking about freedom under a repressive regime is like having sex in the street at noontime. "Be careful, Said. The walls have ears," she said repeatedly, until I had learned the lesson well, writing it out in my notebooks, on my wrist and on my pillow. On the wall I drew big ears to save her the bother of repeating her words of warning. I did all this to put my mother's heart at ease and reassure her that the tragedy would not recur. But I never did promise to stop making fun of Papa Aflaq and his big belly.

Iraqi Jewish Writers

A major feature in Banipal 72 (Autumn/Winter 2021)

Conclusion

At 8.25 a.m. on Friday, the accidents and emergencies department at Oslo General Hospital received a phone call from Barbara, the cleaner in the Venus building, which lies in the middle of the Hellerud district in the east of the city. The caller said she had found Mr Said Jensen lying on the floor in his flat on the ninth floor of the building, inside the library, and that he was having convulsions and unconscious. The paramedics arrived at 8.34 a.m. but it was too late for first aid. Mr Jensen's heart had stopped and he was dead. The next day the post-mortem report said that the cause of death was an overdose of Ketamine.

The manuscript of a novel was found on the desk and Mr Jensen appears to have finished writing it some hours before his death. There was also a letter addressed to Helena Jorstad, the editor-in-chief at *Dagposten* newspaper. The manuscript and the letter were delivered to Ms Jorstad, who proceeded to open the envelope sadly and in puzzlement. There was a short request on the part of Said Jensen – that his story and the fantasies about his trip to Baghdad, which he was deprived of seeing because of a silly joke, should be published, and that he should be given a gravestone so that he should not be forgotten, which would be like a second death.

Helena spent that night crying, with her friend's novel in her hands. He had passed away too soon, without saying goodbye. In the morning, after reading it, she contacted the heirs of Mr Jakob Jondal, the neighbour who had died several years earlier, and obtained their written permission to bury Said there. Said's body spent a few days in the morgue and Helena then arranged a burial under the shade of cherry trees in a ceremony attended by his colleagues at the *Dagposten* and a group of his readers and admirers. Finally, she buried with him the frame that had been hanging in the library, and she had the gravestone inscribed with the words: *Here lies Said Jensen / Glory to those who Lie at Rest in the Cherry Orchard*.

The translator

HASSAN ABDEL MAWGOUD

A Bicycle Brings Back an Old Comrade

A SHORT STORY
TRANSLATED BY RAPHAEL COHEN

As unobtrusively as possible, he scanned the location in every direction until he was sure that no one was watching. Waiting for Monica at the top of Manial Street, he started thinking – a little wryly – that he had two names and that Monica, of all people, did not know either of them.

He often thought about those two names: which of them did he want to last? All his comrades in the Communist Party knew him as Taufiq, or Tau, while only a few of them knew his real name – Abdel Malak. The Party Chairman himself had once forgotten that name during a conversation. He utterly failed to recall it, and in the end had to apologise, given that he had called him Abdel Rasoul. At first, he had not been fond of the name Taufiq, but life helped him make do with it. Apart from a very limited group of shopkeepers on his street, no one in his circle had called him Abdel Malak for years. He had no father, no mother, and no friends outside his clandestine work for the Party. Anyway, he was inclined not to mix colleagues and friends. He liked his comrades, of course, and was ready to die for them, but he was not certain that they thought of him as a friend. They met each other in trembling, stifling rooms. His only friend, the one who had recruited him into the Party, had died some time before in a road accident. Always a road accident.

He did not fear death as much as he feared the oblivion of being forgotten. He did not want fame so much as he wanted his name to endure for as long as possible, even if only in the memory of a single person.

Monica arrived.

He usually waited for her at an intersection that allowed him to monitor all directions without drawing suspicion. Party instructions required him to make sure the location was secure and to leave at once if anything seemed wrong. If he sensed anything like that, it meant something unseen was going on. And sometimes, even though he had no proof that something was untoward, he left the location right away. While waiting for Monica, he amused himself by betting on which street she would come from. He usually won the bet.

After having waited for Monica dozens of times, the bet began to develop. He told himself that she would come wearing a black skirt and checked shirt. That she never wore trousers surprised him, given that trousers would allow her greater freedom of movement. After having met her regularly for two years, he could be sure that Monica hated trousers. Yes, she wore skirts, but he could never understand her taste in colours and never guessed either what she would be wearing – skirt, blouse, or shirt – nor its colour. But he found a reason: she never wore the same thing twice. He imagined that she owned a factory making skirts, blouses, shirts, dresses, and jackets. Perhaps she was from a rich family. After all, he knew that the Party included rich and poor comrades. When she wore very short skirts, that revealed a lot of leg, he was happy. When she appeared down the street he had bet on, he would stare at her legs and study the way she walked. Then, so she didn't notice him staring at her bare legs, he had to look at her pretty face. Those seemed the best moments of his life, the moments when Monica came into view. They were the real reward for his clandestine work. He wondered how he would feel if another young woman turned up one day instead of her. At that moment he realised he loved her, and by chance that day, unusually, she smiled at him, as if she had read his thoughts or as if she loved him too. Looking at her smiling mouth, he thought that perhaps her real name was Nadia.

He had never asked her or anyone else what her name was. He did not care to poke into other people's business, even though he was convinced that might be as enjoyable as poking around the old papers in his desk. He kept a suitable distance from everyone, which kept him sane. He looked around again, then handed her the envelope.

Often, when he thought about this easy mission, which the Party always assigned him, he felt annoyed, but because he respected Party work, he quickly shook off his annoyance. Over time, a one-sided relationship developed between him and Monica. He liked to imagine her always with him as they played heroic roles against the Germans, the Soviets, the Israelis, and the Egyptian police. Master spies at all times, but his fantasy never included who those two spies worked for. No doubt, though, they stood with the other side, the side of the few brave fighters against evil.

All his stories had a sad ending. Monica would die horrifically, shot or under torture. Her torturers would break her fingers and extract her nails; they pulled out her hair with such violence that a piece of scalp would be attached to the roots. He wept and felt guilty for killing her such a vast number of times. He didn't know why, but he thought that such a beautiful woman was not destined to live long. Perhaps part of him wanted her to die; perhaps part of him knew that she was the real threat – possibly the only threat – to his seclusion in his empty apartment, his cocoon that would grow more confining when he later developed cataracts. Despite killing her countless times in his head, he waited impatiently for the Party to assign him to meet her. If the Party cancelled his mission – he thought once – or entrusted it to someone else, he would object, even if the order came from the Party Chairman himself. Yes, he would object, and openly, hierarchy be damned. Were the Party Chairman to decide to stop assigning him to meet her and deliver the money, he might object openly. Then he began to think, in all seriousness, that he might give up clandestine party work if they forced him to not see her. Then it struck him that he shouldn't be so melodramatic.

He had never once tried to talk to her, perhaps afraid of her reaction, perhaps to maintain a certain distance. Until at the next meeting after her smile, he unexpectedly found himself saying that he loved her. She smiled again, and seemed so angelic and good, but did not say a word. Then she moved off, as always, as ever.

He met Monica practically everywhere in Cairo. She exhausted him. When he wanted to meet her, he had to take the tram from Heliopolis to the Ramses Street extension and then walk to the far end of Sakakini. Sometimes he took a bus, minibus or taxi to Old Cairo, or sometimes to Helwan or to Maadi or the Giza gardens, other times downtown, at times Rod al-Farag, sometimes the far east of Cairo, then the far west, at times the northern tip, at times the southern. Then the Party decided to give him a bicycle.

They sent for him and told him that there would be a meeting at a villa in Garden City owned by a famous cardiologist. The first time Tau saw him, he was standing with a large cigar in his mouth, and the Party Chairman and two comrades he knew well were standing next to him. The Party Chairman pointed at the bicycle, then started giving a speech about someone called Joseph Rosenthal, the Jewish goldsmith, who had performed valuable services for the Party in the early days. He did not know what the Party Chairman was getting at. Perhaps he wanted to make a link between the goldsmith and the doctor – Tau thought – because of the money and assistance they had given the Party. That's what he thought, even though he knew nothing about the goldsmith, or the doctor, and even though the Party Chairman did not say that either. The speech ended without him gleaning anything useful. One of the comrades handed him a piece of paper and asked him to sign it. He understood that one day he would have to give the bicycle back. The Party Chairman said that they wanted to make things easier for him, especially for places without public transport. He felt grateful to the Party Chairman – everything seemed to suggest the bicycle had been his idea. In the days that followed, everything went smoothly. He would recall Monica's smile and feel such a surge of confidence that it made him take a chance and ask her to meet him in a café downtown. Heading there, he thought about the two married comrades who did not discover that they both belonged to the Party until they were stopped by the police in Suez and questioned together.

He went to the next meeting by bike. All the way he imagined her reaction. True, she had smiled before, but then she had gone and left him without saying anything. This time she would have to say something. A smile wouldn't be enough. She didn't even need to smile. He thought that somehow he would make her talk. It was his right, even if only for her to say, 'No, you're a comrade that's all,' or, 'I'm married,' or, 'I'm a nun.' But she said nothing of the kind. She arrived, appearing in the distance as always, wearing a white dress dotted with tiny dark blue flowers. He didn't need to say anything, for she said, "I love you too."

He did not hand her the envelope and she did not ask him for it. In violation of all security measures and all Party and personal instructions, she sat in front of him on the bicycle, and they set off through the September air along the Corniche in Maadi.

Monica told him that she had fallen in love with him at first sight. Then she arranged everything. They would not talk about their marriage in front of Party comrades – there was a chance they would be assigned separate missions, maybe, maybe not. But she wanted to keep meeting him in the street, and when she told him, he said he would rather die than stop meeting her in the street. So, they would stay loyal to the Party and continue carrying out their missions. He would leave home to pick up and deliver the money, while she would leave the same home to collect it. They agreed not to talk Party business and that each would remain committed to their cell and its instructions. They also agreed to tell his neighbours only that he had got married and that his wife would be coming in a few days. It was a good thing too that she was the only child of parents well on their way towards death with a long inventory of serious illnesses between them. She provided the two witnesses after he had registered his conversion to Islam. On the marriage certificate he saw her name for the first time. Not Nadia, but Hanaa.

The differences between them never bothered him. Differences he soon discovered. Her family owned a large two-storey villa in Zamalek; she owned enough clothes to be able to change twice a day for the rest of her life and had to bring five enormous suitcases-full when she moved into his apartment. She told him then that the rest of her clothes would need at least another ten trips. She had graduated in medicine, while he had graduated in literature. In passing, she mentioned that she had no money worries, while he lived

Banipal Books

Literary translation from Banipal:
from Sudan, Kuwait & Tunisia

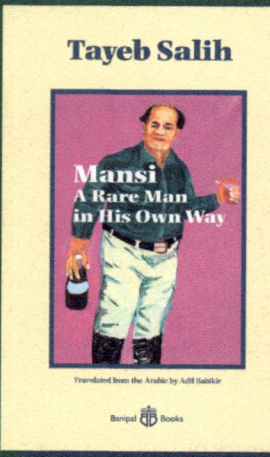
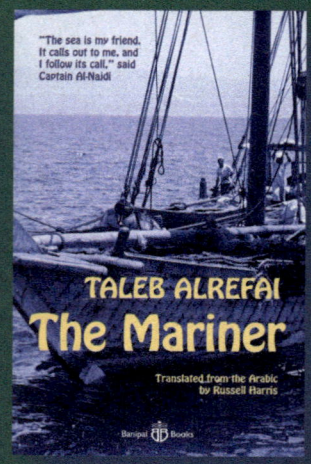
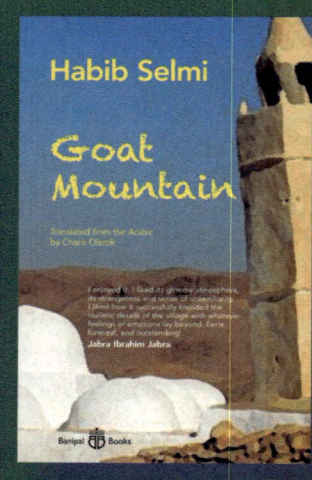

"A flavourful and entertaining memoir of Salih's friendship with a shape-shifting, rule-breaking character who treated life as an "endless laugh." **Boyd Tonkin**

ISBN 978-0-9956369-8-9

A spotlight on Kuwait's pearl-fishing history in an enthralling fictional re-telling of the fateful day in 1979 when the country's famous dhow shipmaster Captain Al-Najdi is lost at sea in a treacherous storm.

ISBN 978-1-913043-08-7

"I enjoyed this book. I liked its gloomy atmosphere, its strangeness and sense of unfamiliarity . . . Eerie, funereal, and outstanding!"

Jabra Ibrahim Jabra

ISBN 978-1-913043-04-9

Available as Paperback and eBook

www.banipal.co.uk

off the interest from the small sum his father had left him in a savings account and, to reduce expenses, only ate twice a day. He wondered what would have happened if his father hadn't bequeathed him the apartment.

Before he laid a hand on her, she confessed that she wasn't a virgin. She had been involved in a love affair with another student at university. They only had sex once, at his apartment, then, when she graduated, he broke up with her. She should definitely have told Tau before they got married, but would he have changed his mind? As she told him, he nodded his head as if to say never mind. Until that point she had not told him how she was recruited into the Party, or by whom. He felt she was very straightforward, but he still had not asked her how they would manage the household expenses, or why she had told him that she had loved him at first sight. He felt flattered whenever he remembered her saying that, and decided to let her tell him of her own accord. There was no need for haste, given that their destinies were virtually identical and neither of them would go far from the other.

Five days after their marriage, the Party assigned them a mission. She planned to go to Helwan and then downtown: he planned to go to Heliopolis, then also downtown. They exchanged a few words in the morning. He wanted to bend their strict rule about not talking shop at home and decided, as he looked at her blue dress with a pattern of white flowers, to tell her about the Party Chairman's speech before he gave him the bicycle. He told her that he still did not understand why the man talked about Joseph Rosenthal. She told him that Rosenthal was one of the Party's founders. He felt slightly surprised as he watched her disappear behind the front door.

He had some time before he needed to leave to meet Monica. He knew what to do with the time: he would put up the pictures she had brought with her, Hanaa's pictures. He went from room to room, putting them up. He felt that her spirit was present in her pictures and he even saw a soft white light emanating from them into every corner of the apartment.

He stood checking and waiting with the same old zeal at the junction of Sharif Street and Adli Street. He guessed she would come, heralded by her blue dress, from the direction of Fouad Street. He was eager to see her face approaching in the distance; somehow, he longed to see her from a distance, rather than a few inches away.

She would appear and he would give her the envelope, satisfied with a smile and the usual password, 'conscience'. Tau wondered why the Party had chosen the word. Did somebody want to remind him of his conscience – he was carrying money after all? Perhaps someone in the Party had doubts about his integrity, or was making fun of him. He felt furious, which shocked him, because they were usually circumspect in their work. As an ambulance sped past, he noticed the commotion of a gathering crowd on Adli Street.

Her dress peeked out timorously from under sheets of newspaper before the paramedics lifted her up. Monica had departed without saying goodbye to him.

Life carried on; it always does. He felt devastated as he placed the envelope on the Party Chairman's desk. He told him that Monica had not picked up the money. He wanted to inform him that he was never coming back to the Party but something indefinable prevented him from doing so. They tried to get in touch with him afterwards, but he did not open the door to those who knocked. The Party Chairman himself came on one occasion. After knocking for a long time the Chairman said in a loud voice that he knew Tau was behind the door (he was right) and it was rude not to let in him. The words resonated, albeit weakly, in Tau, who felt he ought to open the door, but something indefinable kept him rooted to the spot.

His eyes developed cataracts, which was more painful for him than the loss of Monica. His vision became so weak he could no longer see her pictures properly. Each day he took down a particular photo of her and placed it between the images of the Virgin Mary and Saint George slaying the dragon. A picture of her laughing. And he sat crying, imagining that he was shedding blue teardrops into a lake at his feet.

For the next twenty years, Tau met no one except his doctors and the shopkeepers on his street and then their sons. He completely stopped thinking about his real name. He thought about the Party, especially when he heard some news of it. He learned that the Chairman and many of those he knew had died or filled the prison camps. Some of those who had been released set up parties that operated openly. He no longer cared about oblivion after Monica died. She had been the only person who might have remembered him forever. He was no longer afraid of death or of oblivion. He perceived oblivion as something external and distant, connected to others, but he also realised that it was terribly close to us. Oblivion is horrific if it decides to overwhelm us. It ends our connection with the world, even before that world decides to forget us. Alzheimer's crept into his brain cells, blasting them one by one, like kernels into popcorn. He had been afraid that others would forget him, but now he began the opposite process of forgetting them. So, he decided to write everything down in a ledger that was nearly always with him. Monica had left him but her pictures were still pinned to the wall and in the four chambers of his heart. He was scared she would leave him for good as the forces of Alzheimer's marched ever on. Fortunately, so far he had forgotten nothing to do with Monica. He remembered her smile as she received the envelope after saying the usual, hated password, 'conscience.'

Speaking of that word, Tau felt worried one day when he read a piece of paper concerning a bicycle that he had received from the Party. He thought that some comrades might accuse him of theft. Who knew? He felt it wrong to think like that, but he couldn't stop thinking about the bicycle. In his youth, old Tau had never feared death. Only one thought terrified him – abandoning his conscience. In Monica he had found a mirror for his conscience. If conscience had been a coin, they would have been its face and obverse. But the Party never stopped making him doubt himself, otherwise why would they have chosen 'conscience' as the password? Tau did not remember where the bicycle was, but after a search he found it in a room that had been locked for years, a room thickly layered with dust, that he had set aside for things he did not want to see again. He had to return the bicycle to the Party. It was the only thing that had been entrusted to him. Yet his conscience – he realised – was not the main reason pushing him to return it. With difficulty he recalled that the Party no longer existed, and that the comrade who gave him the receipt to sign had become Chairman of the Stalinist Party. He did not know, or more accurately did not remember, anyone else. He cleaned the bicycle again and thought about taking it to the Party offices, but he told himself not to overcomplicate things. No one was going to comment on the dirty tyres, that's if they even were dirty. The point was that the bicycle seemed in good condition overall. He asked the information officer if he could see the Party Chairman and, pointing at the bicycle, added he was returning something lent on trust. The official burst out laughing in a way that greatly annoyed him. He ought to have asked the official what had prompted his raucous laughter, but instead he decided to avoid that and hand the problem over to the Party Chairman's secretary. Politely, Tau asked the good-looking secretary for a meeting with the Chairman. What made him say the man's name prefixed with the word 'comrade', he did not know. She laughed, and again he did not know why. He had only said two words, 'comrade' and the name. Then all of a sudden, and for unknown reasons as usual, he recalled the Qur'anic story of Ahl al-Kahf. He quickly tried to get it out of his mind while observing her lips that were in constant motion. She seemed to be repeating herself: "The chief is at a conference in Ukraine until the end of the week." Followed by, "Please, how can I help?" Should he tell her? She might laugh like the other official. Certainly, that guy had made fun of him, and perhaps she was doing the same. Even so, he abruptly told her that the Communist Party had entrusted him with the bicycle and he wished to return it. The astonished secretary, still smiling, with what he took might be ridicule, told him that that party no longer existed. "It's been gone nearly a quarter of a century," she added. Very well, what did she want him to say? He knew that fact. She had to do something, fetch the deputy Party Chairman or another official. But she said she could sort it out herself, if he liked. He thought for a moment, then gave a nod. The secretary called in a photographer and said she would keep the photograph for the Party Chairman, and that he could come back later. She left him to the photographer, then came back shortly after with two young men, who she said were journalists on the Party newspaper. He gave a nod to return their greetings, trying through the fog of his vision to figure out which of them was taller. They asked him, in a manner he found strange, about his story and about the Communist Party and the entrusted bicycle, and why he had disappeared for such a long time. He found it hard to remember and was incapable of answering their questions. Honestly, he did not remember why he had left the Party, and found nothing that could be said that wasn't silly regarding what he'd been doing for all those years. He was careful to say nothing about Monica. Despite the simple fragments he came out with, the two journalists embroidered a long tale that they published along with a picture of him and the bicycle.

A week later, the Party Chairman met him with a great deal of fanfare. Tau looked at him. Something fundamental about him had changed. Perhaps in his features, he did not mean the effect of aging but the obesity of his face and body, the obesity puffing out his shiny black suit. His cataracts did not prevent him seeing his old comrade who spoke, most enthusiastically, happily, and warmly, before leading him to his office. At that moment, Tau discovered he was wheeling the bicycle with him, while the Party Chairman hurried towards his enormous desk and took out the newspaper. He folded it in half and pointed at the photograph of Tau, the one taken by the Party photographer, and told him that the headline beneath had taken him more than an hour to come up with. He read it aloud in the same tone of enthusiasm: "A bicycle brings back Communist Party comrade Taufiq." Then the secretary clapped, and he noticed her presence with them. The Party Chairman pointed at the bicycle and said its return was not enough for him and he would put it in the foyer of Party headquarters as a symbol of the new Party and its principles. Tau, however, did not seem to be paying attention. After a long silence, he said he owed the Party something other than the bicycle: a piece of information, a piece of information about him and about Monica that the Party did not know. "Who's Monica?" exclaimed the Party Chairman. But Tau did not speak and wondered how he had forgotten Monica. How had her beauty not stuck in his mind? Her bravery? Her commitment to the cause? Her martyrdom for the Party? He stood and left the room. He left the Party entirely and went out into the downtown street, taking the bicycle with him, and he tried to take an enormous gulp of the fresh air blowing his way.

From the author's collection of short stories Huroub Fatina *(Ravishing Wars), published by Al-Kotob Khan, Cairo 2018*

Katia al-Tawil reviews
Lam yusalli 'alaihum ahad (No One Prayed Over Their Graves) by Khaled Khalifa

Published by Naufal, Beirut, 2019
ISBN: 978-614-469-436-7
pbk 348 pages

Men who wanted to touch the sun, and burned up

Khalid Khalifa choses to start his novel *No One Prayed Over Their Graves* with a tragedy. A disastrous event afflicts the characters and half of them die. As for those who remain, death is a suspended sentence. The flood of 1907 turns Khalifa's main protagonist, Hanna Gregoros, into a cursed mythological hero, only this time in Aleppo at the beginning of the twentieth century. The author gives his hero everything: women, money, land, influence, youth, strength, and defiance. Then he punishes him and watches him weak, helpless, and destroyed. Heaven and Aleppo punish the hero and make him unable to rise again, even though he has yet to reach his time to die. Hanna, the cursed hero and victim of heaven's anger and Khalifa's fury, says, in his weakness, "I am not a target for robbers and murderers, I am dead, there is no use in killing a dead man".

Khalifa, a leading contemporary Syrian novelist, has chosen to write a three-hundred-page epic with three aspects. First, he relates the epic of Aleppo in the nineteenth and twentieth centuries, a city buffeted by political, religious, and social problems, a city plagued by struggles between bishops, clergy, Muslims, Turks, Armenians, and Jews. On a second level, Khalifa writes an epic of the human

Aleppo punishes the mythic hero in Khalid Khalifa's novel

The Arabic cover of the novel

soul, weak and ruined, as it moves from youth and vigour to old age and infirmity. He tells the story of humanity as it tries to rebel, but fate comes and crushes it. Finally, Khalifa recounts the epic of love when it is shackled in a society that does not pray for lovers. An epic of love sentenced to death in every story.

The narrative swings therefore between Eros, the God of love, and Thanatos, the God of death, while Man, in the form of the novel's main characters Hanna and Zakariya, remains their victim. Together, Hanna and Zakariya form a single hero split into Christian and Muslim characters. Together they form a symbol of the human being expelled from paradise – the hero, whether Christian or Muslim, who faces the wrath of God. Anger and punishment afflict them both and escaping punishment is impossible for them both: "We thought we survived the flood and reached a settlement with death, but death cheated us."

Aleppo, the Apocalyptic City

The novel's narrative space is divided into two epochs: before and after the 1907 floods. This temporal caesura marks a profound and painful change in the makeup, psychological depth, and behaviour of the characters. Their fates change with the situation in Aleppo and the vicissitudes of time. Before the flood, Hanna, the main protagonist, and his friends, Zakariya, Azar, and William, are paradigms of dissolution, arrogance, and profligacy – symbols of wealth, influence, and power. Hanna hosts parties where champagne flows, women are available, and guests gamble. He plans to build a citadel where ladies can entertain the powerful men of Aleppo. Hanna and his circle gain a mythical reputation in the stories spun about them, and the reader first knows of Hanna as "the man who used to set fire to the imagination of the city with his scandals and his ideas".

Then comes the 1907 flood; Hanna's land is submerged, along with his family, his dreams, his recklessness, and his insouciance. All is destroyed. Post 1907 is an age of collapse and weakness, and Hanna is transformed into a cursed hero, the victim of the anger of Aleppo and God. Calamities befall him and he says he is living a time of innumerable and endless losses.

Aleppo takes the lives of its people or causes them to self-destruct. Hence, the men are stricken with anxiety and the women rebel in vain. Times are hard and Aleppo becomes a vast prison, the gallows, or as one of the characters says, "the place that had become increasingly confining". War, civil strife, massacres, earthquakes, famines, follow in succession, leaving all the characters defeated and downcast.

No One Prayed Over Their Graves turns into a novel of decline and fall, a novel of the human inability to escape a deadly place. Stories of decline, nothingness, and disintegration that begin with the flood of 1907, a year that marks the beginning of the punishment. Hanna

A Boat to Lesbos
and other poems
by Nouri Al-Jarrah

This powerful epic poem by Syrian poet Nouri Al-Jarrah, in the form of a Greek tragedy, bears passionate and dramatic witness to the horrors and ravages suffered by Syrian families forced to flee across the Mediterranean.

"The delicate, heart-breaking poems in A Boat to Lesbos *find in Sappho's exile a common bond between the island's most famous poet and Syrians escaping civil war."* Ruth Padel

Translated from the Arabic
by Camilo Gómez-Rivas and Allison Blecker
Cover & inside paintings by Reem Yassouf

The poet's first collection in English translation
ISBN: 978-0-9956369-4-1 • 120pp • £9.99 • €13 • US$15

Banipal Books

says, "We were so powerful, and now I am so weak. I am like a vagrant, walking along the bank of the great river which, with its might and tyranny, killed all those people."

The flood sweeps away youth, power, and defiance. It sweeps away dreams, ambitions, and resolve. Aleppo is turned into a frightening city, a city that devours its people with their stories of love and defiance. Hence the novel's title appearing twice in the text. The curse of lovers is that no one shall pray over their graves; the curse of those who love life, joy and revolt is that they will die in silence and no one will pray over their graves. The title speaks to the injustice of the city and its cruelty to its inhabitants.

Hubris, Curse and Punishment

The flood can be seen as divine punishment that falls on Christian Hanna and Muslim Zakariya to remind them of their true stature. They possessed wealth, influence, women, land, horses, and property; they built the citadel for wild nights of debauchery and champagne in the company of their friends, Aleppo's privileged upper class. Hanna and Zakariya are cursed for their hubris, and become together one complete cursed Sisyphean figure, punished together for their defiance, greed, and sense of superiority just as Sisyphus was cursed by the gods and lost everything. Water, which is usually a synonym of life, baptism and purity, is also metamorphosed in the novel into an instrument of divine punishment that kills and overwhelms Christian and Muslim alike.

Khalid Khalifa's two heroes become Adam expelled from Paradise, the Adam of both the Bible and the Qur'an. Their citadel, intended as a hotbed of debauchery and gambling, becomes the Tower of Babel, whose builders God cursed so that the tower collapsed and the ur-language was confounded into the mass of human tongues. The curse of Hanna and Zakariya is weakness, incapacity, and diminishment. Hanna says of himself, "After the flood, on my first night when I regarded the sight of the destroyed village, I felt that nothing was left of me."

After the flood, Hanna renounces life, people, and wealth. Like Oedipus, he roams, lost, in an effort to atone for his sins. Hanna and Zakariya roam without direction in search of redemption,

KHALED KHALIFA

peace, purification. Hanna changes from the builder of the pleasure citadel into the builder of a monastery, which is visited by pilgrims from all over seeking to gain blessings and intercession. Hanna turns from a myth of dissolution and power into a holy man on his way to sainthood. All of this because of a flood, which stands for the eternal curse of punishment that comes to all those who have the defiance and hubris to dare to believe in their own strength. After the flood, Hanna says of himself, "deliverance from this putrid soul will take a long time".

No One Prayed Over Their Graves, Khalifa's sixth novel, is one of the most outstanding of recent publications. It combines Greek mythology with deep Biblical and Qur'anic symbolism that gives psychological depth to the characters and creates the narrative space in which events unfold in detail and with coherence. Khalifa's novel excavates the stories of Aleppo and its people, their history, with all its massacres, wars and famines, the strife between Muslims and Christians, conflicts between bishops and clergy, extremist movements, sectarian clamour, and conflicts with Ottoman soldiers, as well as stories of love, passion, recklessness, and defiance. This novel poses side by side the tragedy of life and the tragedy of society, along with the tragedy of punishment. Maybe one of its most beautiful heart-breaking narrative moments is a literary echo to the exquisite novel *All the World's Mornings* by the French novelist Pascal Quignard, when Khalifa states "each new dawn was totally unlike the one that had died the day before".

Translated by Raphael Cohen

KHALED KHALIFA

NO ONE PRAYED OVER THEIR GRAVES

EXCERPT FROM THE NOVEL
LAM YUSALLI 'ALAYHUM AHAD
TRANSLATED BY LERI PRICE

KHALED KHALIFA

Chapter One
The Flood

Hosh Hanna – Aleppo – January 1907

The village of Hosh Hanna was completely silent when the storm hit and the Great Flood rose. Within a few short hours, the houses of the small village were destroyed, its inhabitants drowned in their rags. No one survived apart from Mariana Nassar and Shaha Sheikh Musa, wife of Zakariya al-Bayazidi. The two women clung to the trunk of a walnut tree caught between the iron columns of the minaret that guided the boats through the depths of the river. Some fishermen recued them and took them to a house in a nearby village, and then everything quietened down at dawn.

Before Mariana Nassar lost consciousness, she saw the bodies of her mother, her father, and her four brothers and sisters floating on the surface of the river along with the bodies of others she knew: her neighbour and her six children, the rest of her impoverished neighbours. She saw the corpse of Yvonne's fiancé – the girl was currently in Aleppo having her wedding dress made, oblivious to the rumours that her fiancé had deflowered her in his father's mill. The village priest was smiling as usual, and next to him was Hanna's son, not yet four years old, his mother Josephine Al-Liham gripping him tightly. Their bodies rose and fell with the waves as if they were dancing.

Mariana had known most of the drowned. They were her students, her neighbours, family friends from the neighbouring villages, her own friends. All the corpses passed by her. An entire life was buried in the river and she wasn't sure she had survived herself. She closed her eyes in surrender, praying desperately to Jesus as she held onto the sturdy tree trunk caught in the minaret. She noticed Shaha next to her, clutching the body of her son to her chest. Later, the fishermen only succeeded in extracting him from her arms after a struggle.

Mariana saw cooking pots and rugs and beds, shards of large ceramic water pots mixed with roof timber, mirrors, bridal trunks, and other things she couldn't make out. In her memory, there remained an image of Shaha grabbing hold of her dead son when the waves tossed him near her, and the smile of the priest who had dedicated his last sermon to defending the honour of Yvonne and her fiancé, 'the eternal lovers' as the fellahin of Hosh Hanna called them.

Zakariya al-Bayazidi and his friend Hanna Gregoros, arrived in the afternoon after hearing news of the disaster. When the destroyed village appeared in the distance, they were horrified. Zakariya couldn't believe that the unconscious Shaha was still breathing. Their son's body lay curled up in her lap and they were still clinging to each other. Hanna was utterly stupefied and he thought for a moment that he had lost the power of speech. One of the fishermen led him down a narrow, debris-filled lane to the body of his wife, Josephine. She was whiter than she had been in life, her lips closed like the dead, and his son was next to her, rigid, his stomach distended like a waterskin.

Hanna trudged back by the river road, a familiar route to him. He jumped over the corpses of cows, sheep, and people. He climbed the long staircase to his rooms and from the broad window he looked out over his village, transformed into silt and the remnants of things. There was no longer anything that blocked his view over the remote distances. The river, which he knew well, ran along as it had done for eternity, meek and quiet, as if it hadn't done anything. The sunlight glittered on its surface like gold coins.

He reflected that once again he was alone, without a family. Entertainment and pleasure had saved him and his friend Zakariya. If they had delayed being at the citadel with their friends, they would now be two bloated corpses reeking of mass death, that fetid smell which he tried to describe later on but couldn't. He couldn't forget Mariana's reply when she told him that Josephine had been terrified as her soul rose to heaven, raising her hand and clutching at the air while her other hand gripped her son tightly. She plunged and came back to the surface of the river more than once before she drowned and turned into a corpse, meek and smiling, just as she had when she arrived at Hosh Hanna for the first time and all the fellahin of the village saw her get down from the carriage. When Hanna insisted on asking Mariana about their last moments, all she said was that drowned people's features disappear, and they don't look at all like the other dead.

Hanna felt as though he was hanging in a shadowy horizon, hearing the bones of perished beings shattering under his feet. Zakariya couldn't bear to see him so frightened, and so he acted decisively. He arranged the village graveyard anew with the help of the fellahin from the neighbouring villages, and he buried most of the bodies which the river spat out onto its banks. He still knew them, even though their features were distorted. He knew their scars, the colour of their eyes. He buried an intimate part of his life in their graves.

The graveyard seemed the utmost horror to Zakariya and Hanna as they were looking at it from the window of Hanna's room. The graves of the Christians were lined up carefully next to the graves of the Muslims, and the graves of the unknown and the strangers were in a third orderly row. Other graves were left open to receive any corpses that the river had swept away to distant villages. The fellahin had spent three days digging graves according to Zakariya's instructions, who at that moment had no thought for anything other than burying the dead. He kept repeating that the dead would turn into a plague before long. He buried more than a hundred and fifty bodies, and he was never truly rid of their cold touch and the smell that accompanied him forever. He hadn't known that the smell of death hangs in the clothes, and that burial wasn't the least arduous task it had seemed to him when he was giving orders to the fellahin to dig the graves, and sending someone to call a sheikh and a priest to complete the requisite rites. The priest and the sheikh arrived and both refused to pray over the unknown corpses, or those with features too distorted to be recognised. The sheikh said it wasn't permitted to bury a person in the Islamic way or pray over their body if that person might be Christian, and the priest agreed, corroborating that they had to confirm the religion of the body. But Zakariya went on burying them all in his own way without bothering to pray over them, repeating that the dead lost all their religious affiliations and turned into other beings who didn't care about the affairs of Heaven.

After ten days, Zakariya finished burying the bodies. He sat on the steps of the room and heard Hanna sobbing. He felt intensely exhausted as he reflected on their former lives. It was no consolation for him to see his sixty horses whose bloodlines had been lost when their pedigrees were drowned. They had come back to gather at the site of their stable, of which only some wooden fragments and empty stone troughs remained.

Zakariya prepared a horse-drawn carriage and he only set off with

Mariana Nassar and Shaha after extracting a promise from Hanna that he would join them in Aleppo within a few days. Zakariya didn't look behind him when the carriage left what used to be known as the village of Hosh Hanna. He wanted to forget the place that had turned into a graveyard. His horses ran behind him with bowed heads, dejected at leaving the riverbank and their obliterated stables.

Zakariya couldn't believe the loss of his only child. He spent the whole road immersed in heavy silence, and he didn't reply when Shaha told him that the noise was starting to wound her. Before the flood, when she was lying naked next to him on the bed, she would ask him to close the curtain when the dawn light stole in through their window, saying that the light wounded her. They lived, before the flood, in the certainty that everything would be alright, they would have children who would inherit a love of horses, and who would be wounded by invisible things like light, air and sound. But now, after the flood, they entered Zakariya's family home in the new quarter of Aleppo like a pair of orphans. They couldn't explain what had happened, not to Zakariya's father, Ahmed al-Bayazidi, and not to his sister Souad, who knew that the flood hadn't just taken the son of her brother and his wife; it had destroyed what was left of their passion and their love for each other. She said to her father, "We have to get used to them being two ghosts, two invisible people." Her father didn't understand. He encouraged her to convince her brother that he needed to open a mourning tent, and go to Hosh Hanna to bring back Hanna. Leaving him alone with the dead meant he would disappear like withered rose petals.

Zakariya left the business of caring for the horses to his groom Yaaqoub, who was already responsible for his second stable in the village of Anabiya. He didn't reply to Yaaqoub's question of whether it was possible to regain the pedigree records for these horses and paid no attention when Yaaqoub said, "What are the horses worth without a record of their bloodline?" When Zakariya returned to his room in his family's house at night, Shaha was asleep. He sat next to her on the sofa and looked at her for a long time. She had changed considerably. Surely it wasn't possible that seeing death turned you into another being within a few hours? Her laughing eyes were hollowed out, transformed into two pits of clotted blood. Her chest rose and fell with her agitated breathing, her lips were clamped shut as if she was afraid that river water might leak in. Her large moist nipples had shrunk and the gorgeous valley between her breasts had become a shadowless pit. He had never seen her sleeping before. From now on, she wouldn't scold him for perpetually going on trips with Hanna in search of pleasure and women and card tables. She wouldn't laugh coquettishly when he replied calmly that horses love women and gambling and fun, adding, "You won't find purebred horses in the houses of the frightened, and the misers, and the moneylenders." She used to conclude this little flirtation by asking him to describe the women that the horses loved so much, but now she was surrendered to the image of death.

Shaha didn't understand the relationship between horses and moneylenders in the early days of their marriage, but she liked the idea of it. She thought that pleasure and entertainment were the kind Zakariya had introduced her to. When he saw her in the house of her brother Arif, she stole his heart with her slim figure and wide eyes. Zakariya fell in love on the spot and exchanged some lingering glances with her, and that night he whispered to an intoxicated Hanna to ask for her hand on his behalf. Arif laughed when Hanna told him gravely that he was asking for Shaha on behalf of Zakariya. Arif went out of the salon where his guests usually gathered and brought his sister. He asked her, "Do you accept Zakariya the Runaway?" She said, smiling, "Yes." He went on, "You have to know he is utterly shameless and a complete buffoon. He has no respect for married life and he will betray you with the first woman he trips over on the way to Afreen." She repeated her answer: "Yes, I will marry him." Arif had no idea what he was supposed to do in moments like this. He walked towards the cupboard, took out his rifle and fired a shot into the air. He sent for Mullah Mannan to recite the Book and no one disputed any details of the marriage contract.

Hanna felt that this novel event merited drunkenly staggering to his feet in the middle of the party, and he took some gold lira out of his leather zunar to present to Shaha as a wedding gift. Everything was very simple and joyful – "wonderful", as Shaha described it. Arif didn't care about the objections of his wider family who would have preferred a Kurdish groom for the daughter of Sheikh Musa Agha. Arif didn't stint his sister and put on a lavish wedding for her, where he danced and flattered Ahmed al-Bayazidi and Souad (whom he called "arrogant"). Souad was no more pleased by her brother's improvised wedding than she was by his marrying a girl from the country, even if she was the daughter of an agha. But the happiness of the bride and groom was enough to defer her criticisms. She knew, deep down, that this marriage was a declaration of Zakariya's permanent separation from his family. He couldn't care less what his relatives would say and delegated the task of informing them to his father who, for his part, was delighted. Shaha belonged to a large and powerful family, and by marrying her Zakariya had put an end to his father's constant fear that he would be embroiled into marrying one of the prostitutes at the citadel whose shamelessness and licentiousness were the stuff of legend throughout the city.

After the wedding, which carried on for three days, the married couple left Sharran loaded with gifts that were crammed into large carriages: rugs of virgin wool, embroidered cushion covers, Kurdish carpets made specially for Shaha's jihaz many years before, large copper cooking pans, along with earthenware jars of goat cheese, olive oil, cured meats, and small things that Zakariya hadn't even seen yet such as Shaha's anklets and a large necklace of pure gold, along with a carriage just for the married couple pulled by a black purebred stallion which Arif had gifted to his friend and brother-in-law.

On their way to Hosh Hanna, Shaha said to Zakariya that she had loved him since she first saw him three years before. She used to look out for him among her brother's permanently-installed guests and she could relate many stories about the moments he came to light. She said that she had put compresses on his forehead one day two years earlier when he had been struck with a fever. On that night of revelry, Arif Agha had gathered his many friends for a party to mark the end of the olive harvest. In actual fact they were celebrating many things that had happened that year, most important of which was the return of his father's library to its proper place, and the reconciliation that had taken place at last between Arif and his uncle who had beat his nephew with a shoe in front of his servant Mabrouk Al-Habashy and called him ignorant, after learning that Arif had sold the library to an Englishman who, in the company of a translator, perpetually wandered the region that extended from Kilis to the Cathedral of Saint Simeon Stylite. This Englishman was interested in the theatre of Nabi Houri, the ruins of the destroyed temples and churches in Barad, and the villages of Mount Simeon. Arif only regained the library after no small exertion. He travelled to Aleppo where the Englishman was staying in a residence belonging to the English Consulate and paid substantially more than the price he had been given for it. Leaders of Arab tribes and Kurdish aghwat mediated on his behalf, and they succeeded in striking a bargain for the return of the library which was still in trunks in preparation for being sent to London. But three ancient texts written in Kurdish were missing, most important of which was a manuscript of Mem and Zin copied out by Abdel Latif Bihzad, an adherent of the work's original author, the Sufi poet Ahmed Khany.

The returning library was welcomed with a raucous celebration. Munshidun recited the odes of Ahmed Khany and Mullah Jaziri for three days straight. Arif's uncle and Mullah Mannan scrutinised the books which Mabrouk Al Habashy rearranged and rehomed as they had previously been. Despite mourning the loss of the three unique texts, they were content that the library had once again returned to its place in the house built on a hill within Arif's estate known as "Grandfather's house". It was an isolated residence composed of two large rooms that overlooked his vast olive groves.

At that party, Zakariya drank a lot of arak. At the end of the night he was exhausted and suffering from sharp stomach cramps, his forehead was sweating and his body wouldn't stop convulsing. Arif summoned a doctor from Azaz and it didn't require much effort on his part to diagnose Zakariya's condition. He said that Zakariya had drunk arak like a mule and his malady was just a fever that needed complete rest and some compresses soaked in a herb tisane and he would soon be cured. Arif conveyed Zakariya to a large room in Grandfather's house and instructed Shaha to change his compresses. She was delighted with this task and found herself so close to him that their breaths mingled. When the servant Mabrouk went to bring the firewood brazier, she seized her opportunity. She looked at Zakariya for a long time, she inhaled him slowly, she took hold of his fingers and rubbed them, she wiped his forehead with her palm and when he opened his eyes he saw her as an angel hovering overhead. Mabrouk came back and placed the wood in the brazier. Shaha was embarrassed, rose from her place and left, lingering at the door and looking at Zakariya with a smile.

The road to their house in Hosh Hanna was filled with the stories that Shaha was skilful in retelling. Half an hour before they arrived at the village, he pinched her chest. She leaned against him and said that his smell was the cause of her desire for him. Smirking at her, he asked, "What else apart from that?" and she replied, laughing and reaching coyly towards his sex, "Don't you know that smell wounds my heart?" It was the first time she told him about the invisible things that wounded her.

A year after their marriage, her happiness was overflowing. She joined in telling stories and daydreams, and Zakariya loved her generosity and her imagination when it came to love. He would always surprise her, and she responded enthusiastically to his imagination and his peculiar stories about horses and women when he narrated the details of his trips with Hanna, her brother Arif Agha, and the rest of their companions who adored uproarious parties at the citadel. Arif was the most resplendent of all the visitors there, obediently losing everything he won throughout the days of his stay. He would say that the gambler was a creature of eternal losing, and he liked this phrase so much he would reformulate it and repeat, "Gambling is eternal losing." He would roar with laughter, as usual, and add, "A winner is a cowardly gambler, and he should be ashamed."

Zakariya and Shaha led a cheerful life in the few years before the flood. Whenever he went on a trip with Hanna, he missed her. She enchanted him. She wasn't hostile towards the citadel, she didn't ask him to remain at her side, but after his marriage he didn't spend much time loafing around. Leaving Hanna drunk in one of the many houses they were both familiar with in every city, he would leave at dawn and return to her weighed down with gifts and desires. She loved it when he called her by the names of his horses, and his trade in them began to expand considerably after he added nine purebred Arabian stallions to his stable. A travelling broker displayed them to him, saying that he was selling them on behalf of the sheikh of a large tribe who didn't want to declare his name. Zakariya, who knew everything about the horses of his region, dispatched his groom to the sheikh who was staying in Khan Al-Wazir during his visit to Aleppo. Without mincing his words, the groom asked the sheikh if it was true he wanted to sell his nine horses, swearing to keep his secret. On receiving an affirmative reply, they agreed a price and the agent's percentage, and the sheikh surrendered the horses' deeds. Zakariya never forgot the moment they made their lofty entrance into his stable. He had dreamed of the day that such horses would be in his stable to fill out its shortcomings and make it into one of the most important stables in the Vilayet of Aleppo. Horse traders made a beeline for him, along with Bedouin sheikhs who loved horses, princes of distant regions, and hobbyist foreigners who couldn't believe this outstanding collection could be found in a single place – and enjoyed such a high degree of care. Their mangers were spotless, their saddles were hung in designated places like new clothes for Eid, and the spurs had the pleasant smell of gazelle leather. The place was always clean, as the four grooms (who also drowned in the flood) used to take it in turns to mix the dung with straw and muck out every six hours. The horses drank water from huge copper basins inlaid with tin, just like the rich people in the city. A long passageway separated the stables and the horses' overnight shelter from the large office composed of several rooms, its walls filled with walnut cabinets. Lined up on the shelves of these cabinets, the complete files archived in a single register, were the biography and the bloodline of each horse which Zakariya delighted in writing out in his splendid calligraphy. Alongside this was a special cabinet where the pedigree of every horse was lined up, written on gazelle leather, signed and witnessed by seven people of good standing. (Per the custom, Zakariya had memorised the lineage of the horses.) There was also a guesthouse attached to the stables, which were expanded several times over ten years. And in the stables in Anabiya he kept the several rare horses for breeding and crossbreeding. Everything was overseen by Yaaqoub, the most experienced groom in the vilayet.

On their first night back in the family home, Zakariya stayed seated on the sofa all night, watching Shaha drowning in uninterrupted nightmares. She had lost her magic, she aged suddenly. He had always believed that coming back to the family home was a bad sign, a man losing his dream, especially if the place was tumbledown, dripping the chronic illnesses of its elderly inhabitants, stinking of rot from being crammed with old furniture and his father's files, which he hated.

After the departure of Zakariya, who considered his friend's conversation about regret to be an evil omen, Hanna woke at dawn. He reflected that he didn't want to think about his new life. Instead, he let it seep away into the river that he had begun to see as a new river at every moment. He brightened at the thought that very little would suffice for him: a couple of cotton thobes and some garments he could gather in a single bag if he wanted to leave suddenly. Gone was his wardrobe that had contained sumptuous English suits and European hats, custom-made shoes and perfumes and rich objects that reeked of his adoration of the good life – all drowned. He thought that the Lord wanted him to have a new life, one he could touch with his hand and heart. Hanna resolved not to regret anything he was going to do from now on. Nothing would go back to how it used to be, no matter how many times Zakariya repeated it; he himself was wagering that Hanna wouldn't be able to bear living among the meek, those who feared a bit of buffoonery.

Hanna wouldn't listen to his friends who came from villages and cities, far and near, to assist and condole with him. They brought with them carts loaded with enough provisions for hundreds of people: clothes, cured meats, lambs and cages filled with chickens, bottles of wine and cognac, excellent tobacco, and money. Hanna was silent, wouldn't reply to any questions, and wouldn't listen to condolences. After a few weeks he would no longer receive any of them. He pondered the meaning of death by drowning and wouldn't permit anything to enter his room. He asked his servant to take everything to the caretaker of the church in the nearest village so he could distribute it among the few families that had stayed by the river. He begged Zakariya to tell their friends not to bring anything with them, as what he already had was sufficient for him: a little bulghur wheat, olive oil, and some dried vegetables. But their friends wouldn't allow him to turn into a vagrant (or an imbecile, as they termed it), an ascetic renouncing property and uproarious living. Everything could be replaced as long as there still existed the thousands of dunams of his fertile lands, the olive groves that extended huge distances over the territory of Anabiya, along with his great citadel and its gardens of one hundred and twenty dunums planted with all types of trees, and the khans in the souq, and the four splendid houses in Aleppo that was only half a day's journey from this room that he kept informing everyone was enough for him.

Hannah felt like the flood hadn't just drowned his wife and son; it had drowned his sordid and uproarious past, his entire life. A wish welled up inside him for a new life. An image came back to him of Father Ibrahim Al-Hourani, the wanderer who came to Aleppo every now and again and stayed in a large room attached to the Syriac Catholic Church. Hanna would greet him silently at Sunday Mass which he was assiduous in attending, compelled as he was to prove that he was still Christian and hadn't turned into a Muslim, as the rumours went. Once, Father Ibrahim blocked Hanna's path and said, "You won't feel the power of weakness until you fall to the lowest point." Back then, he didn't understand why this man so venerated by the other worshippers had stopped him. Hanna didn't leave the church after the prayers were over. He knocked on the door of Father Ibrahim, who took him by the arm, and together they went out into the city's streets. They sat in a nearby coffeehouse and Father Ibrahim told Hanna that he had known his father Gabriel Gregoros very well. He had lived his entire life afraid of being massacred, of being forced to abandon his religion and convert to Islam. To be safe, he hid the money for the jiziya tax in a place no one knew apart from Ahmed al-Bayazidi, despite Sultan Abdel Majid I's 1865 proclamation of the Humayuni Edict which relieved non-Muslim citizens of the Ottoman empire from paying the jiziya. Gabriel hadn't believed that he would never pay the jiziya again and lived his whole life resigned to the idea of his death, so when the massacre took place, he was expecting it.

Continuing to address Hanna, who was unusually submissive, Father Ibrahim said, "You are not like your father but you will gradually transform into an exact copy of his original, and your wicked soul won't be saved unless you sink to the very lowest point and realise that everything you have ever done in your life is just meaningless ignominy." Hannah asked for his address and Father Ibrahim replied quietly, "You may consider me a person with no address. I walk this earth waiting for my death." He wouldn't permit Hanna to question him further. He rose smiling and left Hanna alone, turning into the street that led back to the church.

"This is the lowest point that Father Ibrahim was talking about," Hanna said to himself as he felt that life was passing before him, slow, pleasant, and lightened of material things. Death was walking lightly alongside, invisible, reaching out his hand to help if life stumbled. Hanna left his room at dawn, walking slowly over the flat ground that used to be the village his father had founded more than thirty years earlier, and which he had named after his youngest son. Hanna wished it would fall into oblivion forever, he didn't want anyone to remember it, he wanted to go back to the image of the first world. He felt himself to be a child, reborn into another life without a past. He was a blank page expelling a memory burdened down with the uproar and gaiety and pain of an entire life that was finished with now. He felt guilty and longed for his son, and the face of the gentle wife who had endured her life with him. From the first day of their marriage, Josephine had placed no reliance on his presence in their family life. She had gifted him to the distant wilds and the citadel of Shams As-Sabah with its uninterrupted caravan of women selling pleasure, with the troupes of musicians who played for days without stopping at the order of a group of landowners passing the winter immersed in gambling, and in sumptuous feasts prepared by Aleppan cooks who were adept at catering for the tastes of the band that Hanna and his friend Zakariya presided over. From Aleppo, Damascus and Beirut, they would invite women who had been hand-selected by a group of pimps throughout the year. In the middle of December, the women would arrive at the citadel on the small hill overlooking the ruins of Barad, accompanied by trunks of sumptuous, exorbitantly expensive clothes, all paid for by the men. They were shared out among the rooms of the citadel and would wander half-naked through the passageways, the large salon, the rooms, and the cellars tightly packed with bottles of fine wine and foreign drinks brought back by the men from their trips to Beirut, Baghdad, Damascus, Venice, Paris, Istanbul. They bought the finest alcohol from the Jews in Aleppo and sent the bottles to the cellar of the citadel whose every detail had been deliberated over and chosen by Shams As-Sabah herself: feather pillows, embroidered silk sheets, tall copper bedsteads furnished with mattresses of combed wool. She had gone to the trouble of selecting individual colours for the bedcovers in each of the nine rooms. The card table had been imported from London by a Jewish cotton trader from Aleppo. He had thought to open the first casino in Aleppo only for his plan to fail before it began when the men of religion attacked him in a Friday sermon and his friend Raoul the goldsmith asked him to abandon his project. The Jewish trader forgot the idea and sold the ebony table to Arif Agha, who donated it to the citadel along with a china service, copper saucepans, and cutlery fashioned from pure, unadulterated silver.

INTERVIEW

Lebanese novelist **Alawiya Sobh** speaks to **Katia al-Tawil** about her new novel and exposing religious fundamentalism in the Arab world

"To love life" means to be implicated, involved, to glow, to persevere in the face of illness

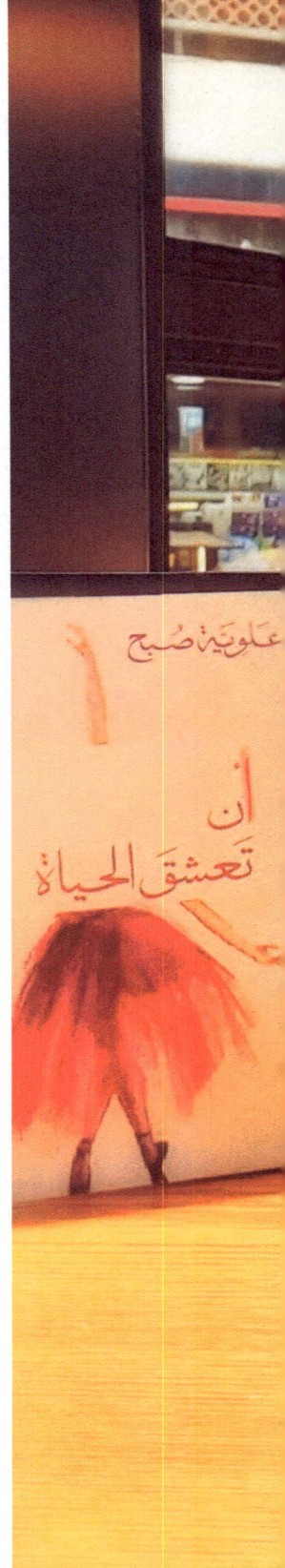

Lebanese novelist Alawiya Sobh is known for her deliberate, unhurried approach to publication and her ability to mould her texts and her characters with leisurely composure. In her artfully created novelistic spaces, Sobh fearlessly tackles issues relating to women, women's bodies and their thoughts in the context of our patriarchal Arab societies. After an eleven-year absence from the limelight, Sobh presents her readers with her fifth work, *An Ta'ashaq al-Hayat* (*To Love Life*) a novel in which, armed with art, love and beauty, she exposes the various forms of religious fundamentalism in which our Arab society continues to flounder. Out of the violence of ISIS and Hezbollah has emerged a meaty novel teeming with symbols and

Alawiya Sobh recently released a fifth and long-anticipated novel, *An Ta'shaq al-Hayah* (To Love Life). Her four earlier works are: *Nawm al-Ayyam* (The Days' Slumber) (1986), *Maryam al-Hakaya* (*Maryam: Keeper of Stories*) (2002), *Dunya* (2006), and *Ismuhu al-Gharam* (It's Called Love), (2009).

allusions which, making its way past censorship and national borders, delves deep into the stain of violence that sickens the Arab psyche. The novel is based on a conflict between art, love and life on the one hand, and disease, violence and religious fundamentalism on the other. The battleground on which the conflict plays out is at once the human body and the body of Arab society, where deliverance is found only by those who cling to their passion for life, art and freedom.

In this novel, Sobh exemplifies the disease afflicting Arab states that languish beneath the weight of violent religious fundamentalism through the body of her protagonist, Basma. After developing a severe neurological disorder, Basma's condition deteriorates whenever she witnesses news broadcasts showing the orgies of rape, murder and torture being indulged in by the blind followers of tyrannical, criminal organizations. At one point in the narrative, Sobh compels her heroine to wonder: "Did I make myself ill, or is it my country that's made me ill?" (p. 20).

Sickened by ISIS-like organizations (Sunni and Shia alike), Arab citizens have been robbed of their passion for freedom, culture and beauty. So long as these sightless, brutal entities exist, there will be no well-being, safety or health for anyone. The Arabs who are sick and imprisoned today are the same Arabs who once enjoyed centuries of flourishing creativity, art and culture. Aimless, displaced, and disease-stricken, life is as much a curse to them as death is. Describing her condition, the protagonist-narrator says: "Sometimes I'm lost to myself. I lose track of when I was born, of how old I am. I even lose track of my here and now. I can't tell where I am: am I in some wrecked, blood-stained room in Syria, or Iraq, or Libya, or Yemen? Or am I in a country where this room is all that's left?" (p. 10).

To Love Life is a narrative cry of rage in the face of alien, absurd religious fundamentalisms. It is a novel in search of the Arab soul, and in search of a way to cleanse it of the stains of blood, violence and obscurantism that have taken it over in recent years.

In the following exchange, conducted in Beirut, Katia al-Tawil interviews Alawiya Sobh about her newest novel and the ideas she hopes to convey through its characters and events.

KT: *How long did it take you to write this novel? And what are the main difficulties you encountered in the writing process?*

AS: This novel took me around ten years to write. In fact, I started it while I was working on another book. Then I developed a neurological illness, and the only thing I felt able to write about was my body and the spasms and pains I was enduring. The first five years of the process were extremely difficult, as it was hard for me to concentrate. I was determined to write every day, but because of my inability to concentrate, I didn't produce anything coherent. Some time after that, I came across more than thirty notebooks filled with disjointed words and phrases. The novel had been forming itself in my head during that period, and my imagination had been ignited in a powerful way, but it was only later that I wrote what I did.

KT: *In his review of your book, literary critic Abdo Wazen refuses to call it an autobiography. Do you agree with him on this point? And to what extent does your heroine Basma resemble you?*

AS: Abdo is right. It isn't an autobiography. Everything beyond Basma's physical suffering is fictional. I used to wonder to myself: if I'd developed this illness as a dancer, what would have happened to me? Consequently, I chose to have Basma be a dancer who suffered from the same health issue that I had. Everything having to do with the Lebanese war and the Arab wars in general, as well as with Basma's pain and her struggle with illness, is the outcome of my own experience. The ugly, devastating wars that were ravaging the Arab world had shaken me deeply, and I detected a resemblance between my pain-racked body and the cities collapsing around me.

KT: *The sick body in your novel becomes a battlefield between the passion for life and destructive religious fundamentalisms. In other words, it represents today's sick, exhausted Arab states. Are you drawing a parallel between betrayal by the body and betrayal by political parties, religions, states and societies? Do you intend for the pain of the body to enter into a struggle with the pain we experience in Arab countries?*

AS: In this novel, I express my anger at ISIS and Hezbollah equally, since, in my view, these racist, doctrinally bigoted parties are what have brought us to the mess we're in now. The killing and forced migration that have afflicted moderate Muslims, Christians and Yazidis fall on the shoulders of all these fundamentalists, Sunni and Shia alike. Practices and attitudes that violate women's bodies, their lives and their mere existence – treating them as public property – not to mention the fatwas that support these practices and attitudes, are bound to make a person angry. I am personally infuriated by both men and women who go along with the fundamentalist way of thinking that's landed us where we are now.

Bodily pain is a mirror of the pain being experienced by this sick society and its systems. My critique of our current reality is woven into the fabric of the novel. Furthermore, it is a critique of all political associations, from the Syrian Baath to the Iraqi Baath to Communism; similarly, it is directed against fundamentalism, despotic regimes, militant religious systems, Shia Islamic courts and sheikhs whose fatwas shackle Arab people as a whole, and women in particular.

The sick body in my novel is simply the outcome of all the heinous acts committed by these despotic regimes and these parties, whose leaders' only aim has been to profiteer from this cause or that. I've tried not to neglect any of the factors that have contributed to the ruin of Arab people's lives on the physical, emotional and mental planes alike. All of us are sick, oppressors and oppressed, slayers and slain. We're a sick society that suffers from serious disabilities and dysfunctions, and the lives of individuals have to be seen in relation to the political, religious and social systems and patriarchal values that surround them.

This novel isn't some ideological manifesto, but a cry of rage released through the creation of an angry novelistic world. Of course, my country has made me ill, and I say this emphatically. How could I not fall ill when I see Arab society collapsing around me in worn-torn countries such as Lebanon, Syria, Iraq, Yemen and Libya? We live in a state of madness unparalleled in history as Christians, Yazidis, neutral Muslims and others are raped and murdered. Whatever makes Syria, Iraq, Lebanon or any other Arab country ill, makes me ill too.

KT: We're accustomed to seeing you take up women's concerns and issues in your writing. In this novel, by contrast, you burden your characters with worries relating to issues of politics, party and religion as well. Why this new direction?

AS: In all my novels there's an obsession with giving courageous voice to taboos: religious taboos, bodily taboos, and political taboos. I don't believe there can be any creativity without freedom, and writing is freedom. A novel has to address human concerns. It conveys a vision. It makes a statement. It holds space for preoccupations, fears and worries. Unfortunately, however, most of the novels I encounter read like news reports.

In this novel, I've spoken of all the things that cause me pain. However, I don't feel I've weighed my characters down with the things I've given them to carry. The political voice in my novel isn't rhetorical or moralistic. Rather, it's woven into the fabric of a narrative whose characters are flawed and incomplete. A political preoccupation may be more evident in this novel than it has been in my other works. If so, I see this as a reflection of the political and social experiences of those living in the Arab world, and as a way of criticizing laws, systems and popular beliefs that impact Arabs and the course of their lives.

My novels are banned in most Arab countries. But I can't write if I try to restrict myself to what the censors would allow past their desks. I don't even know how to censor myself. My anger in the novel is directed against all systems, especially those that hinder the woman's freedom, contribute to her enslavement, or disregard the violence and tyranny she endures.

KT: *Throughout the narrative, readers encounter the horrific violence going on in Arab countries. There is such cruelty and bloodlust that you even liken the Arabs in one place to prisoners, saying: "At that moment I felt as though we were all trapped in a giant prison whose doors were impossible to open, as though one of the prison guards had thrown the key to the bottom of the sea. And here we are, imprisoned, as though we were dying" (p. 288). Why this narrative violence?*

AS: Of course there's cruelty in the novel. However, it's a cruelty mitigated by irony and poetic language. This is precisely what I put to use in my previous novels, including, for example, *Maryam al-Hakaya* (Maryam: Keeper of Stories), or *Dunya*.

ALAWIYA SOBH

Together with the experience of maturing as a novelist, my illness prompted me to tone down the shrillness of the text. My novel has been strengthened, rather than weakened, by poetry; fiction can be especially persuasive when its characters allow for this type of poetic language. I treat all characters and their cultures with the utmost respect, making sure that they have the artistic justification necessary to speak out of their own culture and their own natural inclinations.

As for the presence of violence and illness in the novel, the reason for this is my sense that our society is ill. Consequently, the characters embody the presence of death, imperfection and incompleteness. The body in this novel takes on a different dimension than those highlighted in my other works, since the stories of our bodies resemble the stories of our cities. The individual body and the country bear some resemblance to one another. These are the basic ideas posed by the novel in narrative form. The anger I felt and the pain that would come over me in response to the scenes of violence I used to witness led me to imagine numerous characters, most of whom suffer from some defect or dysfunction while being targeted by the arrows of violence that whizz about them.

KT: Your novel is filled with art. The main character is a dancer and a choreographer, her sweetheart is a painter and a poet, her best friend is a writer, and the man to whom she tells her story is a director. You say somewhere in the narrative that "writing, music and art generally can rescue a person from suicide" (p. 258). Do you actually believe that a return to art can be a kind of salvation?

AS: Art is a kind of therapy that causes us to grow deeper, more aware and more in tune with ourselves. Art is a key to discovering yourself and your surroundings; knowledge and culture enable you to be freer, more beautiful, more conscious. Knowledge changes people, and when they possess the capacity to read their inner states and express themselves, they change. This is why our Arab regimes are afraid of knowledge. They're afraid of the arts because they confront the brutality of society and, in particular, its brutality toward women and humanity as a whole. Our societies fear knowledge and, instead, promote the vacuous and the trivial. They fear knowledge because it's knowledge that introduces people to themselves and brings them freedom. That's why we see them popularizing 'the dark word', 'the blind word'. They promote human blindness because, if our society changed – if knowledge became a part of who people are – they would be sure to reject tyranny and darkness and begin to think about justice.

No entity on Earth fears knowledge more than our dark, tyrannical societies, especially those whose tyranny is directed toward the woman. I deal in my writing with the fact that, despite the ruin that's been caused by the failure of attempts to struggle against religious and political regimes, there remains a passion for life, for art. I share in my protagonist's passion for life, in her will and fortitude, and in her adamant determination to overcome illness. The character's passion for life, her resolve to resist illness and reclaim her body belong to me, too, and these are the things that will rescue us all.

KT: At one point in the narrative, Amina's character says: "Don't beautify me. Don't make me an attractive, sophisticated, strong woman like you. I'm afraid the man will run away" (p. 282). Why does this novel present us with male characters that are so deficient, and with female characters that are both weak and content in their weakness? Why these truncated models?

AS: Amina is aware of the fact that Arab men are afraid of strong women. So, not wanting to risk her chances of getting married, she prefers to appear weak. Women in our Arab societies are raised on the idea that the man's violence represents protection, strength, and a symbol of manhood. Viewing herself as men have portrayed her, the woman then becomes the fiercest advocate for the very patriarchal mindset and patriarchal social constructs that oppress her. But this terrible fear of women is something I don't understand.

I'm not against men, and I don't always portray men as bad in my novels. What I am against is the concept of male domination. Youssef, for example, the sweetheart and the husband, has a positive presence in the novel and in Basma's life. When he is a painter, and before becoming a member of Hezbollah, he believes in and promotes women's freedom. He encourages and embraces it. But when, as a reaction to his disappointments, sorrows and losses, he joins Hezbollah, he changes. Youssef is a dramatic character par excellence. He is a painter who, in a dramatic shift, joins Hezbollah. However, given that he is, in fact, a true artist, he must of necessity return to his art. When I describe Youssef's perception of the bedbugs in his house, this is a symbolic way of saying that a fanatical, closed society (a society of darkness) exudes "bedbugs" and stinking corruption. After his decision to join Hezbollah, Youssef continues to feel alienated from this decision, and love for life still lives inside of him. As a consequence, his final painting turns out more beautiful than anything he has painted before. However, it remains without a signature. Youssef's end is a symbolic one. Youssef's involvement with Hezbollah and the way of thinking associated with it is bound to be temporary, its flame bound to be extinguished. This is why I view this work as my most powerful novel in terms of symbolic meanings, imagination, and the issues it addresses.

KT: Why do we never learn anything about the man addressed in the novel – the "you" to whom Basma speaks throughout the book? Who is this unnamed man, this reader concealed behind the second person pronoun 'you'?

AS: Basma is in need of a neutral, anonymous figure; someone to whom she can reveal everything, pour out her story. What draws her to this person is the fact that he is a producer and a playwright who treats people with art, and because she needs to talk, to be healed. Narration is necessary for her recovery, in order for her body to heal and retrieve its memory.

Consequently, I wanted the person being addressed to be present yet absent: a mere reader, a listener. I wanted him to be a new hope, an open horizon that wouldn't interfere in events. Expressing things inevitably frees us from those things, draws us closer to ourselves, makes us stronger and more transparent. I didn't want this novel of mine to be just a personal cry. I wanted to put a finger on the pain experienced by Arabs as individuals, and specifically, the women among them. I wanted to strip bare the regimes of tyranny and the 'ISISes', both Shia and Sunni, of anything with a connection to extremist, tyrannical organizations, religious and political alike, within a narrative framework. And the result was this character.

This unnamed listener becomes Basma's physician, her book,

her healing. Basma is transformed into a Shahrazad who treats her pain by telling her own story, just as Shahrazad treated her beloved Shahriyar by telling him other people's stories. Nevertheless, Basma doesn't meet her listener in the novel. Will she meet him? We don't know. The answer to this question would require another novel. As Basma says at the end of the book: "Love holds many possibilities."

KT: Every one of your novels is a hymn to love, an expression of longing for love and a call to embrace it. Tell us a bit about the title 'An Ta'ashaq al-Hayah' – 'To Love Life'. What's the secret behind it?

AS: *'To Love Life'* means being implicated in life, glowing with life, letting life fill you. It means feeling the tremendous power of joy, resisting illness, riding out the bumps in life's road. Passion for life gives us all this beauty, and a sense of pride in our existence. It makes us feel alive. Nobody with a passion for life can be a religious fundamentalist. But it's a passion that's quite costly in our societies. *To love life* means to pay a price.

If Basma didn't love life with a passion, she wouldn't be able to triumph over her illness. Her passion for life is what seals her victory. Likewise, my own passion for life is what has enabled me to write, to recover my memory and my body.

On the personal level, I'm someone who believes in love, and I'm filled with love for all things beautiful. Life has no meaning without love, whether in the sense of romantic passion or of simple platonic goodwill. I believe in love's ability to heal not just this or that illness, but all of humanity. In this respect, I believe heartily in the expressions of Christianity that focus on the concept of love in the humanitarian sense.

My own experience in life has taught me that anyone who lacks love is incomplete. Love really does heal many conditions. It heals bitterness, hatred, despair, envy, fanaticism and all things ugly. Love changes the details of both the person who loves with a passion, and the object of that love. Love changes everything. In the words of my protagonist, Basma: "I'm a passionate lover of life, a passionate lover of art."

Translated by Nancy Roberts

ALAWIYA SOBH

THREE CHAPTERS FROM HER NOVEL,
AN TA'ASHAQ AL-HAYAT

To Love Life

TRANSLATED BY NANCY ROBERTS

Chapter One

"I've told you a lot so far, but I don't remember anything anymore. I can't tell my story in chronological order, but where was I? Can you remind me? Since getting sick, I've developed a habit that I don't know how to break. When I'm talking, and even when I'm not, I keep pressing on my wrist, as if I think that will keep my memory from slipping out of my head from all the sedatives and other meds.

"All I remember is that whenever I finish the first chapter, I find myself starting a new, different 'first' chapter. Then I start a second one, or a third one or a fourth . . . I've lost count of all the 'first' chapters in my story! My delirium, my forgetfulness, scares me to death, not because beginnings are so difficult and confusing, but because they've started to get mixed up with endings, like sleeping getting mixed up with being awake. There are no boundaries between things anymore, no separation between one time and the next when the present burns up the past and turns to ashes. The present's stained with blood. Even Nature's seasons have started to overlap and get all confused. Their names have changed as though they'd lost their memory, or as though they were sick and delirious like me. Time itself has become ambiguous.

"Please listen to me the way you do when we have long talks over the phone and we never run out of things to say. You don't have to rearrange the story to however suits you, or the way a novelist would do, or the way my friend Anisa does after she finishes the first draft of a book.

An Ta'ashaq al-Hayat, Dar Al-Adab 2020

"Let my story wander around lost, the way I do. When my body gets its memory back, my life will catch its breath, recover its chapters, its seasons. But for now, leave my words scattered just the way they are, and just the way I'm able to recall them on my own. Imagine what a struggle it is, what a war I have to wage with my memory, and how much I agonize! As if the war my body is waging against me weren't enough. I have so many thoughts, but they evaporate in a flash before I can tell you about them. I strain to recall this idea or that, or to grab hold of the thoughts that cross my mind. I'll be determined to put them in your hands, but they escape from me. It's like trying to fill a basket with water. Because of the sedatives, my memory is encased in a thick, white fog that feels as hard as iron.

"Sometimes I'm lost to myself. I lose track of when I was born, of how old I am. I even lose track of my here and now. I can't tell where I am: am I in some wrecked, blood-stained room in Syria, or Iraq, or Libya, or Yemen? Or am I in a country where this room is all that's left? I'll be so disoriented that I can't even conjure an image of my own face, and I need to look in a mirror to remember what I look like. I often don't recognize this woman with the spasm-contorted face, her features destroyed.

"I wander through the rooms and down the corridor, trying to recognize a place that seems unfamiliar to me. All my homes feel alien to me now: my body, my memory, Youssef, my country. When I get up in the morning to make my coffee, I often put two cups on the tray: one for me, and one for my mother, who died fifteen years ago, and swallow the lump in my throat. Sometimes I've got up off the couch at night, fighting off the convulsions racking my body, and danced around the room. Its walls feel like mirrors all around me, and my body is the audience clapping for me. I've become a friend of the night, even though that's when the pains are the worst. Sometimes I look out the window at that time and wonder: am I the shadows of its darkness, or a star in the sky? And it's such torture! When I walk down the street in the hot sun, I don't know which one is me: my body, or my shadow? I look at my body and I feel afraid of it, and I get the urge to cry. Other times I feel as though I've disappeared. I can't perceive my presence even in my own house. I'll imagine that I'm behind me. Then I spin around and around as though I were trying to find myself. Other times I've looked outside and wondered in a whisper: is that me in the dress hanging on the clothes line? And at those moments when I'm broken up over the breakup with my boyfriend Youssef and his betrayal of me, I feel as though I was born from a hot tear once shed by my mother who, although it was her nature to be harsh, even to herself, was pure-hearted and affectionate deep down. That tear is the womb that bore me.

"I don't know why, but there's one thing I'm sure of, namely, that I wasn't made from a man's rib. Rather, I was made from the ribs of my mother and my grandmothers. This conviction was solidified when, one terrifying, pain-racked night, all these women appeared before me. I was lying in bed, and my body was trembling like a feather being buffeted about in a storm.

"Our area was being ravaged by devastating wars at the time, and hearing terrible reports of things going on, I decided to darken the room, thinking mistakenly that the darkness would block out my pain and stop the convulsions in my body. But instead, I was seized by a fit of delirium from the high dose of sedatives I'd taken. I felt as though I was fading away into nothing, as though the darkness had completely dissolved me this time. I was absent from myself. Even Youssef was absent – Youssef, the one person who had never left my memory or my body for a single moment. I wept bitterly, but even my tears, copious though they were, started evaporating and collecting as vapour on the ceiling.

"Then, all of a sudden, at the peak of my out-of-body experience, I saw the spectre of a woman wearing a long, white robe and headscarf. Sensing that she must be the fairy godmother, I said to her: 'I'm sick, O Good One, and I'm being made sicker still by the oblivion that's devoured my memory. I don't recall my life. How can I

Alawiya Sobh, Beirut 2010 ©Samuel Shimon

recognize it when it's been lost to me, just the way my body has? I'm hurting, O Good One. I'm hurting.'

"Then I heard her voice ringing in my ears, saying: 'Stand up, woman, the way you used to. Dance the dance of the dervishes, and of the people whose hearts are pure. Dance all you can, and after reciting the Fatiha, repeat the words: "Your provision, Your provision, O God." Then light will come to you. You will feel it radiating from you, and you'll become as transparent as a crystal. When this happens, place your ear to the ground, and you'll hear your story. Remember that from dust we came, and to dust shall we return. Beneath the dust of the Earth lie all the stories of our lives, both present and past. You should know that every bit of time that passes of your life, be it a minute or a day, everything you experience, whatever you lose or whatever passes you by, takes part of your spirit and goes before your body to the dust. And when you die, your departure is simply your final story buried beneath this soil.'

"I trembled at her words, which sparked a longing in me to hear my own story. Doing as she'd instructed me, I spun and danced the dance of the Sufis until I felt a powerful light radiating from my chest and driving the darkness from the room. It wasn't long before my whole being was pure light. As I pressed my ear to the ground, I heard moans and tearful gasps coming from bones hidden away in near and distant layers of the Earth. I heard the weeping of the slain and kidnapped who had been buried alive. I heard cries of distress from women who had been raped and their throats slit. I saw children's severed limbs longing to be knit together once more and folded in their mothers' arms, their tiny hands never having developed to the point where they could grasp the dolls and toys that had awaited them on Earth. I heard countless stories of mothers in pain, and beautiful tales of love that brought joy to my heart, filling it with more light still. The stories were being told by waters that welled up from the depths of the Earth, as though love had been transformed into life-giving streams. But what I heard most frequently were stories of passionate love, followed by painful farewells that rang out from the Earth's depths. The accounts meshed and intersected, as though every particle of soil was now a story that I was hearing together with every other.

"Then I felt dizzy again, my sick brain about to explode. I pressed my ear more tightly to the ground in the hope of hearing about me. I heard my name and Youssef's being repeated over and over. Then everything went silent. Before I'd heard my own story, my light went out, and I entered once more into my dark delirium.

"I'd like to be able to remember my life in my mother's womb. If my body could obey me and repeat its journey through love, dance, and life, its rhythms could tell the whole story. I don't know how I ended up choosing you as the person to tell my story to. You aren't the only person who's urged me to talk!

"One time, Anisa said to me: 'Stories are what birth us. Stories are our mothers, Basma.'

"And now I want to be birthed again by my story."

Chapter Three

"The next morning, I trembled as I read about what the storm had done the day before. I tried to get Youssef to talk to me about the state he'd found me in, but he put me off.

"However, I don't want to do that to you.

"I'll finish the story for you, although words are like threads that get wrapped around each other. I think you really do want to know about my life, which makes me feel safe. It also strengthens my determination and my ability to express myself and remember the things I've been through. I need that kind of safety to be able to tell my story. It's so odd to feel you need somebody neutral, or possibly even a total stranger or passer-by, in order to be able to tell all. But this way, you don't feel you're being censored or judged. I long to be able to hear my own voice, with you listening, and to hear my own confessions, totally uncut!

"When I turn on the TV at night and see scenes of death, I think of a Hollywood horror flick I saw once where werewolves turned into wolves that came out of caves when the moon was out. I also think of a legend I read when I was a teenager about a man who turns into a wolf when the moon is full. Back then, I loved reading things like that, and I'd imagine I was experiencing them myself. I dream of writing a marvellous legend with my body some day.

"But Youssef was never a wolf. To me he was the moon, and he did a number of paintings showing the moonlight reflected off the night sea. Missing him, and feeling hurt and abandoned, I headed yesterday morning for the seaside spot that had brought us together for the first time.

"My eyes wandered lost in the blueness of the sea, causing me to forget my spasms. There was a small wave lapping against a boulder, the sound of which reminded me of our first kiss.

"That was the first time Youssef had called me by name: Basma. Up until then, we hadn't been close, and he'd addressed me as 'Madame' or some other formality. After finding out how crazy I was about a certain folksy seaside café, he'd invited me for breakfast there. We were sitting at a wooden table together and I was talking to him about a project that involved turning poetic texts into a dance performance. His interest piqued, he got excited about the idea and started asking me all sorts of questions. He encouraged me, telling me he believed in my talent, and offered me any sort of advice or help I might need in deciding which texts to use. His enthusiasm gave me a sense of warmth and intimacy that I'd never felt with anyone before. I noticed that poetry was a point of connection between us, and before I knew it, I was drowning him in details, even though I'm usually the type to keep mum about a project until it's performed on stage.

"He had an attractive, confident, sonorous voice, and a calm, balanced temperament, despite his wild and wonderful creativity. Then there was his flirtatious grin, and those shoulders that made me want to come at him full speed and leap on top of them. The details of his face, his entire aura – everything about him, actually – was familiar to me somehow. It was as if he wasn't just close to my heart, my imagination, or my memory, but lived inside them. How had this happened, and why? I didn't know. In spite of the ease I felt with him, I felt flustered and confused. Yet, it was an ease I hadn't experienced in a long time. I realized, of course, that it was the spirit of my first love, Ahmad, who had led me to Youssef. But why to Youssef in particular? He said to me once: 'Who can say how spirits connect and why some are attracted to each other?' Another time he said: 'Don't be fooled. The body is a person in its own right. It has a voice. It speaks. It goes silent. It loves. It hates. It cries. It laughs. It longs. It understands and feels confused. It accepts and rejects.'

"I kept thinking about whether Youssef was the man of my dreams, or someone I'd loved in a previous life. Then again, I thought: maybe he's the headstrong force of love that tries to bind the present and the future to the past, including even the distant past, and, just possibly, to the realm of the unseen?

"When I told Anisa later about the questions that had my head spinning, she said: 'Sudden passion generates all sorts of feelings. And they might all be genuine.' Then she added: 'Listen, girl: forget the questions, and just be happy. You're lucky. There are people who grow up, marry, and become grandparents without even once knowing what passion feels like.'

"We were sitting by the seaside, and I was wearing a bronze-yellow blouse with a golden sheen to it, its top buttons undone. (I knew he adored this colour. One day when we were in his studio, he'd given it a number of different names, one of which was 'the colour of ecstasy.') I was sitting there jabbering away at him excitedly when suddenly I was seized by the gleam of desire in his eyes. They felt like a pair of wings that had swept me into an ardent embrace and taken me soaring. Without thinking, I reached out and took his hands in mine. Ablaze with the heat of passion, they gave me a sting that shook me to the core. So, hands have their own kind of embrace, one that engraves love's tattoo in the beloved's for as long as time shall endure.

"What else can I tell you? I don't know if I mentioned it to you in one of the first chapters, but I always used to feel as though there was a thick layer of frost between my ribs. It would be there even in the height of the summer heat, and no matter how profusely I was sweating. After I came to love Youssef, I felt as though it had melted and been replaced by a tiny sun whose intense warmth seeped into my entire body.

"Youssef! How could he have erased himself the way he did? How could he delete the old Youssef and become somebody else? Turn from a spring into a turbid swamp? Commit murder in the first degree against his own soul? What scared me the most was that his eyes took on a lustful gleam that was more absent than present. Had he become like the bloody world outside? It was a question I was afraid to ask myself. I didn't want to be unfair to him. Lots of other questions crossed my mind too, but I refused to answer them."

***

"I'm going to tell you about something strange that happened to me. And please don't think it's some fiction born of my delirium.

"It was one in the morning as I recall, and I was thinking about Youssef. I noticed that the television was blasting, but I was so distracted that I couldn't see or hear a thing. Then my attention was arrested by a fundamentalist preacher on one of the religious channels. He had a long, hennaed beard that came down to his belly. I was afraid of him. He looked like a wolf that had come out of some cave to prey on viewers' minds, devour their lives and their bodies. All I heard was his last sentence, which was a fatwa allowing a husband to have sex with his dead wife. I was so revolted, I sank into a funk.

"I felt the need to read some poetry, the way I do sometimes after hearing and seeing reports on the appalling wars that are doing my body in. Turning off the TV, I randomly picked up a poetry collection by Mayakovski that had been lying on my desk. I had the urge to read something that would carry me away to distant orbits, where I could enjoy the fruits of a lovely astonishment, the kind of warm-hearted delight that would bring sleep to my eyes. I imagined the lyrical words carrying me to bed and laying my body down to calm its worsening convulsions, at which point I would slip into a peaceful slumber. Poetry gave me the sense that I was closing my eyes to the image of Youssef, who had absented himself from me. He used to read me amazing verses that he'd composed. I encouraged him to publish them in a collection, but he rejected the idea. 'I'm a painter,' he said, 'although every now and then, when I feel as though a painting has been saturated with colour, I have to resort to words to convey what I need to.'

"After reading a few pages out of Mayakovsky's collection, I came to a passage in the middle of the book where he says:

> If you prefer,
> I'll be pure, raging meat
> Or if you prefer,
> as the sky changes tone,
> I'll be absolutely tender,
> Not a man, but a cloud in trousers!
> ....
> I'll cherish and love your body
> as a soldier,
> mutilated by war,
> useless,
> alone,
> cherishes his one leg.*

"When I turned the page, I came across two pieces of paper, folded up and badly creased, inside the book. I unfolded them and began reading what was written on them. Their contents were hard to make out, as the handwriting was tiny and uneven, and some of the letters had been swallowed up due to an unsteady hand. But here is what I read:

I'm surprised at how alien my body feels to me. I feel crippled, unable to stand. It's abandoned me, and in its place it's left something that bears no resemblance to it, as though I were walking on crutches of air. I'm vexed by a feeling that I'm inside of something resembling the body, but that I can't fully trust.

"These words brought back the memory of Youssef's abandon-

---

* John Glad and Daniel Weissbort (eds), *Russian Poetry: The Modern Period* (Iowa: University of Iowa Press, 1978), pp. 9, 27.

ment, as though my body and Youssef had united inside me. On the other hand, it wasn't an abandonment. It was something I didn't know how to name or describe. I'd have to figure it out on my own.

"My body doesn't allow me even a moment of quiet. When I was little, I struggled to overcome my terror and hatred of it. It was like an enemy that taunted me. I worked hard to be reconciled with it. I wanted us to live together in peace. So I taught it, and it taught me how we could be one. As I learned to listen better to my body, I began to understand what was happening to it. I would stay away from anyone it didn't like, and we stopped heaping abuse on each other, my body and I. I pampered it, showered it with love and affection, especially after dancing, when I'd be flying with elation. When I took a shower, I would scrub it with soap and a loofah. I would pass them over its every part, taking delight in each one. As the shower head sprayed down on me, rinsing off the soap, I'd feel as though God had opened the gates of Heaven's blessings. After bathing, I would massage it with sweet-smelling lotions and feel its intimate companionship and its gratitude toward my hands. As I gave it the freedom to laugh, it opened up to me. Its potentials were released, expressing themselves even in my tones of voice. They gave me my identity. Then love helped me get to know it even better, discover its true nature, as we exchanged gifts of tenderness and abandon.

"In dance, my body was liberated from the inhibitions that had kept it imprisoned, enabling it its full range of expression. When I danced, I would feel myself soaring above the realms of war and destruction. But now, my body seems caught in the thickets of its pain, or bound by a rope of iron. Its roots go so deep that I can't break loose. It holds the reins now, and lords it over me, preying on me like a wild beast. It's as though it's blind, and blinding me, trembling, and causing my nerves to tremble along with it. The muscles in my body and my face go spastic, and all I can feel anymore is my body's cracks and fault lines.

"What terrifies me is the way it's turned against me, as though it doesn't want me to live inside it anymore. I escape into sleep, and put it to sleep by force. It occurs to me that the painkillers and the sleeping pills might prevent it from escaping, or postpone its flight at least. Even so, it eludes me and disregards my authority, even while I'm living inside of it.

"It's hell to be betrayed by your own body!

"So now I'm entering into a new struggle with it. Maybe I confused it and caused it pain by not listening to its complaints. Maybe I abused it, made it angry. Or maybe it's running away from confusion. Did it want something I didn't? We've always been so frank with each other. We've never held anything back. So why is it doing what it's doing? I ask it, and it doesn't answer, as though it's either gone deaf, or just turned hard-headed. Then, when it speaks through its shudders and twitches, I don't understand what it's trying to say. And it doesn't hear me, even though there was a time when it listened to me avidly.

"My body slipped out of my grasp. Then it dropped me and left, so I have to remember the story on my own. I'm relating the story both to you and to my body so that it can recover the memory it's lost. I tell it in order to heal my body and myself, and to gain understanding. In spite of the muteness that's afflicted it, I know for a certainty that it will recover its memory and seize the ability to speak. Then it will become the narrator of the story: its story and mine.

"What's happened to this body that was so compliant and affectionate with Youssef? It's showing a side that's the very opposite of all the qualities I've ever known it to have. Yet something tells me deep down that I'm the only person who knows what's happened to it.

"I was shocked by what I'd read. Something bizarre was going on. Who wrote these things? I wondered. Might I have written them during one of my bouts of delirium and pain? But I'm not a writer. When I was in school, the Arabic teacher viewed me as a failure at language. As far as she was concerned, I had no talent for writing essays or anything else. My body was the gifted writer, the pen that transcribed through dance whatever I wanted to say. My body was my magnum opus, my only 'book' being the performances I'd done. So, these words must have been a message from my body to me, to help me understand the reasons for my illness and to recover from it. I remembered having a conversation with my body where I'd heard it telling me something similar to what was written on those two pieces of paper. But could a body write with a pen? What I was thinking was crazy, really crazy.

"But who besides you can I tell about the things that go on with me? Anisa wouldn't believe me if I told her. And Amina, who believes in spirits, is sure to tell me that some wraith wrote me the note. At the time I thought: might Ahmad's spirit have written it? Or maybe it was the fairy godmother who used to appear to me as a child when times were hard. Even my mother would see her dressed in her long white gown and headscarf! Is she the one who did it?

"Spirits and angels don't write to people. My mother told me when I was little that we have angels on our right and left shoulders that are constantly on the watch, and that write down all our good and bad deeds: what we do and what we think. At that time, during my childhood, I figured angels were God's scribes and that Heaven was full of books. So I figured I wouldn't know my own story until I got there.

"Whoever wrote those words, I convinced myself that they were a message to help me understand what had happened to me. The strange thing is that even though they were oozing with pain, they made me happy! It was as though they'd taken hold of me by the very thread that had been escaping my grasp. Just then, the electricity went out. I got up, lit a candle, and placed it in front of me on the table. Then my eye was caught by the wings of a white butterfly that had made its way somehow into my room. It hovered around the candle, but without coming too close lest it get singed, its wings forming the number 7 in Arabic, which is shaped like a V. The sight of it thrilled me. If you only knew what that luminous number has meant in my life!

"Then, with my eyes wide open, I saw my body running away, though I didn't know where. Taking advantage of a fleeting moment of pain so acute that it had robbed me of consciousness, it had separated itself from me and escaped. Terrified, I felt myself falling into a vacuum. I was bodiless, my limbs torn asunder and falling away from me. Letting out a loud moan, I peered outside, and what should I see, standing outside the door, but Basma, her body intact, ringing the doorbell. Overjoyed, I cried out: 'There's my long-lost body! It's come back to me after all this time!'

"After wandering for so long in places unknown, it had come back to me. It had come back to embrace me, and to be embraced by me. After all, what place but me did it have? Then I found myself swaying to the rhythm of music that welled up from somewhere in my body's memory. I pondered my legs, how they flexed and straightened with a suppleness I could hardly believe. Meanwhile, my desire grew more and more intense. I myself had become desire, and all feelings of helplessness, pain or weakness took their leave. They'd turned to ashes, and out of them emerged a tremendous will to triumph over my infirmity. I was determined now not to let myself be immobilized by my seizures. I refused to give in to them. The desire to dance and to restore my body to what it had been before charged me with a miraculous, irrepressible energy.

"I wished somebody had been there with me to see what I saw, and to witness my beautiful flight through space. I wished Youssef could have been there to celebrate me the way he used to do after attending my dance performances. He'd take me into his arms and dance around with me, and I'd laugh and laugh, my heart dancing for joy. And he would say: 'You were free as a bird, the queen of space!'

"Did this really happen to me? Or am I getting ahead of myself and anticipating things that are still to come in a later chapter? I get lost sometimes, confusing beginnings with endings."

Chapter Nine

"We hadn't been in the habit of talking about politics, so I don't know what got us on the subject of the 'Arab Spring' in a number of Arab countries, including yours. You told me things I hadn't known, of course, and about the transformations you and your friends had gone through. After recalling our conversation, I peered out into the darkness and heaved a sigh. Then I asked myself: 'Have I become a friend of the night all on my own, or do I have friends I don't know about out there?'

"What do you suppose Youssef's doing now? I wondered. Will a person be happy when his heart takes leave of his hands, his eyes, his memory, and the planet he lives on with the clean air, freedom and love it offers, then goes to some alien planet that he would have completely spurned before? I'll ask his friend Nizar the next time I see him. I'll be delighted if he's happy and at peace even though I'm filled with rage. My loving heart doesn't know how to hate. It's bound to forgive in the end, even if it can't forget the wound or the pain of parting. As I relate things to myself and to you, I suture my wound word by word. But its pain is still ablaze, etched into my soul. What a difference there is between the pain of loving union, and the pain of absence and illness! I remember Youssef telling me once: 'I love you so much, it hurts.' He likened it to the sweet ache spoken of by the Sufis, whose ardent longing is the source of such agony that it sets them wandering through the wilderness. But their pain is the balm of the joyful heart, O balm of my heart.

"Has my disappointment over Youssef become part of my disappointment over the broken dreams of the Arab Spring? It was a slap in the face that forced me to confront the changes he was going through. In my naiveté, I'd thought they were a passing phase, and that he'd come back to me again. But now they've opened up a chasm inside me, a chasm as deep as imperfection.

"Sighing, I sat back down on the couch, trying to figure things out.

"I started recalling the beginnings of the Arab Spring. Around that same time, Youssef had asked to be alone. Then he'd immersed himself in painting. He'd produced a lot of brightly coloured canvases, as though springtime had bloomed at his fingertips. Anisa and I were filled with a new revolutionary fervour as well.

"The only one who wasn't fazed was Nizar, who insisted that there was no 'Arab Spring' anywhere on the horizon, and who went on clinging in silence to the perceptions that had taken up residence in his head. Youssef concluded gloomily: 'When somebody buries his past and his memories, it's as if he's burying himself.'

"When I first started getting sick, even though I would go stiff in front of the screen, my body seemed to rise up and resist its tremors, as if it were saying no to them. Of course, they weren't as severe at first as they were later on. My mouth would go into spasms, and I couldn't control any of its movements. Then, as the condition progressed, my mouth would open all the way and refuse to close again. My tongue would go around and around in my mouth, then start twitching and loll out. I would grind my teeth too, and my voice turned thick and gruff on account of the medications. My chest muscles would tighten until I couldn't breathe, and my wheezing would fill the room. I felt as though the various parts of my body were attacking each other. Then my condition deteriorated even more. It was as if I'd been hit by a tsunami, and before I knew it, convulsions had invaded my entire body. My neck muscles tensed up and I felt as though I was about to choke. Before long, I was having spasms in my ears and every muscle in my body, including even my feet and around my eyes.

"I resisted, promising myself and my body that I'd get well, and that life would embrace me again the way I embraced it. I smiled, looking down at my body to see whether it had really started to live in peace. Then I looked away again so as not to see its convulsions or hear its rage. After seeing the rivers of blood in Syria, Iraq, Yemen and Libya on the television screen, it had started shaking like an earthquake.

"After waking from a long, drug-induced sleep, I experienced a few fleeting moments of peace, but they were gone before I knew it. Without noticing exactly what I was doing, I stretched out my hands in front of me as though I were trying to escape from my body and catch up with those lost moments of tranquillity.

"They'd been like a spirit exiting my body, and all that mattered to me now was to recover them, even if it meant becoming pure spirit and leaving my body behind. I was afraid of losing the spirit that had brought me joy and had remained untouched by illness. Then, remorseful, I resisted the urge to flee and apologized to my body, holding it in my arms like a baby I'd given birth to, and which had given birth to me."

***

"Anisa was busy writing her novel, and had gone a whole week without visiting me. But when she heard how exhausted I sounded over the phone, she rushed right over. My body had collapsed in no time, it seemed. I generally didn't open the door for anyone, but I could tell from the way she rang the bell that it was her. I made my way to the door, stepping slowly and deliberately so as not to fall. When she saw me, she stared at me in disbelief. I laid my head on her shoulder, and she took me into her arms as I swallowed a tear for fear of making her worry even more. Seeing the stunned look in her eyes, I gave her a reassuring smile. I wanted her to know how brave I was. Without saying a word, she sat down on the couch across from me, observing my spasms with a mixture of bewilderment and distress, and periodically turning her head to hide a tear that had trickled down her cheek unbidden. Other times she would bathe me in gazes of loving affection. I don't remember what we talked about. The words were few, surrounded by a silence that joined us in what felt like an embrace. As she was getting up to leave, I blurted out: 'I love you more than anything in the world, Anisa! You're a priceless treasure. Your friendship is healing, Anisa. It's my healing!'

"'Of course,' she said, looking surprised but happy. 'Our friendship is dazzling, abundant, like no other, and it will always be pure no matter what happens. No strings attached.'

"My voice weary, I added: 'My body seems to be sabotaging me on all these fronts, Anisa.' Then I fell silent.

"'No,' she said. 'I want you strong. Don't worry about anything but your health. I want you to face your illness with the power of your will, just the way I've always known you to do.' Nodding, I replied: 'I promise not to give in to being sick. I've always overcome suffering. You know how passionately I love life!'

"After Anisa left, I lay down on the couch, thinking back on how we'd met. It was July 1980, and she'd written a wonderful article on my debut dance performance. We were in the middle of the filthy civil war, but in that performance, my body had glorified life, love and peace. I'd called Anisa to thank her for the article, and we'd arranged to meet for coffee. The day we met, she brought her friend Amina, who headed the archives section of the magazine they worked for. The three of us became fast friends, and we've been tight ever since. (Despite my fondness for Amina, Anisa is the one I got closest to.) We were all so young back then, our bodies explosive and our heads full of dreams, the war notwithstanding.

"Anisa married young. As for Amina, the image she'd conjured of the man of her dreams had been erased by the years. All she hoped for now was some suitor who could satisfy her emotional cravings. However, nobody came knocking, despite her decent looks and her huge heart. Although she didn't dress conservatively, her religious views prevented her from pursuing a physical relationship with someone she wasn't married to. For some time, she'd found satisfaction in making use of her spiritual energy and her prophetic dreams. The presence of an unseen spiritual guide in her life had given her the solace and happiness she sought, a sense of having something special to offer. However, these things didn't satisfy her anymore, and she blamed her late grandfather for not appearing to her in a dream to bring her good news of a marriage proposal in the offing. At some point she had concluded that someone must have produced a magic amulet, tied it to a rock, and thrown it into the depths of the sea, and that this amulet was the source of a curse that prevented men from proposing to her. It was so potent, in fact, that even all the water in the sea had been powerless to nullify its effect by dissolving its pages or erasing its contents. Add to this the fact that her unseen spiritual companion, who could only deliver her from harm on dry land, was unable to reach the amulet in its hidden location deep beneath the sea. This companion would hurt people who had hurt Amina and, tender-hearted girl that she was, tears came to her eyes when she told us about this.

"Once, when the three of us were having dinner together early in our friendship, Amina told Anisa and me how her grandfather had pampered her because she was the only girl among six children. After he died, she said, his spirit had attached itself to her, and he'd started appearing to her in dreams. He would tell her things that would happen in the future, and his predictions would come true. Anisa and I were inclined to believe it, too. Many times she'd predicted things that actually happened. That same evening over dinner, Amina told us that after her first night vision came true, everyone in her family and even her entire village stopped dreaming altogether. Whoever did happen to have a dream would forget it as soon as they'd opened their eyes. She was the only person in the village who both dreamed and remembered what she had dreamed, as a result of which she'd been dubbed 'the dream snatcher.'

"She told us that lovers, young women anxious to find husbands, married women hoping to divorce or fearful that their husbands would take another wife, people dreaming of recovery from some illness – in short, all those with wishes they wanted fulfilled in their lives – would knock on her door and ask her if she had seen her grandfather in a dream, hopeful that he might have told her something about them. Whenever she answered this question in the negative, the inquirer would leave crestfallen, hoping and praying that the hoped-for nocturnal visitation might still come. Her grandfather's spirit had thus become the village clairvoyant, the one who could discern their secret hopes and fears and tell them what the future held for them, whether for good or for ill.

"I smile when I remember Anisa's rounded belly during the fourth month of her first pregnancy. On my way home from her house one day, I ran my hand over my own belly, wondering if I could put up with having a tiny life growing in my womb, and whether I'd look as beautiful pregnant as Anisa did. Thinking about such things sent a tremor of fear though my whole body – fear of the dilemma of unplanned motherhood. To this day, I haven't been able to identify the real reasons for a fear like this, except for the fact that I didn't want to tie myself down with any commitment that might rob me of my capacity for art. Dancing – like freedom, like love – had always been my most passionate pursuit.

"After Anisa married Riyadh, she was shocked to find out what he was really like. One day she said to me: 'If Jahiz had been Riyadh's contemporary, he could have written the entire *Book of Misers* with examples from the life of Riyadh alone. And if you compared him to Molière's miser Anselme, the latter would come out looking as generous as Hatim al-Ta'i*. Riyadh's fingers are like pincers – all they know how to do is grab. For all I know, he's never opened his hand to give anybody anything in his entire life! Even when he shakes somebody's hand, he extends his fist instead of his palm. He brags about the fact that he's never been to a café, even for a cup of coffee, unless one of his friends picks up the tab, since frequenting such places is, according to him, a sinful extravagance. I've caught him counting the eggs and packages of cheese in the refrigerator to see how many of them have been used up, and when he finishes doing the count, he goes berserk. He puts his head in his hands and wails: "O my God, there are monsters around here eating us out of house and home! Nobody has any fear of God, not even my own kids. What kind of a life is this!"'

"Once when we were sitting in a coffee shop, she told me: 'Sometimes Riyadh acts in unpredictable ways. So, for example, I don't tell him how much I make at the magazine, because he might take it from me. I hide some of it away for my personal expenses, though it isn't enough for me. But if I ask him for money to buy a dress because the one I've got is faded and worn out, he yells in my face, saying: "I swear to God, my grandmother went on wearing the same

---

* A sixth-century Arabian poet, Hatim al-Ta'i is remembered for his proverbial generosity; thus the expression "as generous as Hatim al-Ta'i".

dress for fifty years! What's wrong with your dress? It's pretty enough. It'll do just fine!'"

"Shaking her head with a sigh, she said: 'No miser will ever know what love is, Basma.'

"When I told her about the love and affection Youssef showered on me, she looked away dejectedly and said: 'Imagine. I take a bath and spray myself with perfume before getting in bed with my husband, but he couldn't care less. Believe it or not, I often catch him sniffing dollar bills, especially new ones. He'll take a big whiff and say: "The scent of a freshly minted dollar is sweeter than all the women and flowers in the world! After all, what good can they do me?"' He would say things like: 'If you got used to sniffing money, you'd fall in love with it too. Isn't there a perfume made from dollar bills? If you put some of that on, I'd love the way you smell! I swear to God, if there were a cologne out of greenbacks, it would take over all the markets. People would kill to get their hands on the stuff. They might end up having to close down all the perfume factories. After all, the perfumes they make now are just a waste of time.'

"Riyadh's emotional and physical stinginess tormented Anisa, turning her body cold and callous. His hands never caressed her. She never knew the feel of a loving kiss. His lips never once approached hers, or if it happened once by chance, they barely grazed them. Then in a flash, he'd take her from below. Never once had she felt herself transported by his glances the way a woman is by the gaze of her beloved. Never once had he kissed any part of her body. Instead, he would bite her all over with the appetite of a ravenous man, as if her body were some meaty delicacy. When she chided him once for his emotional and physical coldness, he cried: 'Aren't my sperm enough for you!? They'd fetch quite a price on the market these days!' Little did he know that as far as she was concerned, his precious sperm were little more than filth with which he polluted her on a regular basis.

"Before she fell in love with Musa, a well-known film critic, the light had gone out of Anisa's eyes. Even their whites looked jaundiced. But then she started to come back to life. Love awakened laughter she'd forgotten she was capable of. Musa was her window onto life, especially after the loss of her eldest son due to a medical error at the hospital. The pain of the shock had shaken her to the core, casting her into a state of paralysis. But by the power of her will she managed to heal, and she learned to love her body again after having developed an aversion to it with her husband. She was so in love, I started calling her 'Musa's mad woman.' She would have given that man her very soul, yet she refrained from giving him her body: throughout the years of their love affair, Anisa refused to sleep with Musa. Even so, she went on loving him despite her realization that the sensual prolongs love's lifespan. She told me she trembled at the thought that if she broke God's command by committing adultery, she might pay a price for her sin by one of her children falling ill, for example, or even dying. At the same time, she refused to call her feelings for Musa platonic. On the contrary, it was a love so passionate that it was neither dulled nor diminished by their abstention from physical pleasure. In fact, Musa grew more attached to her with every passing day. And for her part, their love was an earthquake that had turned her life upside down. Her ardour for him gave her the sense of being riddled with beautiful wounds of body and soul alike, wounds she referred to in her novel as 'love pangs.'

"Once, I asked her how all this love had gone on living in her heart for so many years without a physical relationship. And her reply was: 'Love is one thing, and sex is another. Love is there all the time, whereas physical intimacy takes up only moments of that time. I don't deny, of course, that those few moments are when love is ignited and intensified. But believe me, my relationship with Musa fills my heart with love's intensity. Love is the pulse of life. It's expansive enough to accommodate sex and lots of other wonderful things along with it. But for lots of people, sex may not be expansive enough to accommodate anything but itself. It's quite narrow, actually, and only appears otherwise to people who are obsessed with it alone to the exclusion of love.'

"Shooting me a reproachful smile, Anisa raised her finger in my face and added: 'Besides, its real name isn't sex, but lovemaking!'

"'In that case,' I objected, 'why won't you do it with Musa?'

"Her face tightened and she looked away before replying: 'Adultery is sinful, Basma. But you can train your body to obey you. My body has absorbed my fear of harm coming to my children were I to give in to its desires. In this sense, the body can be tamed and domesticated. But at the same time, it's transcendent and beautiful. So, in spite of my physical urges toward Musa and my desire to complete what's missing, my body responds first and foremost to my fears.'

"She and Musa would often get together in a coffee shop on Hamra Street that was a hot spot for intellectuals, journalists and writers. Other rendezvous points included the cinema, the theatre, a deserted sandy beach, or under a tree they happened to pass on a mountain road. After parking the car on the roadside, they'd sit under a tree for hours, engrossed in conversation. Their mutual exchange never stopped, even when they were pondering each other in silence. Musa loved her children and, knowing how attached she was to them, he would ask about them one by one. They knew everything about each other's lives and would phone each other several times a day, so there was a sense in which they were never apart. She didn't feel the sun had risen until she had heard his 'good morning'. 'And to you, sweetheart, the best of mornings', would come her reply. Then, before getting up to begin her day, she would pass the telephone across her face as though his morning greeting were his fingertips' gentle caress. As for their good night greeting, it began with his: 'Sleep peacefully, my gazelle'. Feeling herself a true gazelle resting in his arms, she wouldn't notice her husband's snoring.

"Both of them were cinema buffs and huge fans of Ingrid Bergman flicks. Later on, they also fell in love with Meryl Streep and Clint Eastwood. They watched nearly everything these actors had starred in, and they would get into long discussions of what they'd seen. Sometimes when they disagreed, one or the other of them would stick doggedly to this opinion or that, but no matter how vehemently they differed, it never ruined the mood between them. They were especially fond of the movie in which Meryl Streep and Robert De Niro meet on a train while De Niro is having problems with his wife, and *The Bridges of Madison County* starring Meryl Streep and Clint Eastwood. Anisa said to me: 'We identified completely with the two main characters. I'd imagine I was Meryl Streep, and Musa would imagine he was De Niro or Eastwood.'

"One day, Riyadh's younger sister, who was married to a rich Emirati, invited the family to spend the Eid holiday with them in Turkey. She sent them the tickets and made them reservations in a fancy hotel in Istanbul. Well, Riyadh was over the moon, dreaming about the cash she was going to shower him with and all the free food at posh restaurants. But life has a way of crossing us. Anisa called me from Turkey and said: 'I can't believe it, Basma. Musa's died of a heart attack. I'm devastated, but I can't cry, and my body's aching for release. So, can you let me hear you sob out loud, Basma? Let me hear you bawling. I feel like I'm screaming on the inside, so I need you to scream out loud for me. Let your tears flow for me. Cry like you've never cried before, Basma. Be me. Be me, please!'

"Once, after she got back from Istanbul, she dialled his number by accident when she was meaning to call me. She said she felt as though her heart had fallen out of her chest. She lost all her strength and collapsed on the floor. She couldn't walk anymore, or even stand up. 'Basma,' she said to me, 'His number's still here, but he's gone! When it hit me, I started to cry without making a sound. Tears were streaming down my face. When my daughter asked me what was wrong, all I could do was take her in my arms and say: "I'm tired, sweetie. I'm just tired."'

"She said: 'I picked up the telephone and thought: I've got to delete the number from my contacts. But I couldn't bring myself to do it. I tried again, but I felt like I was committing a crime, so I left it on my phone. I felt as though, if I deleted it, it would be like announcing his death to myself!'

"Then she asked me a question that took me by surprise. She said: 'Basma, do you think he would have died if we'd had a physical relationship?' I didn't answer her. She went on to say that she felt as though she was the only person who knew the secret behind his heart attack, just as she'd known his secrets in life. Over and over, she said: 'My love killed him, Basma. If only I'd divorced Riyadh and married him. The reason I didn't is that I was afraid that if I divorced Riyadh, he'd deprive me of my children. They're my life. At the same time, my love for them defeated me. It broke me. You've never experienced motherhood, Basma. But I can tell you this: it's the hardest job in the history of mankind. And it keeps getting harder.'

"Musa had never married, but for ten years had gone on waiting and hoping for the day when she would ask Riyadh for a divorce. So his death left her guilt-ridden. In spite of her usual obstinacy and strength of character, she was stricken with paralysis all over again.

"I'm sure I can go on with my story. Although, so far, I still don't know what will trigger my memory, or what it will come out with. But you can help me by telling me what things you're curious to know more about!"

MAHMOUD SHUKAIR, WRITING JERUSALEM

Mahmoud Shukair was born in 1941 in Jerusalem and grew up there. He studied at Damascus University and has an MA in Philosophy and Sociology (1965). In 1962 he started writing short stories, publishing them in *al-Ufuq al-Jadid* (New Horizon) magazine, whose first issue was launched in 1961.

Since then he has published sixty-seven volumes of works, including fourteen collections of short stories, three novels and more than forty books for children, a volume of folk tales, a biography of a city, and a travelogue. In addition to these, he has written six series for TV, four plays, and countless newspaper and magazine articles, including for online publications.

He worked for many years as a teacher and journalist, was editor-in-chief of the weekly magazine *Al-Tali'aa* (The Vanguard) 1994-96, and editor-in-chief of *Dafatir Thaqafiya* (Cultural File) magazine 1996-2000, when he was also director of literature for the Palestinian Ministry of Culture.

Mahmoud Shukair was jailed twice by the Israeli authorities, spending nearly two years in prison, and in 1975 was deported to Lebanon. He lived in Beirut, Amman and Prague before returning to Jerusalem in 1993, where he has continued to live since then.

Mordechai's Moustache and his Wife's Cats and other stories, (Banipal Books, 2007), was his first collection in English translation.

Collections of short stories

Khubz al-Akhareen (Other People's Bread), Jerusalem, 1975
Al-Walad al-Falastini (The Palestinian Boy), Jerusalem, 1977
Tuqus al-Mara'a al-Shaqiya (Rituals of a Wretched Woman), 1986
Samt al-Nawafith (The Windows' Silence), Damascus, 1991
Dhil Aakhar lil-Madina (Another Shadow for the City), Jerusalem, 1998
Murour Khatif (A Rapid Passing), Amman, 2002
Surat Shakira (Shakira's Picture), Beirut, 2003. Italian translation published in 2014.
Ibnat Khalati Condoleezza (My Cousin Condoleeza), Beirut, 2004. French translation published by Actes Sud, 2008, and Italian translation published 2013.
Baha Saghira li-Ahzan al-Massa' (A Small Courtyard for Evening Sorrows), Beirut 2004
Ihtimalat Tafifa (Slight Possibilities), Beirut, 2006
Maraya al-Ghiyab (Mirrors of Absence), Beirut, 2007
Al-Quds Wahdaha hunak, Beirut, 2010. English translation, *Jerusalem Stands Alone*, by Nicole Fares published by Syracuse University Press, USA, 2018
Madinat al-Khassarat wal-Raghba (City of Loss and Desire), Beirut, 2011
Suqouf al-Raghba (Roofs of Desire), Haifa 2017

Three novels, published with Naufal Books, Beirut.

Faras al-'A'ilah (The Family Mare), 2013
Madih li-Nissa' al-'A'ilah (Praise for the Women of the Family), 2015, shortlisted for the International Prize for Arabic Fiction 2016. English translation by Paul Starkey published Interlink, USA, 2018
Dhilal al-'A'ilah (Shadows of the Family), 2019

Mahmoud Shukair's latest work

Tilka al-Amkina, Sira Thatiya (Those Places, An Autobiography), published by Naufal Books, Beirut, 2020

MAHMOUD SHUKAIR

Three short stories
THE WAY NAOMI CAMPBELL WALKS,
PABLO ABDALLAH'S SEAT,
RUMSFELD'S BANQUET

TRANSLATED BY SAMIRA KAWAR

The Way Naomi Campbell Walks

Her father saw her passing through the large gate as she came home from university. Her body was crammed into blue jeans, she held her mobile phone to her ear as she took a call she had apparently just received, and her long soft hair fluttered across her forehead and on her shoulders. He found out only a short time later that her trousers had provoked a problem in the neighbourhood.

Nahla knew that an unintended problem had occurred. How she hated that neighbourhood! She hated it for forty-one reasons (but didn't have the time to list them). She would go to university in the morning, crossing three military roadblocks and sometimes four, to get there. In the early afternoon, she would leave university, taking the same route she had taken in the morning. She would join the crowds at the roadblocks with different kinds of people, entering Jerusalem after an exhausting effort, and head straight home in a city suburb, feeling that she was entering an area where the rational and irrational lived side by side.

Nu'man al-Mahboul had triggered the problem, and Rabah al-Az'ar had been the reason. As Nahla walked down the road leading to her home, she caught the attention of the young men congregating on the pavement. They stared at her body with a greed that was intensified by Nahla's eye-catching clothes, or at least that is what they felt: various soft exciting dresses, wide slacks, and this time, blue jeans in which Nahla seemed to be appearing for the first time, or at least that is what her ardent admirer Nu'man thought. Nu'man was head over heels in love with Nahla, but she was not in love with him, or that is what his friends told him. He would not believe them, or be convinced by their words. He insisted that Nahla was in love with him, but that she was hiding her love, and would only reveal it once she had completed her university studies.

Rabah al-Az'ar was unable to control his impressions as he caught sight of Nahla, the daughter of the animal feed merchant, swaying down the street, her full hips swinging left and right. He thought that a quick comment on the bewitching spectacle would score several points in his favour: it would draw Nahla's attention to him, so that she would consider him as she thought about young men. It would give her the impression that he had a certain degree of culture, and it would please her, because he reckoned that girls liked to hear praise for their beauty and pleasing looks. And he would gain the edge over his friends, who would be unable to keep up with his ability to flirt with girls. In a voice that assailed Nahla's ears without permission, he commented on her gait, "My word, just the way Naomi Campbell walks, Mashallah."

Nahla walked away from the young men towards her home and said nothing. She continued walking in the same way, and Rabah al-Az'ar received a massive punch to his nose from Nu'man. Provoked, Rabah yelled, and Nahla turned round to see what was going on, then continued walking. Rabah al-Az'ar and Nu'man al-Mahboul got into a big fight, which did not only affect the two of them. Nu'man's family and relatives came to his rescue and joined the fray, as did Rabah al-Az'ar's family and relatives. A huge fight broke out in the neighbourhood because of Nahla's trousers, in which she had paraded herself before the neighbourhood's young men, swaying as she walked like Naomi Campbell, or at least that was the creative way that Rabah al-Az'ar had described it, taking Nu'man by surprise.

Nahla's father caught wind of the news, and realised that he was facing a three-pronged problem. He reckoned that keeping quiet about it would shame him till his death! And who said he was willing to keep quiet about such news. He thought about getting into his Mercedes and driving along the street, running over any member of the al-Az'ar family he found before him, because it was not acceptable that his daughter should be likened to a woman, who, according to the context of what was being said, seemed to be dubious, or to be following an irreputable shameful path, and he could not possibly allow his daughter's honour to be injured.

But the animal feed merchant thought better of going to battle in his Mercedes, because it was new. He had bought it a few months earlier, and members of the al-Az'ar family might be able to jump aside to avoid it, so that he wouldn't be able to run them over. Then they would stone his luxury car, which would become an easy target, and he would come out from such an ill-considered and improperly planned round as the loser.

The merchant glanced at his grandfather's sword, which was hanging on the wall. It occupied its space calmly and unobtrusively, having turned into an ornament that no one carried or dared take out into public places, because that would lead to its confiscation and land the carrier in prison. He brought the sword down from its place on the wall, paying no heed to what might happen. He wiped off the accumulated dust from it, and went to the enclosure where he kept the mare that he had bought from a poverty-stricken Bedouin. He used to ride the mare on holidays and feasts to show off and remind the neighbourhood folk that he was the scion of an old, well-established family. Calling out to members of his extended family, he shouted "Where are the brave noble men?" His call was met by responses from every direction, "We're here for you, take heart."

The merchant went out to battle with forty members of his extended family, armed with clubs and chains. One of them was the young doctor, who had graduated from a Turkish university. They congregated in the public square, looking like an army in a poorly produced Arabic TV serial. The merchant couldn't find any members of the al-Az'ar family in the street or around the houses, and felt a relief that he held back from expressing. Addressing his relatives, he said, "It seems someone told them that we were advancing on them." He pulled the sword out of its scabbard, waved it about to announce the start of the battle and spurred the horse, and it galloped quickly ahead. But his relatives stayed put, because they couldn't see anyone to fight. Members of the al-Az'ar family did not want to intercept the merchant as he drew near their homes, for some reason or other. They let him ride around the street on his own, although they could have smashed his head in with stones from their hiding places on the roofs. But they did not. The merchant rode around close to their houses several times, pretending to defy them daringly and effectively, then decided that his assault had achieved the desired results. Not wanting to take things too far, he thought it best for him and his relatives to withdraw quietly. But the arrival of a military jeep took him by surprise before he could announce this to his relatives, although it seemed as though they had divined the plan before he could inform them of it, and had withdrawn as though nothing had happened. The merchant was unable to withdraw, because the military jeep drove up close to him, blocking his path. He was unable to return the sword to the scabbard, fastened to his right side beneath his cloak, because that would have required raising the arm of his hand holding the sword to point in downwards so that it could be slipped back into its scabbard. By then, the soldiers would have disembarked from the jeep and seen the sword. So he hid the sword under the leg that was pressing against the horse's belly, and drew the cloak over his body. The soldier said, "Has there been a fight over here?"

"No, there hasn't been a fight."

"Are there any arms here?"

"No, there aren't any arms."

"You, have you got a revolver with you?"

"No, I haven't got a revolver with me."

In the meantime, the mare did not feel like standing still, so it moved its neck proudly, dancing around on its hooves. With each dance step, the sword hit the merchant's leg, causing it to bleed in several places. He bore the pain, waiting for the military jeep to leave. The soldier walked around the horse once, surveyed the horse and its rider, then turned around and got back into the jeep, slamming its door shut. The merchant went home with his leg dripping blood.

Members of the animal food merchant's extended family, led by the young doctor who had graduated from a Turkish university, tended to his wounds, as he complained and showed his ire. They bandaged his leg and sat around him in the reception room, trying to soothe him. He tried to recall the incident from its very beginnings in the hope of finding out something reassuring.

"What's her name? Naomi."

The young doctor responded, "Yes, Naomi Campbell."

"And pray who is she?"

"A well-known fashion model. I see her on TV."

"And does she behave in a way that impugns her reputation?"

"God knows! But I haven't heard anything bad about her."

"Where is she from?"

"From England."

The merchant's half-brother, Abdul Baset, who claimed that he knew the genealogies of the entire city and its various neighbourhoods did not like what he was hearing, because he thought it undermined his own knowledge and information. He said to the young doctor, "You're imagining things. She's neither from England, nor from Italy."

The young doctor fell silent, blaming himself for having spoken.

The merchant said, "So where is she from, Abdul Baset?"

Abdul Baset responded to his half-brother, saying "D'you remember, Abdallah, the young man from Jaffa who used to work at Mohammad al-Khalili's bakery on the way to the valley?"

"Yes, I remember him. His name is Kamel."

"You're right. Kamel Abdul Hay. He had a dark little girl called Ne'mah.

"Do you mean to tell me that Naomi is the daughter of the bakery's errand man?"

"Yes, and her name is Ne'mah Kamel Abdul Hay."

"Naomi Campbell! The daughter of the bakery's errand man."

"That's right, her father emigrated and took her and her mother and her brothers and sisters abroad. They emigrated."

A loud argument erupted over the surprise that Abdul Baset had sprung. The young doctor, who was a TV addict, couldn't bear to keep silent about such incorrect information, and tried to find an opportune moment to say something, but he could not get a word in edgewise, and he blamed himself for getting involved in a miserable, meaningless row. But he then rationalised his self-blame, realising that he had to keep up with his relatives for fear of being branded a coward.

Abdallah complained about the loud jumbled conversation, and said, "Let's change the subject, let it be."

The voices fell silent and no one left the reception room out of respect for Abdallah, as everyone attempted to comfort him.

Abdallah remained silent, and secretly cursed his daughter Nahla, who only took his advice with difficulty. He had suggested to her that she should get married when she had received several proposals, but she had rejected all of them, saying she wanted to pursue university studies. OK, she had gone to university, and we started hearing talk. Talk about whom? About Nahla. Today, Nahla was out in a short dress, today, Nahla was out in a blouse that revealed her bosom, today, Nahla is wearing jeans. And now, Rabah al-Az'ar says that she is like Naomi Kamel Abdul Hay, the bakery errand man's daughter. Worse still, the idiot Nu'man is very attached to the girl, and watches her whenever she leaves or comes home. And what's the story? Nu'man is in love with Nahla and wants to propose to her once she has finished her university studies, and Nahla is not even aware of him and doesn't care. The bastard! If only he hadn't punched the other bastard. If only he had pretended not to have heard what al-Az'ar had said, the problem would not have happened. But no, he had to go and punch him in the face, and then there would be a problem, and the whole neighbourhood would hear about what happened, and everyone would ask, "What caused the problem?" The cause was the daughter of the merchant, Abdallah. It was caused by the jeans of the merchant's daughter, the cause was that she did not walk the way other girls walk, she had to sway while she walked, like Naomi Kamel Abdul Hay, the daughter of the bakery errand man.

The merchant could no longer control his emotions or hide his anger. He felt it eating at his insides. He got up to walk towards the sword, but his wounded leg let him down, and he walked with difficulty. His relatives stood up and surrounded him including the young doctor. They thought he wanted to launch a new attack on the al-Az'ar family, or on the family of Nu'man, who had caused the scandal. They almost yelled in unison, "We're here for you, take heart." But he said, "Bring me Nahla's trousers, they're the reason for what happened. I will shred them with this sword and be done with it."

The merchant thought that such an act would make him seem like a merciless killer to his extended family, and would somehow help restore his reputation, and would scare Nahla.

Three of her brothers headed to her bedroom. She was holding her mobile phone to her ear, immersed in taking a call that she seemed to have just received. The three brothers busied themselves searching her cupboard for the jeans, while she continued to utter sweet words on the phone in a low voice, laughing intermittently. The three brothers kept looking for the jeans, but couldn't find them. Then they looked at their sister and noticed she was still wearing them. They waited a while until she finished speaking to her girlfriend (or so it seemed). The older brother pointed at her jeans and said, "Take them off."

"What did you just say?"

"My father wants to shred them with the sword."

There was a look of surprise in her eyes, and she said with a sudden calm, "You just relax, I will go to him myself."

She headed for the reception room, oblivious of the consequences. She walked in on the men crowding around her father, and stared at their faces in surprise. They started at her curiously. They saw a pretty girl with a docile expression, and they felt embarrassed. Her father surveyed her in amazement, because he had not expected her to walk into the reception room when it was full of men, since that broke a principle followed by all the women in the family. The animal feed merchant felt that his hands were tied. He threw the sword into a corner, unable to do a thing. The young doctor bowed his head in respect for that decision. The merchant said to his daughter, "Get out of here, get out!"

Nahla walked out and went back to her room. She took her trousers off, got into bed and went to sleep. But neither her father, nor the men in the family, including the young doctor, could sleep till daybreak.

Pablo Abdallah's Seat

Kadhim Ali was sad that morning, because certain things were not going the way he wanted. He was sad because the famous footballer, Cristiano Ronaldo, had promised in an internet message to visit him, but had not kept that promise. Kadhim had prepared a room in his house for Ronaldo, his wife and their child. Kadhim's wife had remained on high alert as she continued to await the guests. She had told her husband that she was very keen to meet the young woman who had become famous on football pitches. She also said she was keen to meet Ronaldo, and to embrace their child, who lived in luxury under the care of the most famous male and female football players.

Kadhim Ali was hurt, and began to look for an alternative to Ronaldo, encouraged to do so by Ronaldo's greed and love of money. Kadhim would never forgive Ronaldo for that scandalous dinner with a group of rich Asians in exchange for one million dollars, which Ronaldo was paid in full. "Imagine," Kadhim said to his fellow taxi drivers, he earns one million dollars from those idiots just for sitting with them at the same table for dinner at a restaurant."

He added, "Ronaldo made his attendance conditional on them not exploiting the occasion in any form of advertising, so that the companies that have a monopoly over advertising him would not get upset. Imagine, he doesn't know their language, and they don't know his. Their only concern was that Ronaldo should be at their table, sitting with them as they ate dinner, that's all."

Still talking to his friends, who were puzzled by the bizarre goings on in the world, Kadhim continued, "Worse still, one of those rich people said that he and his friends had actually been winners, because they had been willing to pay one-and-a -half million dollars had Ronaldo played hard to get, but they won the deal at one million dollars that went to Ronaldo's pockets, and they were able to save half a million dollars."

Kadhim shook his head with disapproval, then quickly went to his car, and roughly pulled off Ronaldo's pictures, replacing them with pictures of Pablo Abdallah, the Argentinian player with Palestinian roots and one of the stars of Palestine's football team.

For the first time, the neighbourhood folk were interested in news of the star Pablo Abdallah, and began to believe what Kadhim was telling them about him, and his bad temper while playing. "It's true that this is unacceptable on the pitch, but I feel comfortable seeing Pablo Abdallah behaving angrily and losing his temper, for a simple reason. We Palestinians have experienced a lot of injustice, and it's our right not to keep quiet about any offence, even if it comes from another player on the pitch," said Kadhim.

So Kadhim Ali kept talking about football player Pablo Abdallah with admiration, and one morning, announced that he would reserve the front seat of his car for him "because he's coming to our neighbourhood in a few weeks." He would visit his friend Kadhim

Ali, and would stay with him at his home for a week or two. Kadhim Ali confirmed that his communication over the internet with Pablo Abdallah had led to this wonderful result, which could not be in any doubt. Some people in the neighbourhood threw doubts on what Kadhim Ali was saying, and they recalled similar things he had said and often repeated about the visit of another football player (they meant Ronaldo, but could not remember his name.) But others in the neighbourhood believed Kadhim Ali, and they admiringly surveyed the pictures of Pablo Abdallah that Kadhim had stuck to his car windows, and asked some questions about him.

"Are you sure he's Palestinian?"

"Of course, I'm sure. What insolence, by God."

"So why is his name Pablo, not Mohammad or Youssef Abdallah?"

"For goodness' sake! Haven't we got names like Nehru Ibrahim, and Guevara al-Budeiri?"

"So why does his hair hang over his shoulders like a girl?"

"You call that a question? Pablo Abdallah is free to do as he likes with his hair."

Kadhim was faced with other questions, some trivial and others reasonable, which he found it incumbent on himself to answer. Then, one of the political organisations in the neighbourhood decided the situation in Kadhim Ali's favour, by publishing an analysis in its weekly newspaper praising the inclusion of several Palestinians born abroad in the national football team and considering a move that had symbolic connotations, as well as evidence of the need to observe the unity of the Palestinian people everywhere. Kadhim Ali was overjoyed by that analysis, and brought it up at every opportunity, continuing to reserve the front seat of his car for Pablo Abdallah and spreading the news that he would be coming to the neighbourhood soon.

Kadhim Ali thought he was about to forget Ronaldo, but his wife, Nawal, brought him back to the forefront of his attention and problems.

Within the first weeks of her marriage to Kadhim Ali, she began to take an interest in sports to keep up with her husband and his interest in sports. Nawal watched many televised matches with her husband. Kadhim Ali and his wife had never been to watch a game, for the simple reason that women in our neighbourhood don't go to football fields to watch games. Kadhim Ali and his wife limited themselves to watching matches on TV, and they gained quite a bit of enjoyment out of it. That pleasure deepened when some of the terminology used on the pitch moved into their bed, taking on new sensual connotations. Kadhim Ali would play the role of one of the competing teams, and Nawal would play the role of the other team as well as the referee, blowing a whistle to announce the start of the game. Kadhim Ali would give and take with her and she would give and take with him, and a number of direct and indirect strikes would be made. The game would continue, light and easy at times, and rough and noisy at other times. The effects of Israel's cultural invasion would soon make its way into the details of the match, and Nawal would say "Atah sahkan metsuyan (You're an excellent player)," and Kadhim Ali would respond, "Gam at sahkanit metsuyenet (You're also an excellent player)."

Nawal would commit a playing offence during the game, Kadhim Ali would get a free kick, which he would successfully deliver, and the match would end. The enjoyment did not stop there.

Kadhim Ali came home one evening and was taken by surprise to see his wife wearing black shorts that revealed her white thighs, sneakers and black knee hight socks. Kadhim Ali saw her moving the ball with her feet, then kicking it towards the space between the front edge of the house and garden wall. Kadhim Ali felt an overpowering sense of pleasure as he watched his wife playing with the ball. Two or three minutes later, he asked her to stop, and led her smoothly through the front door into the house where calm and the outbreak of desires prevailed. She said, "I want to become a football player."

"I have no objections, as long as you play here in the garden."

"No, no, when the time is right, I will go to the neighbourhood playground."

"Is that reasonable, Nawal?"

"I want to be like Ronaldo's wife, she's no better than me."

Ronaldo's name was once again giving Kadhim Ali a headache, but he had made a comeback this time because of his wife's fame on the pitch. Nawal wanted to plan a path for herself similar to that of the famous player's wife. "Is that possible Nawal? Where do you think you're living? Do you want to create a scandal in front of the whole neighbourhood?" Kadhim Ali couldn't even bear the thought of his wife going out onto the pitch in black shorts that would reveal her thighs, which the teenage neighbourhood boys would stare at. Kadhim Ali couldn't bear what the gossipy women would say. Their long tongues would slay Nawal, they would coin attributes and names that would catch everyone's attention and dog her throughout her life, possibly continuing to spread years after her death, and some of those names and attributes would include him: the football player's husband, the husband of the woman in shorts. "Oh, may God cut open your belly, Nawal, may the raven of ill omen play on your head! You will not become a football player, even if you go to the pitch in a long abaya. I will prevent you from realising that wish, I will prevent you even if things get to the point of divorce." Would Kadhim Ali split with his wife? Could he really do it? He was in love with her, very much in love with her. But she would expose him to massive humiliation if she insisted on going through with her decision. Kadhim had not expected to be subjected to such test. He felt fragile, fragile to the point that the slightest step by his wife that would be unfamiliar to the neighbourhood folk would expose him to humiliation. But who would be the wiser? He might find an opportunity to avoid the crisis awaiting him. He would conjure up all his tact and foresight as he tried to convince his wife to abandon her wish, because he did, in fact, want her to stay with him and could not get over his love for her, or her love for and devotion to him.

Kadhim Ali came home as usual in the evening, and was surprised to see his wife with three other women in the small front garden wearing sports clothes. The ball moved amongst their feet smoothly and briskly. For a moment, he was unable to take it in, then he let loose a nervous laugh that the four women could see no convincing reason for, and he said weakly, "Those who are like us come to us."

The four women said nothing. They kicked around the ball with coordinated, confident movements, and Kadhim Ali watched them at the edge of the yard. The ball deviated slightly from its course and rolled towards him. He moved towards it, and stopped it with his foot. He thought about cutting it open with the kitchen knife to end the disturbing nightmare, but he realised that this would complicate things even further, particularly since he was familiar with his wife's stubbornness and insistence on going through with anything she thought was appropriate. He decided that the situation required flexibility, and that this would give him time to find an acceptable solution. His wife said to him in a flirtatious, affectionate tone, "Kadhim, kick the ball."

Kadhim remained silent and hesitant, with his foot on top of the stationary ball. His wife called out to him again, "Come on Kadhim, darling, kick the ball."

Trying to sound hopeful, Kadhim said, "I will kick it on one condition: that going to the neighbourhood field is postponed until Pablo Abdallah comes."

"When is Pablo Abdallah coming?"

"I've already told you, in three weeks' time."

"What if he doesn't come, just like Ronaldo?"

"Then we'll think about it all over again and come up with a solution."

Nawal responded without too much thought, "I agree, kick the ball."

Kadhim Ali kicked the ball so forcefully that it went over the wall and rolled down the street. Nawal made ready to go after it, but Kadhim was quicker than her. He picked up the ball and walked with it, as the four women waited for him inside the walled yard.

Rumsfeld's Banquet

My great uncle woke up before dawn, and began preparing for the expected banquet. We said, "It seems like he hasn't slept all night, or that he dreamed about the banquet in his sleep."

For weeks, my great uncle had hallucinated during his waking hours and his sleeping hours, repeatedly brining up Rumsfeld's name as though it were a magic charm. My cousin Talha asked his father several times to close the subject and not reopen it. He told him, "You aren't on Rumsfeld's mind, and it is impossible that he will accept your invitation."

Provoked by his son's words, he responded, "And how would you know about that, boy?" And he went on to tell us how his late father, who had been the neighbourhood's sheikh for many years, had invited Glubb Pasha, the well-known English military leader, who had accepted the invitation with thanks and had come to the neighbourhood with a group of his soldiers. The neighbourhood folk were dazzled by the spectacle of the soldiers surrounding the commander, and the soldiers who had taken up positions on the rooftops to protect him. My uncle said, "That day, Glubb Pasha ate mansaf covered in meat. Believe me, he ate the mansaf with his hand just like us Arabs. He didn't use a spoon." My uncle added that Glubb Pasha had drunk the sauce from a small saucepan, wetting his chin and moustache.

My cousin said mockingly, "He pretended to be like you to fool you."

My great uncle told him off, saying "OK, just keep quiet, clam up," and then added, "I'm sure Rumsfeld will accept the invitation, and will come to eat mansaf in this neighbourhood."

My great uncle seemed sure of his words, as though Rumsfeld, the defence minister of the strongest country in the world, were in his pocket, or ready to obey his slightest command. But my cousin Talha continued to doubt his father's words. He whispered in my ear, "My father is losing it." I immediately asked him not to say such things so as to avoid a falling out between him and his father.

The days went by, and it seemed that Rumsfeld would accept my great uncle's invitation, and during that time, many rumours spread. For example, it was said that my great uncle had visited a well-known fortune teller in some village. The fortune teller had started out as an immoral and capricious person, then God had guided him and improved his fortunes. The fortune teller had told my great uncle, "Good news, Abdul Razzaq, the guest whose name is Ramsfeld will come to you on the wings of the wind." My great uncle had overlooked the mispronunciation of the minister's name, and had forgiven the fortune teller for it, because he was a simple man, and had come away certain that his efforts had not been in vain, because he had resorted to many mediators to ensure that Rumsfeld would accept the invitation. My uncle (according to the narrators) had contacted some embassies, unintimidated by the suspicions that doing so would create, with only one thing on his mind: inviting Rumsfeld to lunch. Some of the narrators said that some ambassadors had considered my great uncle's invitation as weird and thought that he was unhinged. But others had deemed the invitation to be infinitely wise and sensible, and had made some efforts to support it. It was also said that my great uncle did not stop at enlisting the efforts of ambassadors. His late father had taught him that God

THREE SHORT STORIES

The Complete Short Stories was published by Raya Publications, Haifa, 2012

entrusted His secret to the weakest of His creatures, so he had gone to see the fortune teller, who had been immoral, but had been guided towards virtue by God. Later, he had gone to see the mukhtar of a nearby village, who was well-known for dealing hashish and forging the title deeds of lands so that they could be sold to Israeli companies specialising in stealing Palestinian land. My great uncle mentioned the minister's name to the mukhtar several times. The mukhtar had said, "Ah, Ramfield. I have come across that name before." It was subsequently said that my great uncle had overlooked that unintentional mistake, and kept listening to the mukhtar, who affirmed that he would ask his friend, the director of the Israeli company, to get involved in the matter. He said, "Rest assured, the company chief is an important man, and he's very influential." He asked absentmindedly, "Where is that guest of yours from?" My uncle responded with a note of distaste in his voice, "He's American. Rumsfeld, the minister of defence. Haven't you heard of him?"

The mukhtar responded, "Oh yes, Ramfield. I told you the name sounded familiar." After a moment of silence, he added, "OK, fine, you can count on me."

But my great uncle did not stop there. He kept contacting various quarters until Rumsfeld responded to the invitation.

News of Rumsfeld's impending visit spread throughout our neighbourhood and adjacent ones. My cousin was completely taken aback. How could Rumsfeld accept an invitation from a prominent person in an unknown neighbourhood somewhere or other on this vast planet? My cousin said he would have to revise his ideas and attitudes, which he had painstakingly and gradually built up, but which were now threatening to collapse inside his head just because Rumsfeld had accepted his father's invitation. Had William Burns, or Mitchell (author of the report), or the US consul in Jerusalem accepted the invitation, we would have said this was to be expected and was reasonable. But that Rumsfeld, the strong, mighty defence minister, had accepted it was something that called into question everything that he had taken for granted.

My great uncle had aimed his strike, and it had hit the target exactly. He did not over-think things like his son, Talha. His late father had taught him a piece of wisdom that he had never forgotten: "Befriend the lion even if it eats you." When Rumsfeld became famous and my uncle began to follow news of his triumphs on the radio stations, he decided to form strong relations with Rumsfeld as a way of getting his protection and asking for his help when calamities struck. My great uncle did not think about wider political issues during those times, or of confronting Israel, for example. And Rumsfeld was not an opponent of Israel anyway, so he could not call on his help against it. After we had sustained many defeats and the occupation that controlled us had dragged on, my uncle had retreated to his earlier position as one of the neighbourhood's prominent personalities, hostile to other prominent personalities and engaging with them in unpleasant clannish conflicts. My great uncle and his family would attack some neighbour or other, and at the same time would come under similar attack. Once, he had become embroiled in a bloody fight with the neighbours, had been wounded by a stab to his arm, and he and his clan had been roundly defeated. So it had occurred to him to form an alliance with a mighty strongman, and no one had seemed stronger than Rumsfeld.

My uncle began preparations to welcome his important guest. He chose a large square in the middle of the neighbourhood and ordered that tents should be pitched in it, leaving some space for helicopters to land. Then he sent for the neighbourhood's local pop song expert. (she wasn't an expert in the literal sense of the word). She hurried over. She was tall, and her eyes were still beautiful enough to capture men's hearts, even though she was several years past her youthful prime. She was still able to entertain guests at weddings with her vibrant voice. Looking at her with admiration, my uncle said, "This will be your day, Maliha."

Drawing on her significant experience, Maliha said, "I thought about this before you asked me over, and I have one condition."

My uncle said, "Tell us your condition, Maliha."

"Let's remove the last letter of his name."

My uncle was surprised by what she said, and a crisis of a linguistic nature was on the brink of erupting. Maliha insisted, "His name is strange, as though it hadn't been created for singing." An Arabic language teacher from our neighbourhood laughed and said, "That's actually true, this good woman has a good instinct, because saying his name is as painful as swallowing a nail." My uncle got angry and scolded him without heeding his scholastic status. "Shut up, you bearded guy. I don't want you to turn this into something political. I don't want any politics." After a long argument, my uncle gave in to Maliha's condition.

My cousin Talha went along with his father's initiative, which almost undermined his ideas and beliefs. But he subsequently began to use it to support his ideas. He said, "This is the new world that is being born right before our eyes. The most senior official is not above visiting the most ordinary of people, for a simple reason: to strengthen trust between the ruler and those that are ruled. Our world has become a small village, just like saying "God is One."

I did not comment on my cousin's words, nor was I surprised by them. He did not stop making excuses for himself until my great uncle walked in on us and caught sight of a dozen expensive shirts piled in one of the corners of the reception room. My cousin said, "I will give these shirts to Rumsfeld as a gift." My uncle responded, "Who told you that Rumsfeld is in need of any shirts?" My cousin said, "Rumsfeld always appears on TV in crumpled shirts, so I will give him these expensive shirts." The only thing that saved my cousin's gift from my uncle's definite rejection was the word "expensive". The word had a special ring to it, prompting my uncle to give in and agree that the gift should be presented to his honoured guest. This encouraged my cousin to suggest to his father that he should serve modern food to his guest: A steak for example, or chicken fillet. My uncle was displeased by his son's words, and responded sarcastically, "Steak or chicken fillet! Is there anyone who would turn down mansaf to eat chicken fillet, Talha?" Defeated, Talha fell silent, and my uncle prepared to receive his guest.

The guest arrived on time.

Three helicopters landed at the edge of the large square. Rumsfeld disembarked from one of them and looked around him several times, adjusting his prescription spectacles with his fingers. He smiled broadly and confidently, and the women's singing rang out:

"Rumsfel boarded and went to Aleppo

They offered him baclava in plates of gold."

Rumsfeld walked towards the tents, surrounded by a large retinue. My uncle popped up in front of him, surrounded by a crowd of neighbourhood men, and shouted out his greeting: "Welcome, welcome."

The women sang on:

"Rumsfel boarded and went to Toubas.

They offered him baclava in plates of copper."

Rumsfeld and my great uncle embraced like long lost friends. My uncle took him by the hand and led him to sit on two woollen mattresses. He kept beaming out his smile, which seemed like an indirect response to anyone asking, "Pharaoh, who empowered you?" It was a conceited, disdainful smile floating in its own elitist domain, and it was only interrupted when Rumsfeld took a sip of bitter coffee out of the cup offered to him. He frowned and his face took on a painful expression as though a thorn had stuck in his throat. His smile only returned after my great uncle quickly handed him a glass of water to drink, thanking God in prayerful tones that his guest was smiling again.

The trays of mansaf arrived, carried by members of the clan, who placed them before the guest and his retinue. In very respectful tones, my uncle said, "Welcome to our guest Rumsfeld and his party. Please help yourselves." No one got up to eat, and Rumsfeld directed his glittering smile towards the meat piled over the rice, and remained in his place. My great uncle was confused, and whispered in my ear, "Talha was right. I wish I had offered them chicken fillets." But Rumsfeld put an end to my uncle's thoughts by uttering a few words, and the translator said to my uncle, "You go first, eat a mouthful from each tray of mansaf."

My uncle understood the import of those words, and anger welled up within him like a volcano, but he did not allow it to explode. He said to one of the boys, "Bring the dog over here quickly, boy, go like a shot." The boy brought the dog, and my uncle threw it some rice and meat that he scooped up from the big tray in front of Rumsfeld. The dog wolfed down the food greedily, and Rumsfeld smiled as though he were watching a comic play. The dog began to choke, coughing intensely. His eyes bulged, he twisted in front of everyone, and then fell the ground and died.

My uncle was terrified and thought that he had fallen into an unexpected predicament. Rumsfeld stood up angrily (although his smile did not completely disappear), and several of his fierce bodyguards attacked my uncle, and manacled him with cuffs they seemed to have brought with them in preparation for a surprise of this nature. People broke up in panic, and Rumsfeld walked towards the helicopter.

My uncle was taken away to prison in Guantanamo Bay. (One TV station said that he was being held in a luxurious villa on the outskirts of New York.) He was accused of belonging to a terrorist cell. A neutral international agency examined the dog that had eaten the food and found that it had died because a bone had become stuck in its throat. Several international organisations intervened to demand my uncle's release. (The Arab League intervened, although it is not an international organisation.) The mukhtar who forges documents also intervened, and swore that my uncle was innocent of the charge levelled against him. The fortune teller, who had been immoral and then repented, prophesied in front of a crowd during a visit to the neighbourhood, "When there is a full moon is in the sky, Abdul Razzaq will return."

That prophecy was not incorrect, or so thought some of those who were dazzled by the fortune teller's abilities. Three full moons and nine days after that, my great uncle returned from detention in Guantanamo Bay. He told us everything that had happened to him from beginning to end, and he still repeats it today like a broken record, as he receives those who visit him at his home to congratulate him on his safe return. As for those who have not heard, I am now telling the tale, as God is my witness.

From his collection Ibnat Khalati Condoleezza *(My Cousin Condoleezza), published by al-Mua'ssasa al-Arabiya lil dirassat wal Nashr, Beirut, 2004.*

FAKHRI SALEH

On the Literary Achievement of Mahmoud Shukair:
A Nuanced Reflection on the Losses of Palestinians

Stories mobilizing levity, ironic paradox and a sense of play

Throughout a creative career that spans about six decades, the Palestinian novelist and short story writer Mahmoud Shukair (b. 1941) has sought to give voice to his sufferings as a Palestinian battered by constant attempts to expunge his identity and appropriate his land and the place where he was born, lived and developed emotionally and culturally. The trauma he suffered at the age of seven in 1948, when Palestine was divided and the state of Israel was established, is central to the stories found in his narrative work about the city of Jerusalem, only a few miles from his own village, Jabel Mukaber, which escaped occupation in 1948 only to fall under Israeli control in 1967. Shukair faced the hardships of making a living, of daily life and political and party work, and of being affiliated to the left and to the Palestinian resistance movement, to which he devoted several years of his life. This led to the Israeli occupation authorities detaining him after 1967 and then expelling him from Jerusalem, though he returned to the city after the Oslo agreement. Yet despite those hardships, Shukair's literary achievements, firstly in the form of short stories and later in novels and children's writing, makes him a founder of Palestinian fiction. In the first five decades of his life he produced little work, but in the following decades, when he was free of his day job especially his political work, he produced a large number of narrative writings, including stories for children and young adults, using his memories of childhood and boyhood to examine the village – about which he wrote his best short stories and novels – striving to describe how Palestinians reacted to the disaster that struck them when their country was lost and parts fell under the control of other states – the West Bank annexed by Jordan, and the Gaza Strip placed under Egyptian administration.

Mahmoud Shukair started to have short stories published in the newspapers that sprang up in the eastern part of Jerusalem after the Nakba in 1948, as well as in *al-Ufuq al-Jadid* (New Horizon) magazine, which released its first issue in 1961. But his first collection of short stories, *Khubz al-Akhareen* (Other People's Bread), did not come out until 1975, when it was published by a small Jerusalem publisher called Salaheddin Publishing after one of the streets in the holy city. The collection includes several stories that Shukair wrote before the occupation in 1967 and others written after the occupation that addressed the shock of Palestinians when what remained of Palestine fell under Israeli occupation. They also describe the development of the first seeds of resistance inside Palestinian society, which in twenty years had not yet fully digested the loss of Palestine. But the distinctive feature of this collection is its wit and humour and Shukair's ability to portray village life in all its paradoxical diversity. He describes villagers who are shocked when they travel to the holy city and see a world that is different from their quiet, simple village where time seems frozen in comparison with the bustle and crowds of the city. There are country boys who go on pilgrimage to the city for pleasure or to work, young women ground down by life and forced to the city to sell the eggs, fruit and vegetables they have gathered in order to feed the hungry mouths in their families, and men who insist on visiting the al-Aqsa mosque but are shocked that the Israeli occupation forces prevent them from praying in the mosque sanctuary. Through a mosaic that contrasts the world of the village with the world of the city, the village boys and girls with the greed and cruelty of the city folk, and the Palestinians with the Israeli occupiers, Mahmoud Shukair seeks to portray the ordeals of Palestinians of all classes, without imposing any specific interpretation on the lived experience of his characters, whether as individuals or as a group. The occupation and the class struggle between the rich and the poor explain the suffering of Palestinians, men and women. The Israelis steal the land while exploitative bosses are responsible for the poor Palestinians who die of hunger or who collapse and die in the workshops of the city's tall buildings. A class interpretation of the struggle, fed by the imagination of a storyteller who is armed with Marxist theory and a member of the Communist Party, does colour the world of Shukair's short stories. But the stories seem more lively, more playful and humorous, and more able to capture the sense of paradox when they break free from this theoretical, scholastic and highly politicised approach, and set about portraying the characters as they are – women and men who want to live, love, enjoy themselves, progress, flourish and escape from the captivity of the small world that the village represents in contrast to the city, which is open-minded and noisy and promises pleasures and temptations.

In his next collection of short stories, *Al-Walad al-Falastini* (The Palestinian Boy, 1977), Shukair moves on to portray the incipient Palestinian resistance, both peaceful and armed, after Israel occupied the West Bank in 1967. At this stage, his work includes didacticism and a polemic that glorifies resistance and the refusal to abandon the land and go into exile, as happened in the Nakba in 1948 – equally a feature of the stories he wrote for children and young adults. But it also includes expressionist, symbolic language that is of a poetic nature and raises resistance to the level of Christian salvation and the prophetic spirit manifested in Christ's sacrifice for the sake of humanity, the poor, the destitute, Palestinians and others – a Palestinian Christ in this case, who with his blood waters the land and makes it possible for the crops to grow. In his symbolic story "A Man Rose from the Dead", which strikes me as central to his second collection, Mahmoud Shukair combines this Christian salvationist vision and a messianic vision of the world that is full of hope for the future, with the victory of good over evil and of the oppressed over those who dominate and humiliate them. In this salvationist vision we can detect a kind of belief in the peaceful resistance that Christ represents or the man who rose from the dead to spill his blood into the ground, which then turns green and fertile. This symbolises in a way the victory of peaceful resistance over armed resistance – at a time when the armed Palestinian resistance was reaching its peak in the first half of the 1970s.

But a sharp shift in Mahmoud Shukair's experiment is detectable in the 1990s, when the writer sets aside the didactic tone that marked some of his stories and escaped from the thrall of the ideologically Marxist approach that had hampered his short-story writing and prevented him from portraying his characters with a lighter brush, as more vital and humane. He then was able to put some distance between them and the cursory, didactic and formulaic vision that turns characters into stereotypes reflecting the surfaces of things, not the depths and the diverse and complicated facts that are difficult to interpret and explain. That's what we find, for example, is his collection *Murour Khatif* (A Rapid Passing, 2002), which contains a large number of micro stories, some of them limited to just a few lines or a page or two, with nothing superfluous or any explanation, interpretation or attempt to ideologise the world or force it into a single defined intellectual or interpretative mould. There are phenomena, events, images, and conversations that take place in front of our eyes, but the narrator does not comment on them. He presents them in a narrative that is hurried and economical and that allows readers to see for themselves what is hidden beneath the surface, or at least to see what the narrator has been through in the way of human experience and suffering in life.

This literary form takes these stories – those in this collection and in other collections in which Shukair experiments with this terse form of short-story writing – close to the realm of poetry, to the haiku form, or to the world of allegory and anecdote. But what matters most in this stage of Mahmoud Shukair's development is that he has broken free from the didacticism of his previous stories and the weight of the ideological vision that they contained, and that he sets off into the wide-open spaces of creativity, where his characters face a puzzling world with uncertainty and ignorance. There is no ideologizing here, no stereotypes, no interpretation of the world, but rather a venture into the mysterious experience of living, in the face of which humans stand impotent, their hands tied as they confront the prospect of death and maybe annihilation, since "death

Mahmoud Shukair

crouches on the threshold like an old dog too weak to bark", as the narrator says in one of the stories about an old man and his wife who are frozen in time, waiting for someone who doesn't come.

In his later collections of stories, which came out in the early 2000s, Shukair reverts to the playfulness, humour, irony, and paradox that marked his first stories in the 1960s, in which fantasy, the exotic and the unexpected are the basic features that make up the events and characters and the daily interactions and conversations between them, with nothing projected from outside. His collection *Surat Shakira* (Shakira's Picture, 2003) is full of stories about Palestinian villagers meeting, establishing relationships with or claiming to have relationships with international celebrities – politicians, singers, actors: Moratinos, Kofi Annan, Shakira, Brigitte Bardot, and Michael Jackson. It is a stinging satire about the reality of Palestinians' lives under the Oslo Accords, which brought them nothing but visits by foreign officials, actors, singers and a few football stars. They visited the Palestinian Authority areas in trickles to express their solidarity while the occupation was building settlements and increasing the number of Israelis living on occupied Palestinian land and entrenching the permanent power of the Israeli occupation. Under these circumstances, in order to make life easier for one of his relatives, a member of the Shukair clan claims that Shakira is from the family in order to win the sympathy of an Israeli soldier who likes Shakira's singing and dancing. The same interpretation applies when it comes to the other stories in the collection, which blend fact and fiction, imaginings and white lies in an attempt to give the mistaken impression that Palestinians have broken free of the occupation which, after the declaration of principles was signed by the Palestinians and the Israelis in 1993 and the Palestinian Authority was set up, continued to weigh on Palestinians, making their lives more difficult; in the meantime the land is being pulled out from under their feet and the occupation entrenches itself day after day.

But the harsh reality of life and the complicated lived experience of the Palestinian community in Jerusalem, the West Bank and the Gaza Strip are addressed in a humorous and lighthearted way that reveals the depth of the paradox, the bitter reality and the deep contradictions forming a deep fissure in the lives of Palestinians. It is reminiscent of another Palestinian writer, Emile Habiby (1921–1996), who adopted humour and the language of absurdity and parody, especially in his great novel, *al-Waqai'a al-Ghariba fi Ikhtifa' Said Abu al-Nahs al-Mutasha'il* (1974) – its English title being *The Secret Life of Saeed The Pessoptimist* – as a way to portray passive resistance and the struggle to survive the Israeli plan to eradicate and appropriate the identity of the Palestinians who stayed within Israel's 1948 borders.

Intertextuality with world literature and major writers and creative artists from the history of human storytelling gives another twist to Mahmoud Shukair's experiment, thus aiming to show that the experiences of Palestinians have much in common with the experiences of other peoples who have lost out in other languages and cultures. This is what we find in his collection *Ihtimalat Tafifa* (Slight Possibilities, 2006), which uses the micro story to express these narrative and existential inter-sectionalities, either through the message that the stories convey or through the parallels that they establish between the protagonist who seems to be central to all the scenes that make up this collection of short stories and the character of Don Quixote (Cervantes, 1547–1616) or of the Good Soldier Svejk in the novel of that name by Jaroslav Hasek (1883–1923). The character whose exploits Shukair chronicles is similar to the knight of La Mancha who tilts with windmills, while the Palestinian knight carries his lance through a modern city in the belief that the war is still raging. This knight, who is reminiscent of Don Quixote, lives in a world of ideals that have disappeared, and roams around in a city where are there no longer any fighters, in a reference to the current reality of Palestinians and their successive defeats. These micro stories are explained by a quotation from *Don Quixote* at the start of the first part of Shukair's collection: "Yesterday I was king of Spain, today not of a single town; yesterday I had towns and castles; today I possess none". At the same time, the stories have scenes in which Don Quixote in his guise as a modern Palestinian meets the Good Soldier Svejk in a street in Prague and the latter confides in him that he is busy stealing dogs, which he sells in order to make a living.

Elsewhere this collection of stories sets up an intertextual parallel with Habiby's novel *The Pessoptimist*, in a clear allusion to the fate that awaits the Palestinians in their territories occupied after 1967. The Palestinian knight, who carries his lance in a city that no longer wants war, has no other recourse but cunning, humour, passive resistance and keeping a low profile in order to go on living. One of these stories combines all three characters: Don Quixote, the Good Soldier Svejk and Emile Habiby's Pessoptimist:

> I stopped at the first street, looking in all directions. Just at that moment trucks full of soldiers with weapons and ammunition drove by. Don Quixote went by on horseback, with his squire behind him on the back of a donkey. The Good Soldier Svejk walked past, with his thin nose and small eyes. A man passed who was looking around in all directions like me. He told me he had to live by his wits in order to stay in the country. His name was Said Aboul Nahs the Pessoptimist. I shook his hand and said, "I'm called Said too!" Then he walked on and I kept looking around in all directions.

Translated by Samira Kawar

AIDA FAHMAWI WATAD

Palestinian Writing, Inside a Closed-Open Cage

When one begins to read Mahmoud Shukair, questions about the horizons that are opened up by a Palestinian writer living in a rural neighbourhood annexed to Jerusalem come to mind. Those horizons are condensed into short stories that are a few pages long, or into micro stories that are the size of one's palm. However, they can represent and interpret the reflections of the human soul as it interacts with a society in crisis, with an authority that is both docile and controlling, and perhaps most importantly, with the occupation. These are the three taboos that Mahmoud Shukair's texts tackle with the professionalism of a narrator who masters his tools – thematically and aesthetically – through his rich human experience. Anyone reviewing Mahmoud Shukair's personal and literary biography will find that he has undergone the Palestinian experience in all of its facets, and has internalized the scenes and histories of the things he has lived and that are worth writing about.

Mahmoud Shukair was born in Jabel Mukaber in Jerusalem in 1941, seven years before the Nakba. At the age of seven – which is pivotal to children, since that is when their relationship with their first home has usually strengthened – he first experienced homelessness and being forced away from his home. That childhood trauma created lines that time could not subsequently erase. He says, "A terrible fear of what we had experienced that night infiltrated my bosom and has remained hidden there [. . .] till the present." That was not the last departure from home. Shukair has been forcibly removed from his home by the occupation and returned to it since 1967: "I felt great pity for that house where we used to live to face its fate alone, and then return to it. It would forgive our abandoning it during hard times [. . .] It is my diminutive homeland that has witnessed all the upheavals that my family and I have been through."

In 1974, following a ten-month period of administrative detention (which, of course was not the first time he had been arrested), he was forcibly deported to the Lebanese border, from where he began his journey of forced exile, which lasted until 1993. During that time, he moved between Beirut, Prague and Amman, where he settled for fourteen years, and he continuously experienced a feeling of insecurity and that he was "suspended", although he says those cities "did not let me down in any way". However, exile opened up new horizons to him that had been inaccessible to him in his homeland. Books became easily available to him, and he was able to read extensively, familiarising himself with the art of literary writing and other works of art. His perspective expanded, and his culture deepened and diversified. Shukair participated in cultural and Arab journalistic activity and wrote for television and theatre. Although exile was a harsh experience, it elevated his perspective, allowing him to see Palestine from the outside, and to think in a new way, which was reflected in his texts.

His return was not easy, and he had to spend a year without writing a word as he adapted to the new life to which he had returned, acclimatising to the society all over again and sorting out his living conditions. Shukair returned to Jerusalem after the Oslo Accords, and following his return, wrote *Dhil Aakhar lil-Madina* (Another Shadow of the City). But his return was incomplete, and the seven-year-old child's anxiety about being forcibly removed or driven into exile remained with him. He says that the ending of occupation is what would "give me more reassurance that my life in the city would continue in a manner that would safeguard my dignity and protect me from the prison or exile that I experienced before. Only then would I feel a definite sense of security, and find time to meditate, isolate and write: I will roam all parts of the city and its centre without fear or anxiety."

Such variety in Shukair's human and literary journey – despite suffering and instability – allowed him to see the Palestinian and human experience from wider and deeper perspectives, enabling him to sharpen his artistic instruments away from direct ideological influences, and with a greater focus on text as an aesthetic form first and foremost. Although Shukair's literary experience includes various genres, including the novel, children's writing, writing for television series and journalism, he is considered one of the most important Arab writers to have developed the vision permeating his literary works and has been able to qualitative advance his writing of short stories and micro stories.

Most of Shukair's micro stories can be read without prior knowledge of the context of the writer or the narrative for several stylistic reasons, giving the story the freedom to break free from recording actuality while remaining strongly immersed in it. However, this does not completely do away with the identity of the texts, because they indicate the situation that gave rise to them. Shukair seeks to shatter icons, turning the Palestinian individual into a human being that has his own small space and genuine feelings. He highlights political corruption, economic hardship and social exploitation. His micro stories can be read, not only in a Palestinian or a gender context, but in any global context of repression under similar circumstances.

Shukair also employs the technique of "separate connected" narratives in some of his micro stories. Each story can be seen as an independent text, but at the same time it is connected through an internal narrative relationship with other stories that precede or succeed it. The reader can also glimpse in his micro stories poetic tendencies that appear more like poetic flashes than narrative. At times, he is capable of condensing the narrative of an entire people into a few lines.

Shukair's post-Oslo work is characterised by capturing scenes from the complex actuality experienced by the Palestinian individual from a salient perspective. He is able to transform the mundane and ordinary into a surrealistic multi-faceted collage portraying a Palestinian society that still tries to live and dream, despite being suffocated by poverty, introversion, repression, isolation and occupation. In his own words, "I try to go towards modern writing [. . .] that sheds light on daily life, in all its bad and good aspects, writing that avoids excess rhetoric and provoking feelings of pity, [. . .] writing that expresses the essence of the

Palestinian situation, that reveals our faults as human beings, not angels [. . .]. We are entitled to write about a real woman that literary criticism does not interpret as being Palestine."

He uses several tools to form such a collage, one of the most important of which is satire, which serves an important role in facilitating the narration of the tragedy without cancelling it. Shukair employs ridicule as a double-edged defence mechanism. On the one hand, ridicule allows him "to focus on the executioner, ridiculing him and making light of him and all his repressive measures." On the other hand, "ridicule of one's own deficiencies and mistakes [. . .]

Qalandia checkpoint

seeks to create a morale that allows a Palestinian to remain steadfast," according to Shukair, who understands that ridicule is his means of remaining away from direct ideology. Hence, Shukair explores the immorality of the occupation and its frustrating daily practices, using private experience to turn to a collective experience: perhaps Shukair's daily wait at the Qalandia checkpoint provided the material for several of his stories, allowing him to highlight the Palestinians' daily suffering because of the occupation without directly describing it. All that Shukair does – by means of an omniscient narrator – is to reverse the direction of the camera lens. At the same time, Shukair does not hesitate to turn his sharp sarcasm on the very heart of Palestinian society itself and its paternalistic mentality. His work reveals the situation of crisis and complexity that a Palestinian lives through at a time of globalisation and consumerism within his own society and under occupation, and the difficulty of Palestine's closed-open relationship with the world. His writing also includes implied references to the crisis of Palestinian heroism, in both the literary and social senses.

Ultimately, it can be said that Mahmoud Shukair is a writer who is part of the Palestinian situation, not through direct slogans, but by remaining committed to critiquing the situation from its deeper aspects, presenting what is attractive and what is less attractive about it with the loving intimacy of one who belongs, with the mentality of one who has seen, and with the skill of a narrator who is in command of his tools and is intent on pleasing his reader. He transports his reader lightly through his texts in flowing and flexible language, sometimes inserting spoken dialect. He moves the reader from fantasy to reality, and from reality to fantasy without creating the feeling that this is forced. The reader believes it and experiences both worlds, causing him/her to laugh at times and to cry at others. But through it all, Shukair allows the reader to enjoy the text and think beyond its confines, which reflects a diminutive world that comprises Palestine here and now.

Parts of this article draw on information from literary testimonies by Mahmoud Shukair published by the Journal of Palestine Studies, and al-Karmel, as well as on conversations that the writer had with Mahmoud Shukair in June 2020.

Translated by Samira Kawar

Fayez Ghazi reviews
**Dhilal al-'A'ilah
(Shadows of the family)
by Mahmoud Shukair**
Hachette Antoine/Naufal, Beirut,
December 2019
ISBN: 9786144692868,
Pbk, 336 pages

A journey into internal Palestinian alienation

Shadows of the Family (*Dhilal al-'A'ilah*) is a novel of broken mirrors, both in content and in form. A Russian-doll narrative structure, a journey into internal Palestinian alienation, a tale of a closed city in the time of open borders and globalization, and a story of the psychological, cultural and intellectual transformations which have stormed Palestinian society in general. A journey that shifts between wakefulness and dreaming, between the conscious and the unconscious, between the boundaries of reality and imagination, culminating in a multifaceted tragedy – as much a result of internal issues as external – which pours into Palestinian society and engulfs it in a vast sea of crises.

Although it is the third part of Mahmoud Shukair's trilogy, *Shadows of the Family* equally possesses the ingredients to stand alone as a novel. Its shadows sprawl out from the confines of a small family across the entire Jerusalemite community, which suffers from the Israeli occupation on the one hand and the internal occupation on the other, alongside the emergence of destructive, reactionary ideas.

The novel is based on a narrative philosophy through which reality and dreams are represented almost equally. This tendency pushes the reader to feel the depth of the real tragedy that both the characters of the novel and the Jerusalemite community must live. Far from just a narrative technique, however, this escape to the realm of dreams evokes a painful content filled with sadness, humiliation and the absence of solutions.

The novel is divided into four sections – 'A shadow'; 'Another shadow'; 'As if it were a shadow'; 'As if it were another shadow' – similarly structured in their oscillation between reality and imagination. Subject to the broken mirror effect, both time and narration in the novel are fragmented: narrators change and sometimes even encounter their mirror image, defying time and circumstance. The real characters, the couple Qais and Layla, are thus mirrored in the figures of Mohammed and Sana, though they do not resemble them; they also find their parallels in lovers from classical and modern literature: Layla and Majnun, Jabra Ibrahim Jabra and Lamia al-Askari.

"I kept watching her while the water was overflowing from her dream."

The main plot of the novel comprises a familiar, age-old love story between Qais and Layla: the taxi driver and the school teacher, the son of an originally Bedouin family and the daughter of a successful bourgeois family, opposite ends of the social class system.

Despite the simplicity of the love story itself, the narrative creates a space for depicting the atrocities that take place in Jerusalem on a daily basis – the racism of the occupation and its dominance, the destruction and burning of homes, arbitrary arrests – and for examining different perspectives on events, on life, on reality, on the past and the future. Moreover, it casts light on the Salafist group (known, ironically, as the "Guardians of Honour") who forgot about the occupation and began targeting women and mixed places, and whose ideas are reflected in prestigious Jerusalemite families such as Layla's.

"My joy over Layla was greater than the pain of the siege."

The novel's characters vary. Besides the main duo is the pragmatic, indifferent Rahwan, who lives from day to day and searches for opportunities for "potential happiness" in the arms of women; and

Lamia, the quiet, straight-talking young woman who is martyred before her helpless brother. Other characters include Layla's father, a strict bourgeois businessman; her brother Mustafa, owner of the "honour" pistol; Feryal, the wife of a spy and pimp; Maria Zakharova, spokeswoman for the Russian Foreign Ministry, who features in the narration as the object of erotic fantasies; and Emil, his wife Maryam and his daughter Mary, Christians from Jerusalem who, as a result of the radical ideology among some of their community, are forced to close their café, a space in which both men and women can socialize.

> "I was afraid that one of the extremists who had set themselves as agents of God on earth would approach her, and whisper in her ear to express his dislike of her elegant dress."

The language of the novel enhances the sense of tragedy: clear, sharp prose like a blade, interspersed with crude street talk and colloquial expressions, as well as moments of poeticism and poetic quotations.

Known for his mastery of narrative technique, Shukair's choice of embedded stories in *Shadows of the Family* enables him to fully embody the chaos, confusion and loss experienced by his characters. This wandering structure cannot be conveyed by one informed narrator, so Shukair divides up the narration amongst the characters, voices overlapping across the novel in its sections, chapters and nightmares.

All the crises, upheaval and dispersals, however, do not prevent Mahmoud Shukair from communicating a message of hope, as represented in love's victory over fear, in Layla's victory over her family, and in the victory of her love over the barbaric blade that took out her eye. Layla is the symbol of the beautiful Jerusalem that will live on, despite the external and internal challenges; the Jerusalem that will always love and laugh.

> "Love between a man and a woman is possible in a city plagued by the worst occupation."

Shukair offers a substantial list of sources and references at the end of *Shadows of the Family*. More than a novel, this indicates its status as a contemporary documentary testimony for the Jerusalemite community, which is closing in on itself with outdated and reactionary ideologies in the face of a brutal occupation, and the lack of any prospect of a solution.

MAHMOUD SHUKAIR

EXCERPTS FROM THE NOVEL *DHILAL AL-'A'ILAH*

Shadows of the Family

TRANSLATED BY KAREN MCNEIL AND MILED FAIZA

Shadow

1

I waited for Layla for an hour and forty minutes. As I walked towards the café near Bab al-Khalil, I was unsure what our meeting would bring. There was a patrol of soldiers monitoring people there. I thought of all the invaders who had come to Jerusalem and entered through this gate, then went back out from it, or from one of the other gates of the city.

The soldiers stopped me to search for guns or knives. I stayed silent and sullen as they searched me. They let me pass and I came to Omar Ibn Khattab Square, crowded with settlers and soldiers, soldiers who might shoot for any reason. A stray bullet to kill me, making Layla go into mourning for me and not marry for seven years. One of the girls in my family, Maazouza, did that, went into full mourning for her martyred beloved. Would Layla go into mourning for me? Perhaps, although I wouldn't like that. I wouldn't want her to spend years a prisoner of grief.

The evening was spreading its shadows all over, and in this cruel winter Jerusalem was wrapping herself in some kind of mystery and fatigue – a temporary fatigue, I expect, but I don't know how long it will last for. I waited for her in the touristy café, where the voyeurs' eyes wouldn't find us.

While I was waiting for her, I kept myself busy by looking at the café's walls, as if seeing them for the first time. Ancient walls, restored to resist the weight of time. In the middle of the wall to my right was a photo of the great father, the first owner of the café and Emile's grandfather. Next to him was the son, Emile's father. They both have thick twisted moustaches in the photos, and their eyes are full of determination and persistence. I contemplated growing a thick moustache, then abandoned the idea.

There was also a photo on the wall of the square from almost a hundred years ago, taken in 1918. There are British soldiers and a crowd of Palestinians in it. This city's history is filled with invaders who occupied her, destroyed her many times over thousands of years, and yet she manages to resurrect herself time and again. I was born in Ras al-Nab'a, not far away from the walls of the old city. Layla was born in Beit Hanina al-Jadida. I didn't know her and she didn't know me, even though we lived in the same city.

I kept myself busy looking at the square and the sidewalk. This city's writer, Khalil al-Sakakini, walked on that sidewalk. He was Sultana's Majnun . . . maybe Sultana walked with him on that sidewalk, maybe they sat together in this café.

I waited a long time, and Layla didn't come. I felt anxious and worried.

We met here two weeks ago. I told her about the secret that I had been keeping from her, and I was afraid that she would push me away. Layla was taken by surprise that day. We left the café, hoping to meet there again.

Yet here I am for my date with her and she hasn't shown up. I tried calling her, but her phone was turned off. I sent her several messages on WhatsApp, but no answer. And her Facebook page has been silent for days.

We are just like the characters in that old story: she is my Layla and I am her Majnun. Ever since I met her and fell in love with her, I've found myself sporadically inhabiting that poet's character, who remained madly in love with his Layla until he died. I believe that she is inhabiting the character of the beloved, whose name she carries.

I love her in this untrustworthy time, when Palestinian men are striving for their honour to the point of obsession. Because any taint on this honour means scandal, and scandal here . . . well, let's just say that death is easier.

But she didn't come.

Emile noticed my discomfort while I was waiting, and guessed with his delicate intuition that there was a problem. I drank my third cup of coffee and left.

The wind was very cold and the city lights gave the impression of serenity; nothing but an illusion that the wind dissolves and surprises shake.

* * *

I thought about going home, then I dismissed the idea so my mother wouldn't get upset when she saw my disappointment. I stayed up working until late. The winter cold was harsh and the night untrustworthy. I drove all kinds of people to the different quarters of the city. I passed through random checkpoints. I waited. I complained. I cursed. And at 10:00 pm I went home.

My father was watching the news, yelling angry comments at the screen. My mother was worried about me. She said for the tenth time: "I wish you'd find a safer job."

I tried to reassure her, as I did every time: "Don't worry, I'm always careful."

My mother was buzzing around at home like a bee. She opened another window in the living room, despite the cold, to get rid of my father's cigarette smoke. She went to the TV, followed the news a bit; then she turned away, smiling from the comments she heard. My sister Lamia was sitting in the corner of the living room watching the TV on and off, when she wasn't busy with her phone or writing something on Facebook. What goes on in her mind? I don't know.

She's pretty quiet most of the time.

I looked at my mother, father and sister and thought to myself: it's a stable family. Or it would be, if not for the lack of safety and security, and if not for my father's overwhelming anxiety that makes him wake up several times a night to check that he locked the door.

We exchanged small talk, my mother searching my face as if hoping for an answer. She smiled as if she knew where I had been and who I was with.

I lied to her: "Everything's fine unless . . ."

She interrupted me. "Forget the 'unlesses.'"

My father wasn't paying any attention to our conversation; at least, that's what I thought. My father is interested in the news more than anything else. Sitting in front of the TV, with his salt-and-pepper hair, he seems like a man carrying the weight of the world on his shoulders. But he surprised me when he looked over at me and said:

"You're following in your father's footsteps."

He looked at me smilingly and I understood what he meant: he fell in love with my mother when he was a taxi driver. He kept watching the news, and Lamia kept silent, her fingers substituting for her voice as she wrote a comment here and a message there, perhaps for one of her friends.

Meanwhile, I was like an insect crushed underfoot.

I concealed my disappointment until later.

2

I met her a few months ago by sheer coincidence. My colleague Rahwan accused me of setting a trap to catch her in.

It was a late afternoon in autumn – a morose season of delicate feelings, a yearning to penetrate the unknown. The traffic in the streets and around the curves was at its peak. The sidewalks were crowded with women returning home, parading with their different styles of clothes, some in jilbabs and the others in brightly coloured dresses, each of them with a life story and a history. Their histories are all entangled with the history of this city, making it difficult to unwind and weave in a new, foreign identity. The sky was covered with white clouds. Jerusalem doesn't reveal what's in her mind; she bears her destiny without complaint.

I was waiting in my car near Damascus Gate, hoping to find a customer. I was urged on by hope.

She opened the back door and got in. She was wearing a jilbab, her head covered with a scarf. She asked me to take her to Beit Hanina al-Jadida. I drove through the busy traffic, stealing glances at her in the rear-view mirror. My eyes met hers two or three times – I only did that because I was attracted to her. I remembered a relative of mine called Abdel Rahman, whose nickname is al-Qunfoth, who always says: "You taxi drivers don't leave any woman alone without harassing her." Or: "I bet you drivers have had sex with as many women as there are hairs on your head." But I answer him every time: "Enough of that kind of talk," then I add: "People aren't all the same."

"Are you a secretary in an office?"

"I'm a teacher at a Christian Orthodox elementary school in the old city."

There was a light breeze slipping into the car from the window on my left side. I was too embarrassed to continue the conversation, out of fear of some sort of shock or misunderstanding. I took her to her house, a big one with many windows, deeply rooted in the place. She handed me the fare and left. There was a kind of confident self-esteem in her walk. The houses in the neighbourhood were pleasantly adjacent and the gardens and fences around them spoke of comfort and prosperity. I went back to Damascus Gate thinking about her, captivated by her beautiful voice and the modesty in her eyes, and charmed by her tall figure.

She came again three days later, with the same figure and the same modesty in her eyes. Autumn gives the impression that life is full of secrets. The same scene was repeated and curiosity filled my heart. I realized when I drove her for the first time in my car that she was from an affluent family, that much was clear from her family's sedate house. Did I have a desire, hidden inside me, to get near the rich and powerful? I don't think so. I was attracted to this woman because of her delicacy and beauty, and also because of her warm feelings. She couldn't hide those, not from a taxi driver who, over the last few years, has driven so many men and women to all kinds of places, inside and outside of the city.

"What do you teach?"

"Arabic. I majored in it at university."

I remembered my relative al-Qunfoth and his tasteless jokes. If he says them again around me, I'm going to tell him to fear God and to stop disgracing people. I was in the presence of an educated young woman.

"I studied Arabic at the teaching institute, but here I am, working as a taxi driver." After a moment I added: "I'm trying to be a writer. My name is Qais."

My last words caught her attention.

What he said caught my attention and changed the direction of my thoughts. I became interested in him. His name – and the coincidence entailed when added to my name – caught my attention. I returned the courtesy: My name is Layla.

She asked me: "Are you a poet?"

"I'm trying to write a novel."

She expressed her approval with a surprising affability: "Woooow!"

Her fascinating voice resonated inside me for days. Her name stirred up exalted feelings inside me. She came again a week later.

We smiled at each other. I felt like someone who had found a treasure; that moment of connection was priceless.

I said: "I'm glad to have met you."

She thought about my words for a moment, as if trying to avoid falling into a trap, then said: "Taxi drivers can't be trusted."

Her words brought the shadow of al-Qunfoth and put him directly in front of me. I couldn't believe how bad the reputation of taxi drivers was. But then I thought of my cousin Rahwan, a fellow driver, and his endless adventures with women.

I also remembered Mohammed al-Asghar, my father's uncle, and his wife Sana who had asked me two days ago to drive them to the National Theatre. After I dropped them off, I found my Uncle Mohammed had left a thick notebook in the taxi. (Did he really forget it, or did he pretend to forget it for some reason?) Curiosity drove me to read what was in it before I gave it back to him. I read many anecdotes, some of them happy and funny, others confusing and contemplative.

* * *

She didn't stay away for more than a few hours. She came back, with her captivating beauty and the shadows of her affluent family.

I came, not caring about my family's strictness, nor the soldier patrols who were spread across every street. I left my bed. I opened the door and set off with the lightness of a butterfly.

There was a pale moon looking down at us from the clouds. Calm overshadowed the world as we embraced near the dense woods. How did we get here? We laughed as if we were coming from deep inside one of the stories, and said let the nights do whatever they want with us. We heard the murmur of water, which anointed our rendezvous with a kind of splendour. "It is the spring whose waters bathed my body when I was a child," she said.

Yes, when I was a child, I would hike my dress above my knees, then take it off and let the water flow over my body.

She led me by my hand as we approached the spring. Its water was flowing towards the orchards nearby. She submerged her calves into the water. I came next to her and put my calves in the water too. We were like two children having fun . . . Then I dreamed in my dream that I woke up, perhaps because of the cold water, or perhaps for some other reason. I kept watching her while the water was overflowing from her dream.

He was watching me while the water flowed over me.

After a while, I told her: "Let's go back to the city".

She asked in a reproachful tone: "Am I to go back with wet legs like this?"

I pulled out a white handkerchief from my pocket, and kept drying her calves until there was no more water on them, then we went back. We saw them together, him and the woman, next to the wall, then while they were entering the square. There was a thick notebook in his hand that I felt I had already read; she was strolling next to him, holding a book in her hand.

We followed them, a light twilight covering the world. "I know them," I said.

And I said: "His notebook is intriguing – it contains many secrets."

She didn't say a word. But she was interested in the two of them. Maybe she was humouring me.

I was interested in them because it makes me happy to see a man and a woman with such a strong connection.

They went into a café near Bab al-Khalil and we went in after them. We chose a table near them and sat down. We pretended that we were not paying any attention to them.

I whispered in her ear: "It's Mohammed al-Asghar, my father's uncle, and the woman with him is his wife Sana."

He opened the notebook and started writing in it while Sana was watching him, impressed, or at least that was what I guessed. Then, before long, she opened her book and started reading.

Layla and I continued watching them carefully. His thick notebook was a dream or two's distance from us.

3

I awoke in the early morning. I could remember some of my dreams – that Layla was at the heart of them. And I remembered Uncle Mohammed al-Asghar's notebook. I got up and went into the bathroom.

I showered and put on my clothes. I drank my coffee then left the house. Autumn was loudly declaring itself: yellow leaves falling here and there; a light breeze accompanied by a possible chill; pale clouds in the sky. The houses of Ras al-Nab'a were piled up and spilled about without any order, without a thought for aesthetics, hinting at the kind of crowding that's liable to produce a nervous explosion. Personally, I find it amazing: the diversity of people's destinies! And yet there was a painful truth hovering over it all: this city is still under occupation, after so many years.

I opened the car door and sat behind the wheel. I picked up passengers from the quarter: a post office employee named Amal, her hair blowing freely in the wind, and three other passengers. Amal sat in the front seat, her perfume scenting the air, and the other three passengers piled into the back seat: a minor trader named Azzam, wearing a cheap cologne; next to him a farmer named Awwad, who as soon as he settled into his seat started complaining about the lack of rain this year; and my relative al-Qunfoth, the pungent smell of the sheep that he spends all day with emanating from his clothes. Al-Qunfoth kept watch on the traffic lights, sending me his instructions whenever the light turned green: "Yah!"

Apparently a mare was running around in the head of this relative of mine, because that was a word you only use with a horse or a donkey to get them to speed up. It didn't take him long to reveal his longing for the past when he said: "God rest the soul of our grandfather Abdallah, he had a mare that was a legend for generations."

He asked me: "Have you heard of our grandfather's mare, Qais?"

"Yeah, I have," I said.

Al-Qunfoth kept praying for our ancestors, until finally the trader Azzam released his aged wisdom: "Times have changed. We're in the age of aeroplanes now."

Amal, the post office employee, laughed lightly, then said in a sweet voice: "I've never been in a plane in my life."

Azzam took the initiative in a way that worried the listeners and surprised her by saying: "I'll buy you a plane ticket."

She was taken aback by his words and she thanked him.

Then the conversation was interrupted by the voice of the commander as the last traffic light turned from red to green: "Yah!"

I drove until I arrived at Damascus Gate. I dropped the passengers there.

I was still wearing summer clothes: brown trousers and a short-sleeved shirt. The autumn breeze was tousling my hair, putting me in a good mood. I chatted with Rahwan and the other drivers while

I contemplated the city: crowded with people, no one disturbing its peace but the soldiers carrying the blood-shedding pieces of polished metal in their hands. The sidewalks and stairs were filled with cautious men – each with their own concerns and their small joyful moments, at least as I imagined – as well as boys and girls going to school and women on their way to the old city for shopping or for work. Most of the women were hiding their bodies in baggy dresses or jilbabs and covered their heads with scarves – I didn't know what they were thinking about.

Mornings never appeal to me, except when I see Layla coming along the sidewalk with her graceful walk, putting her foot on the first step of the stairs leading to Damascus Gate, on her way to the school where she spends her day giving language lessons to the boys and girls.

I saw her that morning, her pink scarf tied neatly over her hair, surrounding her face with a striking beauty, and her autumn jilbab draping elegantly on her body, yet unable to completely hide its topography. I looked at her and she looked at me. We exchanged two cautious smiles. Our love was still young and tender like a small, dewy plant. Rahwan was not oblivious to what was happening around him. He looked at me with curiosity, then asked: "Did a pretty girl smile at you a minute ago?"

I looked him in the face and didn't answer. I sufficed with a small smile that could mean anything.

He said: "I tell you all my secrets, so you shouldn't hide anything from me."

Then he started talking his usual rubbish.

* * *

I arrived before her at the café where we had agreed to meet.

Its customers are mostly tourists and it serves men and women without discrimination. Our love was still like a toddling baby, trying to walk but wary of falling down.

I walked fast through Omar Ibn Khattab Square. There were settlers, men and women, pouring into the square and onto the sidewalks, and there were soldiers. I felt that the square was groaning under their feet like old wood.

Layla arrived and we had our first date.

We met and I was drawn towards this taxi driver who was more than a little handsome. Not to mention writing a novel, of which I have no idea what it's about, but I am interested in reading it as soon as he finishes. Here I am, coming to meet him in this café despite my anxiety. I mean, it's difficult to justify a young woman wearing a jilbab coming to a café to sit with a man! Of course, I know that I am breaking social norms.

"You only know my first name so far."

"Your first name is enough for me."

I said, trying to reassure her: "I am Qais ibn Mannan ibn Atwan ibn Mannan ibn Mohammed al-Abdillat."

I smiled, sensing that he was very nice and maybe somewhat naive with his rural or Bedouin roots.

Then I continued: "I came into this world in 1989, and they couldn't take my mother to the hospital because of the city curfew from dusk till dawn. It had been imposed on account of the intifada that had spread through the land."

My words encouraged her to open up, so she said: "I am Layla bint Mohammed Hassan al-Qani'. I was born in 1993. My mother gave birth to me in the Jerusalem hospital on the evening of a hot summer day; the curfew hadn't started yet that day."

I listened to her carefully, and we talked for an hour or a little more. It was an enjoyable conversation, more delicious than almonds and walnuts and honey. Then we left the café. We walked on the sidewalk a short distance but we had to part ways, fearing people's eyes, fearing repercussions from Layla's family, with its high honour and prestigious status.

* * *

We met after a few hours, despite everything. I told her: "I'll marry you right now." She demurred, saying: "No, not now." I respected her decision and we walked along one of the city sidewalks. Then we saw the two of them slowly approaching the café. We followed them and watched them from a distance.

She had said goodbye to her youth long ago, but still was not lacking in femininity. She had a pride that was evident in the way she walked and in the straightness of her back. And he was walking beside her, with his imposing stature and his distinguished white hair.

They sat in the café and we sat in the far corner. He opened his thick notebook and started writing.

I approached him as stealthily as a cat. Sana was sitting next to him reading a book, her hair falling smoothly over her chest and her perfume scenting the air. I looked closely at the page of his notebook, but I wasn't able to read his handwriting. Words were flowing from his pen like water in a creek. I rubbed my eyes, hoping to be able to read it, but with no luck. Layla joined us.

Yes, I moved closer and stared at the page of the notebook but couldn't read it. I didn't blame myself at all for this curiosity.

We blamed our dream and couldn't exchange it for another, more obedient one.

I saw him finally stop writing, contemplating a page in the notebook with big handwritten lines. I was able to read some names, and some explanations: "My mother Wadha . . . my brother Fleehan . . . Maria Zakharova . . . Qais ibn al-Moulawah and his beloved Layla al-Amiriya . . . Rahwan???!!! Nafisa, the relative . . . Qais Mannan, my nephew, and his beloved Layla Mohammed al-Qani'???!!!! She is originally from Jaffa. Her family came to Jerusalem immediately after the 1948 Nakba. They came with their money, which they hid in the women's underclothes, so they weren't humiliated like the other displaced Palestinians who suffered bitter hunger and deprivation. They resumed their business in the city and lived in rental houses in old Jerusalem for two or three years. Then they bought land in Beit Hanina, near the street connecting Jerusalem to Ramallah, and built modern homes there. Layla, their daughter, fell in love with our son Qais, a risky love that might not survive."

I was surprised to see mine and Layla's names in the notebook, as well as the other names. Layla too was surprised when she managed to read them. I told her: "This is what writers do when they are about to write their novels: they record notes and names." She asked me about Wadha and Fleehan; I told her they are from my extended family, the al-Abdillats. She asked me about Nafisa; I hid half of the truth from her. "She is one of the members of my family; I don't know why her name is in the notebook."

They stood up after an hour; she was as tall as he was. He put her hand in his and they walked together, perhaps home, or to a restaurant, or for a walk in the city streets. Layla and I watched them until they left our dream.

4

I spent a long day in the city, driving men and women in all directions. A lot of the men were chatty and offered commentary, but the women were, as a general rule, more inclined to silence, perhaps to avoid being taken the wrong way if they talked too freely.

I was wearing a pair of blue jeans and a grey shirt, and proudly displaying my arm muscles and my good looks that all my friends envied me for. When it was almost evening, I sat behind the wheel waiting for more passengers at the stop next to Bab al-Khalil. I wasn't one to waste time.

I took Princesses' Street: Baghdad Memories out of the glove compartment, where I had put it to read whenever I had some spare time. Once I had got some distance from the people around me, I became engrossed in the book; I was taken with the love affair between the Iraqi, Lamea, and the Palestinian author, Jabra.

I raised my eyes from the book after twenty minutes. The foot traffic on the sidewalks was at its peak, and the city was living the day to the fullest, as if announcing her rejection of being a city under occupation.

I put the book back in its place. The autobiographical touches scattered through it were still infusing me with splendid feelings. I looked around me with an impassioned lover's eyes.

Suddenly Layla appeared on the sidewalk, walking towards me. I couldn't believe it when I first saw her. She was wearing her grey jilbab, and as usual covered her head with a scarf; today's was sky blue, decorated with clouds. She was looking straight ahead, trying to avoid unwanted comments from the people passing by. Her statuesque figure announced a woman of superb beauty, as she walked with serene, measured steps.

It wasn't just a coincidence. This was one of women's machinations when they fall under a pressing desire. I opened the back door of the car.

She got in and said: "Take me home, please."

I paid no attention to the curious looks of some of the drivers standing by the fleet of taxis, and neither did Layla.

I turned on the engine and set off down the main street. I could smell the scent of Nabulsi soap emanating from her body. That smell always reminded me of olive trees. I was secretly thanking the coincidence that made the daughter of a rich family fall in love with a taxi driver. That was a sign of good luck and happiness. I sometimes thought that maybe I was living in a dream, that Layla was nothing but a delicious illusion.

On the road, we joked around innocently. I reached my hand out to the back to touch her hand. Our hands embraced.

I said, inhabiting the character of the autobiography's writer: "You are Lamea the Muslim and I am Jabra the Christian."

She immediately retorted: "I am Layla al-Amiriya and you are Qais the Majnun."

I liked her answer. As I watched her expression in the mirror, she seemed a bit confused. She asked me: "Did you mean Lamea al-Askari and Jabra Ibrahim Jabra?"

I slowed down and reached into the glove compartment, taking out the autobiography. I showed it to her and said: "Yes, that's who I meant, and this here is our love story."

The book piqued my curiosity. I asked him to lend it to me when he was done reading it.

I promised to give her the book, then a few moments of silence fell on us. She looked outside then back at me and said: "Fear is constantly ambushing me."

She said that her father had been on edge ever since the early blossoming of her body. When she grew up and became a fully mature woman, her brother Mustafa became convinced that she would, one day, bring shame on the family. He had bought a gun and hidden it in a secret place.

She said: "I was contemplating my body in the mirror, and I can't understand my father and brother's antipathy towards it . . . It's a good body, harmless and capable and beautiful."

I liked the way she described her body but I gulped, feeling worried. I parked close to her house and said: "Here we are, my Layla."

She said, getting out of the car: "Thank you, my Majnun."

I smiled and followed her elegant walk with my eyes until she was out of sight. Then I left, missing the feeling of security that comes sometimes and is absent at others. I said to myself: I am the Majnun of Layla; I must risk everything for Layla.

* * *

She came at night. I was happy to see her. She was wearing neither jilbab nor hijab; there was no one watching. She came near me and we stood together next to the window.

The whiteness of her body shone from under the nightgown, her hair spilling around her face and chest. She said with conviction: I am not afraid.

We stood, silent. I looked around every which way but wasn't able to determine where we were. I asked her: "Do you know where we are now?" She said: "No, but I am still in my nightgown!"

We remained confused, looking for an answer. Meanwhile, we saw Uncle Mohammed heading towards us; he sat on a nearby chair, and we saw Sana sitting next to him, then she opened her book to read. I said: "We are in a restaurant outside the city wall. See, here is the pretty waitress, checking on customers to find out what they are going to eat." She said: "I'll take off the nightgown then and put on a dress." I told her: "Don't worry about it, Layla; stay as you are".

She fell reluctantly silent, and we watched Uncle Mohammed. We saw him opening his thick notebook, writing a few lines, then from between the lines burst out a long scream – a man screaming in pain like a wounded animal. His screams filled the air of our dream. My body shook and Layla's body looked as if it had been somehow violated.

When he finished writing, he closed the notebook and contemplated the face of his wife sitting next to him.

Layla said: "It's like he was writing about something painful."

"Maybe," I answered.

I added: "It's as if I've heard those screams before."

I started to remember where I had heard them. I saw a ghost of an angry girl; I said: "I think it's my sister Lamia", then the ghost disappeared. I was still confused. I told Layla we should leave this place. I held her hand and we ran along the street opposite the city wall. When we got tired of running, we headed to the café and sat down there. Then Uncle Mohammed al-Asghar and Sana arrived. We marvelled at how we had left them in the restaurant and yet here they were again. She was walking a few steps ahead of him. She looked into the mirror hanging next to the café door, perhaps to reassure herself about what was left of her beauty. He did the same thing, perhaps to reassure himself that he was still able to stand strong against time.

I told Layla, searching the paths of a quick dream: "She is his wife, she has lived her whole life with him without bearing a child."

Then I reproached myself for mentioning having children, but Layla didn't seem to mind and didn't comment.

Suddenly a nurse showed up. I thought for a short moment that she was my mother. She seemed like she was coming from her shift at the nearby medical centre, coming to the café for a short break.

Layla said: "If she hadn't been his wife, she wouldn't have been able to sit with him at the café."

I immediately answered: "But you're not my wife and you're sitting with me."

She smiled: "I'm a rebel."

I touched her hair with love, then we continued looking at Uncle Mohammed.

He opened his thick notebook and started writing in it, and the nurse was sitting with her legs crossed, contemplating the whiteness of her knee, no longer covered by her nurse's smock. I stared at her and was soothed by the peace enveloping her face and appearing in her eyes as she drank her tea. I was behaving carefully so as not to make Layla angry with me.

Suddenly, that sound came out from the notebook again, the sound of a man in pain like a wounded animal, then we heard him saying some obscure words: "Daughter, what? Daughter?"

Layla's body trembled. I whispered in her ear: "I think I know what happened. I know that blood has spilled from the edges of this story, but I am not sure of anything now."

5

The morning was impenetrable like old copper, or perhaps I was fearing bad luck for some reason. I looked at the soldiers standing near Damascus Gate, at the ready to shoot as if they were on the front lines. There were only unarmed men, women, children in front of them, walking in every direction with utmost innocence, making for a strange contrast.

The weather was a bit cold, the sky full of clouds, hiding whatever desires were in its mind. We didn't get any passengers for an hour, even though people were continuously streaming down the sidewalks. I thought of my relative Nafisa and felt sad for what had happened between us. I remembered the name Maria Zakharova, the name I saw written in the thick notebook. I typed her name into my phone and she appeared with her pretty face. I read some information about her and watched her dancing in her short black skirt. She was a brilliant dancer. I was amazed by Uncle Mohammed al-Asghar's interest in her, and wondered: what does she have to do with the current situation . . . ?

My question remained unanswered when Rahwan came and stood in front of me, studying me with curiosity.

He said: "You're hiding something from me."

He kept looking at me, not saying another word, probably trying to provoke me or to create a dramatic impact. Finally, he said: "You have a beautiful girlfriend."

Then, after a deliberate pause: "Don't forget, I'm your cousin and friend, and when it comes to women you must tell me everything."

He added: "She probably has a friend she could introduce me to, then we could be four."

I paid no attention to what he was saying. Just then, a passenger and her daughter arrived, and it was my turn to drive them.

* * *

We had agreed I would take her to meet my mother, at my insistent request.

My mother has her own charm, and I wanted Layla to meet her and also for her to meet Layla, hoping this might strengthen our relationship. I was afraid that Layla might fly out of my hand.

We set a date and went to see her. Layla sat on the back seat, her overwhelming presence filling the car. I wanted to see her next to me, a beautiful twenty-three-year-old woman who was in love with a taxi driver and was going with him to meet his mother. Perhaps that will put their young relationship on the right path.

I was feeling like our love story was unparalleled, then I changed my mind. I told myself that no one cares about us, Layla and me, and our love is nothing for this city to pay attention to. Then I felt again that it was not right to belittle it like that — I felt like the city couldn't contain me, and that I was madly in love with Layla.

I drove my car from Damascus Gate towards Herod's Gate, turned left and headed down for a good distance, then I started up the mountain road. The city was compressed in on herself, surrounded by occupiers penetrating from every direction. Despite that, my happiness over Layla was bigger than the pain of the blockade. I felt as if I was flying and was excited for the meeting that was fast approaching.

I came to the end of the uphill street and turned right towards Al-Amal hospital. Layla was anxious about meeting this woman for the first time.

I was really anxious, and I told him I felt shy.

I told her, so as to lessen her anxiety: "My mother is a modest woman; she loves people and will be happy to meet you and get to know you."

We entered the hospital. We smelled the odour of drugs and we liked the tranquility of the place. We sympathized with the patients' dread and the clear pallor of their faces, then we headed to the department where my mother works. We were told that she was in the operating room; she soon emerged with the doctors and the rest of the nurses.

We were sitting in one of the waiting rooms. We had kept ourselves busy watching the people going in and out of the patients' rooms, and looking at the nurses walking around like white doves. We waited without boredom until my mother came out, wearing her nurse's smock. I wondered at her appearance: she was like a rose blossoming in the daylight. Despite the passing of the years, she still retained her beauty and elegance.

She walked towards us calmly and with confidence. I kissed her cheeks and she kissed my forehead. Then she hugged Layla and kissed her, and lovingly contemplated her face, pleased.

I contemplated her beautiful face and her sweet smile. I could see a lot of her in Qais.

We walked together to the cafeteria to drink tea. My mother and Layla walked in front, and I walked behind them like a loyal guard. I felt that this love that united me with Layla was walking on its own two feet, so far without trouble.

Hannah Somerville reviews
**Mordechai's Moustache and his Wife's Cats and other stories
by Mahmoud Shukair**

Translated by Issa J Boullata, Elizabeth Whitehouse, Elizabeth Winslow, Christina Phillips. Banipal Books, London, 2007
ISBN: 9780954966638 Pbk, 124pp, £7.99 / $15

A Master Craftsman

The best satire tap-dances straight over the boundary line between the plausible and implausible without missing a beat: the type that compels a kind of reflexive self-rebuke on the part of the reader when we invariably realise, miles too late, that we have strayed with perfect guilelessness into the realm of the beyond belief. With tightly-written plots that unfurl amid the grinding clutter of day-to-day existence, exploding out from an always painfully-believable root cause, the satirical stories contained within Mahmoud Shukair's riotous and winsome collection *Mordechai's Moustache and his Wife's Cats and other stories* exemplify this technique. The tales that follow – fleeting, ethereal, often sad but never moribund, and infused with humanist sensibility – emerge in turn as a love-letter to the short story and individual striving, and a tenderly-written one at that.

The author is now 80 years old and has been a devotee of short-form fiction throughout his prodigious career. In an interview at the close of this small collection, which was first published by Banipal in 2007 and is one of more than 40 books bearing his name, Shukair recalls how he first became infatuated with the genre after picking up a copy of the Jerusalem-based magazine *al-Ufuq al-Jadid* (New Horizon) in 1961. Nurtured by the Arab novelists of the so-called '60s generation, and also by Western household names such as Steinbeck, Camus and Chekhov – whose influences are detectable

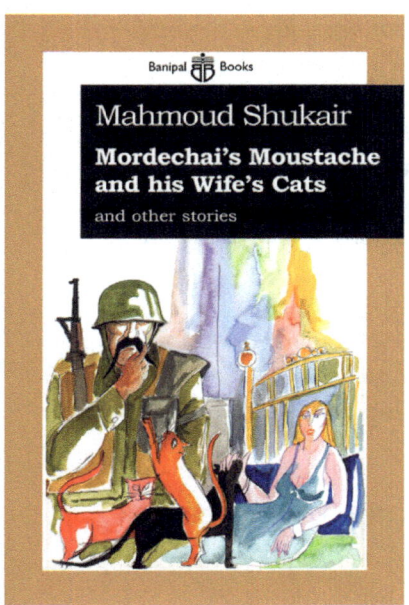

in parts of *Mordechai's Moustache* – Shukair went on to develop a distinctive authorial style of his own, one equally informed by his experiences as a Palestinian resident of Israel (later forcibly displaced to Europe), as a Damascus University graduate in sociology and philosophy, and as a card-carrying citizen of the world.

The first four short stories in *Mordechai's Moustache* explicitly bear witness to the absurdity of this first experience. The opening dance, "Shakira's Picture", portrays a family engaging in a disastrous gambit by attempting to play off their shared surname – Shakirat – as evidence of their blood relation to the voluptuous Columbian singer. By doing so, they somehow expect to secure travel documents from the Israeli Ministry of Interior. In time these discursive acrobatics give way to certain members of the family believing wholesale in the conspiracy, to the point that Shakira's picture is hung up on the wall of their home. Nestled amid the ensuing hilarity are steely reminders of real-world issues such as the generational divide, the objectification of women, the tussle between Islamic orthodoxy and brute pragmatism, and most of all, the grotesque injustice that has compelled a Palestinian family to insert itself into this farcical predicament. The result is a tragicomedy to remember.

The other three 'traditional' shorts in this volume, "Ronaldo's Seat", "Mordechai's Moustache and his Wife's Cats" and "My Cousin Condoleezza", also examine the human impulse toward self-delusion and totemic thinking in times of acute strain. From the mispronunciation of American names to the utter misreading of situations and rooms, the stories are studded with indications that many of these characters do not fully understand the world they are living in; sad, in some ways, that they should have to. Many of Shukair's protagonists try to assert themselves through gestures: a surprising facial hairstyle, a workshop named 'Independence Carpentry', all collapsible and most already in the throes of collapse.

The titular story is an ode to masculinist politics and overcompensation: Mordechai, an ageing and obstreperous Israeli with a moustache comical to all but himself, picks up his M16 and stations himself at a border checkpoint in response to perceived inattentions on the part of his wife. The would-be return to glory is positioned as the counterpoint to their vacillating marital relations, a point explicitly mocked by his wife: "If you want to bombard anything, here is the wall in front of you."

Walls and boundaries are also a central theme of the subsequent three sections, entitled *Vignettes*. These comprise an array of phantasmic 'very short stories': 43 in total, and all beautifully translated by Issa Boullata, Elizabeth Whitehouse and Elizabeth

A STORY FROM THE BOOK

A Piece of Cloth

They arrived in a city known for its quietness. People there were peaceful and did not come to blows in the streets. Life went on quietly and there were no military vehicles at all in the city. They chose a restaurant with tables on the pavement. There was a gentle breeze caressing faces and women's hair. They chose a table for dinner next to a tall tree: the man chose the side opposite the trunk and the woman the side beside the trunk. The night breeze wafted playfully over her hair as though it were its spoiled child.

She looked around her and seemed to feel everything was fine, so she sat down; but as she moved the chair slightly, one of the legs sank into the square bed surrounding the trunk of the tree. She lost her balance and toppled to the ground. Blood flowed from her forehead and drenched the locks of hair dangling over her eyes.

An ambulance arrived. After midnight, a car took her back to the hotel. She entered the room, the man circling her waist with his arm lest another unexpected surprise should happen.

She took off her clothes, and was stark naked except for a piece of white cloth covering her forehead. She examined the legs of the bed, then lay down and fell into a deep sleep as the man lay beside her, guarding her from any mishap, expected or unexpected.

Translated by Issa J Boullata

Winslow. Many of the stories deal with gaps in communication and misunderstandings between individuals, and span a series of seemingly discrete scenes in disparate locations – the markets of Cordoba, King Karl's Bridge in Prague, a backstreet brothel, a hotel breakfast room, rain-soaked city streets – that on closer inspection all appear to be connected with each other, with subtle back-referents allowing the micro-interactions they depict to somehow partly traverse space and time. Enclosed within some of the vignettes are explicit references to the present-day Palestinian condition: "The Martyrs" highlights the indifference of the dead to short-lived mourning, while "A City" gratifyingly satirizes the place-as-a-woman motif that has at times plagued the Palestinian artistic corpus and is despised by this reviewer. In "Vow", the author summons the ghost of Mahmoud Darwish in a song by Marcel Khalifah playing on the radio as if to remind us that, just like his mother's coffee, the voice of a generation has now himself become a signature – or perhaps, an anchor.

In contrast to the more elbows-out, declamatory prose style adopted by some of his contemporaries in 'very short story' writing, Shukair's prose is spare and weighted with human dignity. We are afforded just enough material detail to visualise a scene, and simultaneously the narrative space to perceive the stories, just like their protagonists, as somehow dislocated. Atomization and detachment are also a regular theme in parts of *Vignettes*: notably in "The Bus" and heart-wrenchingly in "A Map". In the latter, a man and a woman find one another after discarding the 'maps' inside themselves – only to be cleaved apart by a bigger 'map' that falls between them: one perhaps symbolising the exigencies and obligations of their respective lives, or socio-cultural contingencies, or even the imaginary dividing lines on a real map, such as the one running between Israel and Palestine.

Whatever they may be, in both their structure and content the *Vignettes* sections stand as a gentle but persuasive argument that interpersonal divisions are conjured-up, grafted-on, opportunistic and inherently unstable – but also harmful, not merely to their intended subjects but to us all. Together with the principal four tales in *Mordechai's Moustache*, they are also testament to the power of the short story in the hands of an adept and lifelong craftsman. It is difficult to recommend this collection highly enough.

Susannah Tarbush reviews
**Jerusalem Stands Alone
by Mahmoud Shukair**
Translated by Nicole Fares
Syracuse University Press, NY, USA, 2018
ISBN: 9780815611035, Pbk, 200 pages,
$19.95 / £14.85
Ebook: ISBN 9780815654469,
Kindle $15.75 / £11.49

Stealing moments of joy

The opening lines of *Jerusalem Stands Alone* transport us to the Old City of Jerusalem, as seen through the eyes of an unnamed narrator: "In the morning I walk to the markets surrounded by the city's history, ghostly layers of people from past eras, men of different ages and women of different times. The living women are careful to avoid physical contact, which the overcrowding all but invites. In this city, soldiers are everywhere."

The narrator was born two years after the 1967 war. "I've been writing about this city for twenty years and I see its past mixing with its present." He is a journalist on a daily newspaper, and is working on a book about Jerusalem.

The year is 2009. At the heart of *Jerusalem Stands Alone* is the predicament of fishmonger Abd el-Razzaq and his wife Khadija who face expulsion from their house in the Old City by five Jewish Israeli settlers with long beards who have moved into the house next door. The settlers have laid claim to the house.

The settlers harass the Abd el-Razzaq family. They erect a metal fence – thus partially blocking the alley – mark the house with red ink and smash the window of the parents' bedroom.

The narrator first meets the family when he goes to interview them for an article about the eviction threat. His eyes meet the honey-coloured eyes of the family's elder daughter Rabab, a college

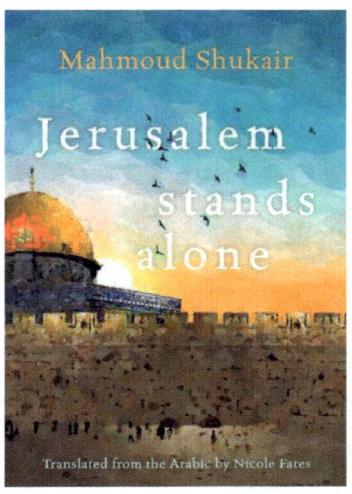

student. "After an hour of taking notes, I become less interested in the soon-to-be evacuated house and more interested in Rabab."

Rabab is an independent spirit who combines her reading of, among others, Shakespeare, T S Eliot and Bertrand Russell, with a fondness for new dresses and excursions with a boy who has a car.

Visiting the narrator at his habitual café, Rabab brings him poetry she has written. Despite their twenty-year age difference, she agrees to marry him. "She tells me there is a mystery about me that the younger guys who go to her school don't have. She tells me 'there is a huge difference between a writer who has read a thousand books and written hundreds of pages and a university student who can't write a single good paragraph.'"

Jerusalem Stands Alone was originally published in Arabic in 2010 by Hachette Antoine of Beirut, under the title *Al-Quds Wahdaha hunak*. The book consists of a series of loosely interlinked short chapters written in the present tense, most of them just one page or shorter. Some chapters are in the first-person voice of the narrator, others are in the third person. They are lyrical and concise, and rendered well in Nicole Fares's crystalline translation.

Despite the grim situation of Palestinian Jerusalemites, Shukair depicts their lives with tenderness and touches of humour as he reveals their loves, desires and fears.

The narrator spends much time sitting in his favourite café writing, or observing those around him. On his frequent walks through the Old City he sees figures from various conquests of Jerusalem. On passing through Jaffa Gate he is frisked by soldiers wearing helmets and swords. "Their spectral commander speaks a Romance language, so I know they're foreign."

While walking towards al-Aqsa Mosque ". . . in my mind I summon a dreadful scene: seven thousand people slaughtered by invaders' foreign swords, their blood running through the markets

MAHMOUD SHUKAIR, WRITING JERUSALEM

Mahmoud Shukair

and squares up to a man's knee. I walk and as I walk the blood drenches my feet." This episode is a reference to the 1099 crusaders' siege of Jerusalem.

At Damascus Gate he sees someone who looks like a terrified beggar, followed by a group of knights from the Ayyubid period, with Yamani swords hanging from their belts. The beggar is in fact Yoram, the Israeli chief of police of Jerusalem, who roams the streets in various disguises.

Yoram is beset by visions of the past, to sometimes comic effect. He reads old documents as if they refer to the present day. They include a secret log from 1817 of gunpowder, bullets and cannonballs hidden by the Ottomans in the Tower of David. Yoram summons the modern-day descendants of Ottoman commander Ahmad Agha al-Qutub hoping one of them will know the whereabouts of this arsenal. Yoram's state of mind declines over the course of the stories to the point where he shoots himself.

The threatened seizure of their house is not the only anguish facing Abd el-Razzaq and Khadija. Their eldest son, Marwan, has vanished somewhere in Europe in pursuit of a woman he loves, and has failed to keep in touch with them.

Their younger son, Abd el-Rahman, is – at the start of *Jerusalem Stands Alone* – in prison for throwing rocks at Israeli soldiers. His family are unable to visit him for two months because he has been put in solitary confinement for assaulting a guard. After his release he is rearrested during a terrifying raid on the family house by Israeli soldiers. The reason for this second arrest is that "he was too quiet, suspiciously quiet, and they suspected he was hiding something".

Jerusalem Stands Alone contains a succession of memorable characters. A room in Abd el-Razzaq's house is rented to Suzanne, a thin young blonde from Marseille. After leaving home due to family problems she had moved from place to place for three years before arriving in Jerusalem, "and the moment I arrived, I said to myself that I would stay here forever if I could". But the Israelis eventually order her to leave the city. Back in Marseille she continues to dream of Jerusalem.

Ghazal, a lascivious hospital administrator, is blackmailed by the Israelis into becoming an informer. After the narrator confides in him about a demonstration planned against the eviction of Abd el-Razzaq's family, Ghazal informs his Israeli handlers. The narrator recalls: "The day after the protest, officers and soldiers surround my house and take me to a hellhole where they place me under arrest for three months."

Despite Ghazal's unsavoury behaviour, a widowed mother of seven, Hanan, who works in an architectural office, succumbs to his sexual advances and is desperate for him to propose, despite his already having a first wife.

The bittersweet tone of the book is summed up by its conclusion, when Rabab and her younger sister Asmahan are invited to the birthday party of their friend Mary. "The girls dance joyfully in their white dresses, like a flock of doves," writes the narrator. "Rabab ties her keffiyeh around her waist and dances for a full hour." But the atmosphere changes when Mary's old aunt Janette starts to weep, perhaps remembering her long-lost lover Mustafa who was killed in the 1948 defence of Jerusalem.

"Rabab cries too, when she sees Janette cry. Maybe she cries because she remembers her parents' house, which they've been ordered to evacuate, or maybe she remembers her brothers, one in prison and the other somewhere in the world. I cry as well because under occupation we have to be thieves and steal these moments of joy. I dry Rabab's tears and dance the last fifteen minutes with her."

MAHMOUD SHUKAIR

26 Micro Stories

TRANSLATED BY MAYADA IBRAHIM

No One

He returned to the city after a period of agonising absence. No one was there, not even stray animals. He entered an illuminated café and found partly finished cups of coffee that looked as though they had been hastily left behind.

He went to the apartment nearby. It was open. A shoe lay by the door. He wandered around. The woman's perfume wafted up from the bottle by the mirror. He opened the cupboard; perhaps her lover had disappeared inside. He found no one.

He looked for her in the kitchen, under the bed, and on the roof. She wasn't there. He roamed the city, from one apartment to the next. No one was there. He sought out the bank's security guard but couldn't find him. He looked for the hapless informer who never tired of his job. He wanted to smoke a cigarette with him, at least, and to ask him what had become of the city after all this time, but he couldn't find him.

In the morning, a man who had cried himself to death was found on the sidewalk.

Love

He has never once said to her "I love you". He is content with looking in her eyes and extending his loving fingers, now and then, to gather strands of hair that the evening breeze disperses without permission.

She has never once said to him "I love you". She is content with walking beside him quietly. In the morning, she returns, alone, to gather traces of their footsteps before the cruel passers-by obliterate them. She carries a large basket on her head – no one knows what she hides inside it.

Sculpture

He laid his weary head on her chest and wept ceaselessly. She combed her fingers through his tame hair.

In the morning, people gathered around on the sidewalk. They stood there hesitantly, their bodies fragile, staring at a sculpture of a man and a woman made of flesh and blood. His head was on her chest, her loving hand on his hair as he lay still. The sculpture stood by the eucalyptus tree, exactly where the lovers had met every evening.

Loneliness

He awoke a little after midnight, assailed by a cold breeze. He walked to the window, scolding himself for not closing it earlier. Returning to bed, he noticed that the cat was missing. She was not in the bedroom or under the decrepit dining table. He walked back to the window and waited. He retreated to bed, overcome by despair, and muttering between coughs, "I warned her against leaving the house at this hour," as though referring to a person.

Maria

I meet a woman named Maria and she takes me to the city centre to see a sacred sculpture frequented by lovers. We gaze at it for a while. Maria and I walk away and find a dimly-lit restaurant. A gipsy band is playing a song, and I sip vintage wine made by local farmers. Suddenly, despair befalls me.

Maria tries to soothe me. She tells me about her house in the village far away. Despair will not release me, especially as Maria sneaks up to my heart like a cat.

We leave the restaurant and walk in the dark unhurriedly.

Strangers peer out of large windows.

The tram approaches. Maria decides to go home, and we make a plan to meet the following day. In the morning, I waited for some time but did not see her delicate blonde hair. I searched for her everywhere to no avail. I could not tell her that she and I should never part.

Detail

She tells him about each member of her family, and he listens intently. Her mother has lost her husband and suffers from asthma and allergies. Her younger sister, who just turned fourteen, spends all day with her textbooks and prays to her god from time to time. Her brother works as a salesperson in a fabric shop. He fell in love with a customer, but their love did not last. Her sister, who is younger by four years, is studying philosophy in a faraway university. In his love's letters, she writes that she dreams of a partner who will not betray her and hopes to become an illustrious writer.

She goes over all the details. She tells him of her sadness that the family rarely gathers at the dinner table. Tears fall from her eyes as she recalls her father, who died before having had enough of life.

They part ways, and he is overcome by a worry that the oversharing woman's heart will break if the mother died suddenly, if the little sister failed her exam, or if the other sister fell in love with another cheater.

A Trip

She puts on a cheap pair of socks and goes out.

She crosses the same street she has crossed for years, passing through the city centre, where crowds of construction workers wait for work.

The bitter cold plagues her this morning. She feels tears gathering but finds nothing when touching her eyelids.

She goes on walking. The icy wind is blowing in the streets, forcing the workers to pull up the collars of their dishevelled coats. She, too, tightens her grip on her coat so that the cold will not seep into her chest, as it has done all morning. She goes on walking.

She goes on walking, but her socks keep slipping down her legs, their wrinkles revealing the utter misery. She stops for a moment to pull them up. Passers-by look at her with pity.

She is on her way to buy bread, as is her custom for many years.

Disappointment

The woman had not finished getting ready when the hotel worker stormed into her room to tell her that the host had stopped paying for her stay.

She cried because the hotel worker saw her false teeth sitting in a cup of water near her bed. She had not finished getting ready.

Life

The pregnant woman is alive by a stroke of luck after a nuclear weapon destroyed everything. She gave birth to a handsome baby. However, when he was born, an atom of nuclear radiation fell on his little nose, making it grow to a horrific length. The woman had to walk three thousand yards to reach the end of his nose to wash it with soap and water, then return to feed him in the morning.

The Victim

They came in a hurry and gathered in the dark. They did not even have time to trim their beards. They danced a bloody song with sheathed daggers hanging across their bodies.

They dispersed in a hurry before sunrise. In the morning, the children found the body of a woman on the outskirts of the neighbourhood. What cruelty! Twenty-seven stab wounds in her body, beginning at her loins and ending at her breasts, filled with milk that will waste away.

Toes

A seventeen-year-old girl returns from the city on her wedding day. She is wearing a spotless dress, her skin excessively white with paint and powder.

The seventeen-year-old girl grows bolder as she watches other brides at the hairdresser's laughing without pretence, impatient for the evening to come.

The seventeen-year-old girl could not stand the moment of undressing on the night of the wedding. Her husband saw that she only had three toes. A few years ago, when she was a child, she dropped a kitchen knife while playing a terrible game.

Misery

The family sits in a dimly-lit room eating silently. The girl is cautious about ruining her cheap nail polish. The boy eats with his left hand and looks at the plate with disgust; he cannot stand his sister's nails and the cheap nail polish. The father thinks about the children's future. The smell of onions from the mother's worn dress is making her uneasy.

The lamp retires before its time. Darkness falls. The family goes to bed, leaving behind a plate of cold food, and a lamp drowning in a sea of shame for its failure.

A Puzzle

For twenty-nine days, the wretched woman diligently washed the stairs in the five-storey building and dried them with shabby pieces of cloth from her distant room. She cleaned before the overfed women peered at her from their doors, their nightgowns revealing their brazen thighs.

On the thirtieth day, the wretched woman left the building minutes after her arrival, without taking her monthly salary. She did not want the overfed women to accuse her of theft. Before washing the stairs, she decided to count them one by one, as she did every morning. Much to her surprise, there were only seventy-four, not seventy-five steps.

A Kidnapping

She brought the horse to her room and tied it to the bed frame. She ordered the horse to stop neighing, lest the neighbours wake up and lose their temper. They might get carried away and accuse her of bringing strange creatures to her bedroom after the traffic dies down and the lights go out.

The horse yielded to her request, as she expected. She slept soundly on her bed as she hadn't done for years. She awoke in the morning, but there was no sign of the horse or her bed, which escaped under the cover of the night.

She could not believe it. The door was still closed from the inside, as it was before the horse had fallen asleep.

Innocence

The family sits in front of the television, eating a simple dinner of oil, olives, zaatar and locally baked bread.

A group of black people are marching down a street holding signs. The food gets stuck in the boy's throat when he sees white police officers blocking the marchers' way, holding sticks and batons.

The camera moves closer to a black boy. Blood is dripping from his shaven head. The boy sitting in front of the television stops eating when he sees that the stick is in the house, in the teacher's hand, under the general's armpit, and on the screen.

Docility

She goes alone to the place where they once sat. She gazes at the small, sleepy village in the mountain's embrace. In the distance, a lone woman stands in front of a dreary house lighting a wood fire; three docile police officers resembling children walk around the station, bundled up in their coats.

How come they came in the dead of night and took him away when they are so docile and peaceful, walking around the courtyard surrounded by darkness, which is sinking into her chest like a disease she cannot fight off?

A Tear

She stands at her father's grave in the morning. Her lover's image floods her. She tells him about university problems, the pains of the body, and the treachery of others. She receives no response.

She meets the young man her heart had chosen in the evening.

While she sits beside him, she recalls the image of her loving father.

The images mingled with each other; an unexpected tear like a broken heart falls from her eye.

Rituals of a Wretched Woman

She goes to the newspaper office to print an announcement of her death, which is to take place on the following day. The child inside her has not stopped crying, and she decided to end her life that evening.

She enters the building, her face as white as wax, her eyes like ash and smoke. The security guard gazes at her. He hadn't yet had his morning coffee because his sleeping wife did not want to tell him where she hid the milk carton.

The switchboard operator gazes at her and thinks to himself that he has never seen a woman glide like a bird.

The bespectacled editor gazes at her with bulging inquisitive eyes. He is certain, for the first time, that what he reads has nothing to do with what he sees.

She disappears inside the advertising office for moments. When she returns, the security guard, switchboard operator and editor announce in unison that the beautiful woman has made their morning as sweet as peach.

She cries tears of joy and returns to the office to withdraw her request. Behind her, the security guard, switchboard operator and editor are bewildered, as is the angel of death peering out from a corner.

A Hole

When they met in the forest, all the beautiful words he propped up like lovely pieces of furniture faded away. He shrank and hid inside himself when she told him about the latest in books, music, dance and fashion.

As the talking came to an end, finding nothing else to do, he carved their names in the oak tree. She admired his skill. Deep down, he was grateful for his kind father, the only carpenter in the village, who had recently been laid to rest in the wood.

Understanding

After days of roaming the distant coastal cities, they returned to their ancient city, which is choked by incense and the invocations of elderly grandmothers. He returned to the clamour of life and thoughts of daily bread; she returned to a room full of books, plants and birdcages.

He did not telephone her as was his custom; he feared losing the faint scent of the days they spent away. She did not telephone him as was her custom; a single word might cause the heart to overflow and drown the world in inexplicable emotion.

A Mother

When he is overcome with sadness and feels trapped he runs to her like a tortured child. She soothes him and recounts stories she had gathered from distant mountainsides. He falls asleep on her tender hip and awakens to the smell of bread and coffee carried in by her small dewy hands.

He exclaims, "What a wonderful mother she is," this anxious woman who is fifteen years younger than he.

An Encounter

He waits on her, anticipates her every move and chases after her like a puppy, making his feelings clear. She blushes, and he knows that she likes him too. But their love was small, their woes far more immense, and so trouble began.

When the rain stopped pouring, her mother sent her to the shop. She dragged along her tattered shoes, which tore on the way and were full of mud and clay.

She took them off, hid them in a field and went on barefoot. The mud covered her feet and soiled her legs and the hem of her dress. She was just a girl, so she didn't mind.

He saw her leaving the shop and followed in a rush. She quickened her steps and crossed the field before he could reach her, realising she was no longer a girl.

He stood at the edge and called out to her. She remained still and red-faced. "How beautiful you look among the plants," he cried. "Go away. Someone might see us," she said. "Like a lovely pine!" he said. "I cannot stand you! Go away!" she said anxiously. Wounded, he hurried away. She picked up her shoes and left, feeling dejected. That night, he could not get to sleep, and she washed her mud-caked feet with her tears.

A Confession

I am in love with a young woman whose sister is a religious studies graduate. The sister is married to an alcoholic, and their son is as pure as a sparrow.

I grow attached to the little boy hearing the young woman's many stories, but she does not tell me about his father, the alcoholic.

She tells me about her older sister's husband who is a painter, and the younger sister's husband who is a language institute manager.

The only person I hear nothing about is the alcoholic brother-in-law. I met him two nights ago in a bar with a group of friends. He told me about the constant quarrels with his wife who is a religious studies graduate. He wept openly when I told him about a little boy as pure as a sparrow.

Nasheed

He encounters her in a restaurant downtown. They go to the golden beach and run on the sand like children. The vast ocean lures her in, she undresses; the delicate waves enfold her. She slips into the water like a fish and calls out to him, "Come in. It's warm."

They swim for some time. They break free from the water's embrace and lie on the sand. They find themselves alone with the murmurs of the sea and the ribbons falling from the coppery moon. He loses himself, and the entire world seems like a full moon.

He awakens despite not wanting to and gazes at her as she sleeps. Fearing his intense gaze might wake her, he looks away at the blaring lights of the city where she's from that sleeps soundlessly at the ocean's edge. Calamity awakens in his heart.

She rises and leans on her arm, made of silver and marble. She senses his pain and notices a trace of sadness on his face. She asks why and he answers, "The city is wandering in the dark."

She sits up. Her naked body shimmers with silver, grass, marble, and stone. She sings: People of the East. He joins her in singing: People of the East. He hungers for more music and feels a kinship with her. They sit on the sand until daylight.

Pieces of Bread

A lamp hangs from the ceiling, its bright light illuminates a small cell and a torn, foul-smelling blanket. Since the iron door was shut, the man inside has been examining his surroundings and relentlessly pacing the two-metre square floor.

There is a piece of bread near the corner. He touches it gingerly. The tomato juice seeps into bread. There is someone else here. Where was he taken? Why did he leave his food behind?

He vainly tries to sleep but the image of the lifeless bread and the lamp will not let him. He hides the bread under the bed and buries his head under the blanket. He still cannot sleep.

They bring him another piece of bread in the morning. He tries to take a bite, but can't swallow it, and he vomits. He puts it under the bed. Now there are two pieces of bread and one man in the cell.

They arrive and lead him out of the cell. Like panic-stricken rabbits, the pieces of bread sniff anxiously, anticipating danger.

In the morning, there are three pieces of bread, a pool of blood, and no one on the bed.

A Separation

She spent three hours cleansing herself, she scrubbed her body vigorously with soap, spent two hours making herself beautiful, and styled her hair the way he likes it. She waited anxiously for the final hour.

In the last minutes she busied herself with changing the bedsheets; he prefers the colour white. Interrupting her wild frenzy, they entered carrying him on their shoulders, enveloped in a terrible white cloth.

From the collection *Tuqus al-Mara'a al-Shaqiya*
(Rituals of a Wretched Woman), 1986

Ibrahim Nasrallah reviews
**Faras al-'A'ilah
(The Family Mare)
by Mahmoud Shukair**
Published by Naufal, Beirut 2013
Pbk 320 pages Arabic.
ISBN:978-9953-267937

Life, Deeply Rooted

In a harsh and difficult environment where life is hard and governed by isolation and the bitter search for a blade of grass or a drink of water, human life seems like the only oasis. As life blooms, its profound manifestations unfold, starting with the family mare and encompassing endless tales of people and their obsession with beauty, a quality which only women appear to embody amidst such a harsh wilderness.

Palestinian novelist Mahmoud Shukair's novel, *The Family Mare*, explores such an environment, meditating profoundly on events about a remote region removed from life and the usual focus of novels. Shukair wonderfully surprises us with his subtle meditation on the spiritual history of the Bedouins in that part of Palestine, and with his marvellous ability to utilise popular mythology, with its strong influence on shaping people's spirits, obsessions, fears, joys and sorrows.

Life there seems deeply rooted. Despite an utterance that connects the Abdallat to an ancient Arab past, the thread that connects people's daily lives with their distant past is clear, forceful and capable of shaping their identity, their self-image and others' perceptions of them.

In this novel, woman is the sole element of life that imbues its characters with vitality and a sensuous, wild, burning love. However, the desire to procreate in pursuit of strength and to reinforce the clan's status are equally important elements which complement the connotations that women evoke in these vast expanses.

At first glance, the novel seems like a love series that keeps surprising the reader with an unending chain of lovers, whose lives morph into other series, because the one thing they cannot stop drowning in is love.

That is how we understand the narrative of Mohammad Abdallah, the father, with Sabhaa, Mahira and others; and that it how we understand the tale of Mannan, the son, with Fatima, Safiyyah, Mathila and Wadhaa; and the tale of Wattaf and his gypsy lover, Murwadah; and of Falha, who dares to elope with her lover, the sweets vendor, marrying him against the wishes of her family. Then there is the story of Nawal and the orator, or teacher, and the tale of Mathila, the wife of Mannan, and the travelling salesman whose grave turns into a shrine and a memorial.

Foreigners do not escape the love trap. Mr. John finds the magic of the East in a woman named Najma, with whom he is desperate to begin a relationship, but he is never able to quench his thirst. He arrives as a soldier with the British occupation forces, and is not part of the heart, soul and body of the land. Hence, in the end, he only finds a Jewish lover on whom he bestows all the clothes and perfumes that he has prepared as gifts for Najma, but she never succeeds in filling those clothes. By contrast, the Turkish officer Oghlu takes refuge with the tribe and seems to become one of its members despite the strict social environment, and he can fall in love and marry. His relationship with his wife, Mahyouba, is one of the main love stories that illuminate the narrative.

The tribe encounters four factors that shake its existence: The small inventions that Othman introduces, such as the portable Primus kerosene cooking stove, rugs, and children's toys; the arrival of the British at the tribe's encampment following the defeat of the Turks; the city of Jerusalem, which the tribe visits at first to then end up settling in its suburbs; and finally, a collision with the harbingers of the fate that awaits their homeland, after discovering that they are ultimately part of a people that has its cities, villages, dreams and aspirations for freedom.

The events around the tribe and within it are shaped by the popular imagination and consciousness of its members. In that regard, the novel is faithful to that consciousness, accurately interpreting it and revealing the great disparity between it and the invader's cunning. The aircraft – or the strange bird as people perceive it – that flies overhead, the Zionist attack, the mare that

Tilka al-Amkinah, Sira Thatiyah (Those Places, an Autobiography), Naufal, Beirut, 2020

appears then vanishes, the dog that speaks in dreams, the lack of rain, the flood that threatens everything in its path and other phenomena are all signs of heaven's displeasure with them. Othman opens an unfamiliar door, acting like something of a mythical voice that is external to the tribe's narrow world. The British appear, and at the outset are received as guests; Mannan, whom they appoint as a mukhtar, has no qualms about collaborating with them.

Much of the narrative is devoted to the city of Jerusalem and its diverse life, and it accounts for the most significant upheaval: its life is different, and the changes, which no one can escape, decisively reshape the tribe's way of life, ultimately forcing its members to accept what they had never been capable of accepting before. A time that is completely unrelated to the innocent previous age begins at the gates and on the streets of the city, and knowledge of what occurs around the tribe and within in becomes the fire that will reshape it. Hence, the narrative's major transformations are inevitable, and they culminate in a courageous clash with the British forces and Zionist gangs.

The narrative has numerous characters, but some are unforgettable, such as Abbas; Adham, with his long ears that resemble those of a horse and his neighing; the loving courageous giant Wattaf; slayer and flayer of hyenas Abdul Jabbar; Mannan himself, and the women and men who share the same names, as though their constrained world had been ungenerous with names. The reader becomes accustomed to the repetitiveness of those names as one facet of the uniqueness of the narrative's individuals. All this is permeated by the spirit of the family mare – a thoroughbred that breaks loose from its rein, galloping away and turning into a myth, becoming the delicate thread that pulls together the narrative's events, and governs the thoughts and obsessions of its characters.

Mahmoud Shukair is rightly known as one of the most prominent writers, innovators and creators of new spaces within the Arabic narrative genre, both as a prolific mini short story writer, and as author of wonderful adventures in his two collections, *Shakira's Picture* and *My Cousin Condoleezza*. *The Family Mare* presents us with a rich work that is in keeping with the horizons and expansiveness of a novel.

Translated by Samira Kawar

MAHMOUD SHUKAIR

The Phantom

A SHORT STORY
TRANSLATED BY PAUL STARKEY

A fine evening, or so it seemed at least. From the roof of his house, Abdel Sami' looked at the quarter crammed with people. He contemplated them for some time then forgot them, without meaning to, of course.

He walked about, reviewing the journey he had made and the effort he had put in, and this was the result: children in jobs and professions, some in the country and some abroad; daughters settled in their husbands' houses, with no problems or scandals; a house of three storeys and a roof floor (one storey and a roof floor would have been enough!), the floors let to decent people and the roof floor reserved for Abdel Sami' and Fattouma to spend there the rest of their lives, and to enjoy some peace and quiet (or that was what they hoped for, at least!).

Fattouma got out of her chair, gathered together the blue robe on her full, well-proportioned body then galloped across the flat roof like a horse (no one seeing her would believe that she had had five sons and three daughters!). She went to Abdel Sami' to convey to him one of her off-the-cuff observations, which never strayed far beyond the field of her sons and daughters: "According to your intentions shall you be provided for! And our Lord, may he be praised and exalted, has provided for us! Our sons have turned out fine, not a drunkard among them, not a gambler, not a spy! And the girls have also turned out fine, virtuous, and sitting at home, God be praised!"

Fattouma looked warily at her husband as his eyes measured the height of the roof from the building's foundations. She was afraid of the return of the fear brought on by the earthquake. "It's time for the bath you take every evening," she said, in a deliberately gentle tone. "You go and take one first," he said, "stretch out under the water, and I'll take my turn after you." She was happy with that and thought that everything must be in order. She took off her clothes and stretched out under the water in the bath while Abdel Sami' carried on calmly watching two Israeli helicopters that had appeared in the sky. Their appearance disturbed him slightly, but after a little the two helicopters disappeared into the distance. A little later the sound of a Phantom aircraft suddenly broke through but Abdel Sami' could only locate it in the sky by tracking the source of the booming noise it was making. The aircraft only remained in his field of vision for a few seconds then disappeared, leaving behind it an ugly, suppressed roar. Abdel Sami' was a little upset then banished the worry from his head and went back to contemplating the houses and residents of the quarter. He saw one of his tenants leading his child back home; he saw that the man was growing his beard long in a way he had never noticed before, and said to himself: 'When I leased him the house five months ago, he did not have a beard!' He didn't dwell on the subject for long but headed inside the house, sat on his bed, opened the Qur'an and started to recite the chapter of 'The Cow'. There was no noise except for the quiet sound of the water dripping on his wife's body in the bath.

Fattouma was stretched right out in the bath with the water dripping from above onto her firm body. Fattouma took advantage of every spare moment in her life to compensate herself for her days of toil in the past. She feared that her situation might change at any moment. She hadn't yet forgotten how Abdel Sami' had been affected at the time of the earthquake that had struck the area just before midnight three months previously. Abdel Sami' had asked her to rest her head on his chest that night and had started to tell her some amusing stories, not because he wanted to tell her stories but because he couldn't sleep. He had felt an unusual movement in the house, which shook to the right and the left, as the clothes cupboard rattled and the windows creaked in an unusual way. Abdel Sami' leaped up in terror, and quickly put some clothes on. "Run, Fattouma!" he shouted. "It's an earthquake!" Abdel Sami' and Fattouma rushed down the stairs. Almost all the neighbours had come out of their rooms, which had been shaken by the earthquake. They all gathered, terrified, in the courtyard of the house. They recited prayers and invocations and begged God to protect them. Abdel Sami' contemplated his house, with its three storeys and roof floor. He was aware that in an instant he could be exposed to danger. He went up to Fattouma and said: "There is no safety or security in this world! Everything can be lost in an instant." "Trust in God, Abdel Sami'" trust in God!' she replied, to bolster his resolve.

Terror crept into his chest and nerves and he stood there. After that he was no longer capable of going near Fattouma. Whenever he touched her body, his fear of the earthquake came back to him. He no longer dared to be undressed beside her for fear the earthquake would surprise him in that state. On the advice of a neighbour she brought him the 'shaking bowl', filled it with water and made him drink from it, in the hope that his condition would improve, but it didn't. She went to the perfume market, bought some ginger and cumin, bought walnuts and almonds for him, but he did not get better. She went to the fortune teller and he told her: "Cook him a cock every morning!" And he gave her an amulet which she put under her pillow. She cooked Abdel Sami' a pound of hot peppers. Her neighbour told her: "I hope he hasn't rejected you, and his eye's on another woman!" "God forbid!" she replied, "anything but that!" After a lot of hesitation, Abdel Sami' went to the doctor who prescribed some medicine, which he bought from the chemist and soon returned to being as strong as a horse.

He finished the sura of 'The Cow' and started to recite the sura of 'Al 'Imran'. She had not yet finished her bath, which revived her every evening. Harmony returned to the marital nest that they shared. Fattouma believed that what had happened would not be repeated, God willing, but once it was repeated – in a scandalous manner. It was after midnight, Abdel Sami' was sleeping beside her and dreamed that the house was shaking him violently. He got up, terrified, and as he made for the door cried out: "Earthquake, earthquake!" As he ran, naked, he filled the stairway with his terrified, quaking voice. 'Get up! Get up!" he shouted to wake the neighbours. The neighbours looked out from the balconies of their apartments and the windows of their houses, men and women alike. Abdel Sami' was totally naked under the light of the lamp, and there was no earthquake at all. As he became aware that he was naked and causing a scandal, he covered himself with his hands, but quickly forgot himself and waved his arms about, shouting: "Earthquake,

earthquake!" The men ordered their wives not to carry on looking at the sight and told them to move away from the windows and balconies. Fattouma raced down to Abdel Sami' and gave him the dishdasha that he'd forgotten by the bed. He put it on and came to himself, then went back up the stairs hiding from the eyes of the neighbours. (Some of the neighbours thought of leaving the building never to return, the only thing stopping them being the chronic housing crisis, and Abdel Sami's solemn oaths that he didn't mean anyone any harm, that what had happened had been well-intentioned, the result of a cursed, overpowering dream!).

Fattouma left the bathroom with a pink towel around her waist and sat combing her hair as she waited until he had finished reciting the Qur'an. "It's your turn now for the bath!" she said. "Take off your dishdasha and get under the water." He seemed confused, in a way she hadn't expected. She looked at him for a long time. "What's the matter, Abdel Sami'?" "I'm upset about our neighbour Mohammad." "Mohammad! He's been the best of neighbours!" "When he rented the apartment he didn't have a long beard, Fattouma!" "Okay, you want to keep a watch on the neighbours' beards?" "What! Understand me, Fattouma! A long beard! The man might belong to Hamas!" "Suppose he does belong to Hamas, Abdel Sami'?" "And the house I put everything into, Fattouma?" "What about the house?" "Have you forgotten what happened two months ago? Have you forgotten the Phantom that dropped a thousand-kilogram bomb on Sheikh Salah Shahada's house? It killed him, and his wife and children, and the neighbours! Have you forgotten, Fattouma?" "Just trust in God, my love!"

At the very moment Abdel Sami' started to take off his dishdasha, he heard the sound of a plane. He quickly rushed outside and looked at the sky. "The nights of misfortune have returned," said Fattouma to herself, out loud.

The nights of misfortune had indeed returned. Abdel Sami' was afraid for the house he had built. Afraid of a bomb dropped by a Phantom aircraft to kill his neighbour Mohammad, who had let his beard grow long for some reason. The bomb would kill Mohammad and his wife and children, as well as the other neighbours and their wives and children. It would kill Abdel Sami' and Fattouma. Fattouma would be taken into God's mercy when she had not yet had her fill of life. "I know Fattouma well, Fattouma has not yet had her fill of life. And the house that I built with the sweat of my brow will become just a distant memory. No, no, cursed be Abu Israel! This is ridiculous!"

Ridiculous! Every day, crimes are committed against Palestinian houses and no one can stop it. What are you to do? Should you ask Mohammad the neighbour to leave the house and go to live in another quarter? Should you denounce Mohammad? Should you inform the occupying authorities that you have a tenant who has suddenly let his beard grow, which means he has a link with Hamas or Jihad? (Or with the al-Aqsa Martyrs' Brigades, sir, so as not to upset the rivalry between the various factions!). Impossible! Impossible that Abdel Sami' should become an informer after all this time! So let him request Mohammad that he vacate the house, telling a white lie, that his son who works as an accountant in Saudi Arabia will be coming back in a month and needs an apartment for him and his wife to live in. But it's the right of a tenant not to be evicted like that. And Mohammad seems a good man, and it's not right for Abdel Sami' to treat a good man badly. Okay, but I don't want him to be the cause of my house being destroyed. Abdel Sami' considered his options for a moment and seemed to be reconsidering his entire situation.

Abdel Sami' didn't take any decision and didn't consult Fattouma about anything relating to the neighbour. Fattouma didn't bother him by requesting an explanation but left him to act as he saw fit. He started to spend a considerable amount of time outside the house, keeping a watch on the quarter for fear that dubious elements might be entering it. Abdel Sami' knew that the Phantom would only strike after receiving notification from an agent who had infiltrated the neighbourhood, who would confirm to the pilot using precision equipment that the neighbour Mohammad was inside the house. Then the agent would withdraw from the target site and the plane would swoop on the house, strike it, kill everyone inside then disappear into the sky. Out of an ex-

The French edition of My Cousin Condoleezza, Actes-Sud, 2008

cess of caution, Abdel Sami' spied on his neighbour Mohammad to set his mind at rest in regard to his actions. He watched him when he left the apartment and watched him when he returned. He watched anyone coming to visit him and anyone leaving. He didn't notice anything out of the ordinary and was ashamed of himself, fearing that his neighbour Mohammad might be suspicious and think that Abdel Sami' had been commissioned by some authority to spy on him and watch his movements – especially after they had met each other by chance at the entrance to the building and near the door of Mohammad's apartment.

Fattouma went back to intervening vigorously in her husband's quandary, and started to give him one piece of advice after another. Abdel Sami' would think about what Fattouma said for a moment, then fall victim to the fear that was growing inside him and just mutter, not knowing how to behave or find any peace. At night, he would stay awake and not remain in the house whenever he heard the roar of planes. He would ask Fattouma to leave the house with him, but she would not respond to his request so he would leave the house by himself, stay away until the planes left and only then return.

One morning, Abdel Sami' was surprised to find that his neighbour Mohammad had shaved off his beard, so that he looked just as he had used to. He was going to ask him about the change (and the change back), but he didn't, because something like that would represent interference in his neighbour's affairs. Abdel Sami' now became a little more relaxed. A week later, Mohammad brought Abdel Sami' some surprising news; he would leave the house at the end of the month because he would be going north to work there! The decision had been made by the company he worked for.

Abdel Sami' agreed to his neighbour's request but he couldn't overcome a new worry that kept working away inside him: perhaps Mohammad thought that Abdel Sami' had been charged by some authority with watching him. "Speak to him about it and get rid of this obsession," said Fattouma. But Abdel Sami' remained anxious and wouldn't speak to Mohammad about it, because he couldn't bear to be an object of doubt or suspicion!

From his collection Ibnat Khalati Condoleezza *(My Cousin Condoleezza), published by al-Mu'assasa al-Arabiya lil Dirassat wal Nashr, Beirut, 2004.*

GUEST WRITER
TRINO CRUZ

Trino Cruz, born in Gibraltar in 1960, is a bilingual writer and translator. He grew up in the Straits region, between Gibraltar, Morocco and Spain, an upbriging which has deeply influenced his personal vision of the Mediterrranean as an inexhaustible crossroads connecting with even the most remote corners of our planet and memory.

After pursuing his studies in Marine Biology and Medical Research at the Universities of Liverpool and London, Trino embarked on a career in the financial industry for over 30 years before dedicating himself fully to writing and other cultural activities.

His writing arises from the periphery of a fertile shore and is driven by a deep conviction that barriers in culture must be overcome by fostering a dynamics of exchange and collaboration between communities, wherever

IN THE GUEST WRITER FEATURE, BANIPAL PROMOTES INTERCULTURAL DIALOGUE BY INTRODUCING A NON-ARAB AUTHOR AND THEIR WORKS TO OUR READERS. THE GUEST OF THIS ISSUE IS THE POET AND TRANSLATOR TRINO CRUZ FROM GIBRALTAR.

they may be. The underlying common ground needs to be uncovered and enriched each and every day, lest we allow other forces to pull us apart.

He is currently involved in a number of regional cultural initiatives, and is on the editorial board of *SureS*, a literary journal published in Tangier (Morocco) and revista *Banipal*, the Spanish edition of this journal.

He has published several collections of poetry including *Lecturas del espacio profanado* (1992) and *Rihla* (2003). *Memoria del Polizón*, a comprehensive collection of his writings to date in Spanish will be published soon. He has collaborated in numerous translations of Arabic and French poetry to Spanish. He has read his poetry in venues and poetry festivals in Spain, Morocco and South America.

TRINO CRUZ

The fertile shore
SELECTED POEMS

GETTING TO PRIMROSE HILL

for frank auerbach

there is no clear beginning to oneself

memory precedes
the deep furrows   the displaced earth

a surface is only depth
the scaffolding unfolds within
the flux stirs the abyss
time to scavenge at last
the bold brushstrokes of a mind

the dregs   the dregs   the dregs

that which has harmed us for far too long
a relentless undertow drags us
we meekly sink inwards

for there is no safe ground
the rubble's alive   the earth our flesh

what is lost
may be what matters most
we are just shards of something else

beneath
another surface breathes

GUEST WRITER

what leaks away
is never lost

the pulse of clay
where memories meet

we are
an awkward edge
scraped off layer by layer
no new scars uncovered

too attached for too long
to that which forgets

between the unmasked and the caressed
we are what remains
the warm ash
the drifting rubble
our mind is our flesh

your hand and my hand
can only be the same hand
that part which must remain unwritten

we are the strandline
neither too shallow nor too faint
just the disarray of another shore.

A LIFE OF CLAY
(a book of shards)

for magdalene odundo

a
river-deep
pulse

our lives of clay
again reshaped

who dares
slip onboard unseen?

who leaves
the dry land so far behind?

(for a crossing of unknown duration
we have been stitched together with words

we are still the same mesopotamian poets writing of
Atra-Hasis, Utnapishtim and Puzur-Enlil

seeds, flesh and words still mingle in the unbaked clay

the gangplanks are still guarded

once darkness falls
the stowaways will slip onboard

perhaps one will be a scribe
or a poet

a story of clay
whispered through the reeds

how else could the unwritten ever drift across a sea?)

SOME IMAGES MUST NOT FADE

he who becomes a stranger
in this world and says what is not
because he wants
to change the world

he understandably
mistakes patterns for meaning
and so desperately mismeasures
"…veux-tu m'emporter dans ta chute?"

entering minds uninvited
seeking what disturbs and betrays
what poisons and decays

he can now hardly look back
without stumbling

we must appease his fear of sharp edges
on which things so precariously balance

some images must not fade

much warmth has already been lost
our strength is being sapped
vanishing figures in soft glow

unknowingly
we tread on crippled snares
buried in the undergrowth

no beeline, crow flying or rorqual diving
just windswept, dragged, drifted
our shadows furtively embrace
where dead-ends meet
and blind-spots blossom

some images must not fade

the mind wedged open
kept ajar for a time
allows
the poor creature
to come and go at will.

TRINO CRUZ

*Six poems translated from Spanish
by Luke Perera and the poet*

THE BOOK OF OUTRAGE

the book of outrage is one of oblivion
as if a river making its headway
changed its name (as it turned)
to dive shark-like once at sea
and resurface hungry and abruptly
at some other shore

just the path which disappears into the brush
just the sky which collapses without birds

the mountains sharpen
clear as words

love made
your back turned to me
you sleep

you ill-treat the night and forget me

is space as fecund as it appears?
is this torn light a scar or a caress?

this language, love
is the tree that forgets.

IN THIS POEM

in this poem
light is a fish gone astray
a man dropping to the ground, riddled
the expectation of final judgment

light is a desert
which no longer recalls that birds exist
which cannot remember that the sea ever existed
and space continues to receive even more light

your lips move transparently and without language
without response

the pigeon delivers a message
its message is a pigeon

you enter a garden of beings who are flowers
which no longer blossom

you enter a luscious space
where what is transparent is legible

in this poem
there are places which have gone insane
windswept sands and unfolding clouds
these paths change us each time they are traversed

we enter the desert
knowing that the sun will wipe out our memory

light has dreamt of its own extinction

the sea has gone wild
it desperately wants to become what she is

our night has been crushed between rocks

in this poem
the chimaera does not die with man
it peers into the abyss and is born.

TRINO CRUZ

IF WE ERASE SOME TRACES

if we erase some traces
and not others

if we erase some shadows
and not others

if we erase some memories
and not others

and we allow our selves to be seduced
by sterile clay
in a fragile space

we will engender a creature which moves traceless
moves so as not to leave a trace
leaves no trace in order to move

a creature which in itself is the trace
it does not leave when it moves
or the hurried ritual of the one who seduced the wandering shadow
to drag itself back into its own lair.

MIDDAY FOR A SONGBIRD

our prow shudders
whispers

the river
which drags you
is me

every slight movement
is music
a vessel in which beings coalesce

GUEST WRITER

                      I am
                 your blind spot

          the water scours in the
               stream's pulse

            we are the unsayable
the indescribable   the inerasable

            the joy of the cosmos
              is its movement

          the river in which I dive
                  is you

          it suffices to be an echo
              volcano of words
            a Babel for outcasts

            on the rim of being
           nothingness blossoms

           the cosmos is a flower
             of a single flame.

NOTHING IS AS IT SEEMS

words
radiating
oblivion

                    words
               shot to pieces

                                      entwined
                              transparencies
                                        wrestle

TRINO CRUZ

     transactions
     without
     intermediaries

nothing is
as it seems

     word-womb-lair

         hollow
         in the form
         of a body

     unfolded
     boundless
     silenced

wounded
syllable

     nothing is
     as it seems

         an arrowhead
         within a
         hollow body.

THE RIVER LURES US

*"but he, who properly speaking does not exist,
pulls the strings." Rafael Cadenas*

the river lures us
craves us

we are nets
cast in the air

> dragged through water
> so much outrage expressed
> frayed   ignored
>
> deep traces throb
> hem us in   make us fertile
>
> we dig up the mud because we are mud
> we plunge into nothingness because we are all
> tirelessly flowing within the current.

GHARB*

Imagine our world 200 million years ago, a single land-mass, Pangea,
anchored to the Equator, surrounded by one great ocean,
   Panthalassa.

65 million years ago, the plates of the earth's crust begin to move.
The Atlantic takes shape as the plates pull apart,
while the Tethys Sea is compressed to create the proto-
   Mediterranean.
A narrow rift remains and the Straits is formed.

The Eurasian and African plates converge to form the Gibraltar Arc,
with the Betic cordillera and the Rif mountains binding it all together
in one sweeping embrace.

Around 5.9 million years ago, the throat of the Straits narrows,
becomes progressively restricted and finally closes.
The Mediterranean basin dries up, and the Messinian Salinity Crisis
   begins.
During almost 600,000 years, there will be open flow between the
   two continents.

Then, just over 5.3 million years ago, an Atlantic trickle gets it all
   started.
Starts slowly, but within as little as several months,
the Zanclean flood reclaims the dried-out Mediterranean basin,
and the Fretum reappears.

TRINO CRUZ

The Alboran Sea, is a transition zone between the Mediterranean and
 the Atlantic Ocean, where both ecosystems fuse into a single
 thriving space.

A large clockwise eddy forms off the North African coast,
as the upper level Atlantic water-flow pours into the Mediterranean.
The Alboran gyre, has been spinning uninterruptedly
for over five million years, resulting in a rich marine environment
which has attracted us to this zone for millennia.
Smaller weak anti-clockwise eddies form to the north along the
 Iberian shore.

The prevailing winds blow along an east-west axis,
tirelessly stirring things on land and on sea.

The stillness, when it arises in the Straits, is deceptive,
everything moves even when it appears to stand still.
Over time, great sea level fluctuations occur as one glaciation follows
 another.

Black kites (*Milvus migrans*) have been migrating back and forth across
 this complex and dynamic ecosystem for millions of years.

For just as long, each February, the first Atlantic bluefin tuna
 (*Thunnus thynnus*), arrive at the Straits as they make their way to
 the warm waters of their spawning grounds in the western
 Mediterranean. The route is snared, the restless sea is a maze of
 deep dark mirrors which multiply without escape.

The time for our arrival comes. We surface and start to meddle with
 things,
in a small way at first.

The first humans, Neanderthals, arrive in the region about 125,000
 years ago,
Homo sapiens follow some 40,000 years ago.

We are late arrivals!

From the fertile land of the buried and the erased we spring forth.
We paint and engrave the walls of shelters and caves:

paintings of deer at the Tajo de las Figuras,

protome of a horse head at la cueva del Moro,
the Neolithic rider and the ship in la cueva de La Laja Alta,
the petroglyph at la Silla del Papa,
the oblique criss-cross engravings on the floor of Goreham's cave-sanctuary.

... and on the African shore, the quarry caves of Hercules, Mugharet El Khalil,
and the cave of Idols at Achakar; the caves of Caf Taht el Ghar, Benzú and Gar Cahal.

Time digs and sculpts with one hand and erases and buries with the other.

Which words did we use then?

When the first Phoenician merchants arrive from the East by sea,
we are already here.

At first, towards the end of the second millenium BC,
we meet and trade on coastal islands, they are kept away from the mainland.

80 years after the fall of Troy, according to classical tradition,
the Tyrians found Gadir and Lixus. Temples are built in honour of Melkart.
These sanctuaries for seafarers become economic centres,
regulating trade and exchange.
They establish their trading posts and their fish-salting factories
in strategic locations in river estuaries and sheltered bays.

A commercial system is established which we can call, the Circle of the Straits.
The extreme ends of the Mediterranean have now embraced.

The ruins of large garum fish-salting factories remain today at Baelo Claudia, Carteia, Gades, Malaka and Septem Fratres, Tamuda, Rusadir, Cotta, Lixus and Mogador on the southern shore.

The mines of Rio Tinto and Tharsis are part of the Iberian Pyrite Belt, formed 350 million years ago. It is a vast geographical area stretching 250 kilometres across much of the south of the Iberian Peninsula, from the edge of the Guadalquivir basin to that of the Sado in the Portuguese Alentejo.

This is the largest concentration of massive sulfide ore deposits in the world.
A significant reserve of the planet's copper, zinc, tin, lead, gold and silver.
The mining activity in this region goes back far far in time.

The Phoenicians do not arrive empty-handed, they introduce the potter's wheel, agricultural metal tools, the yoke and animal traction for the plough,
exquisite craftsmanship of jewelry, weaving and architecture.

They bring their tales and mythology, their language and alphabet, their vines and their songs.

Myths mix within our deep memory.
We begin to grasp the dynamics of this complex environment that shapes us.

The rich mythological substrate of the Straits, captures an underlying essence which challenges reality and unsettles it.

The underworlds of the region have long shadowed the physical reality
of its jebels, rivers, marshes and shores.

The people of the Straits, those who inhabit, have inhabited and will inhabit,
its shores and hinterland, give rise to a diverse and grand community.
Our words have been flowing back and forth across the Straits for
many thousands of years and cannot be contained in any tidy narrative.

Our unstoppable movement will always challenge boundaries.
We cannot be contained in tight space, a time arises when we are forced
to move elsewhere.

Over time, the shores move closer, then certain forces again pull them apart.

The Straits region has, only rarely and for a time, been a single dynamic space,

during the Roman Empire and Al Andalus perhaps,
but Al Andalus was no paradise, endless power struggles and tensions
between the various communities could not provide for anything
else.

Coexistence is never painless.

We know that the all-encompassing infinite text is out there never to
be written,
so many episodes are silenced, just disappear from memory or never
make it to the records. We will make do with a handful of precious
fragments.

Enkidu, what has held you up so long?

Do you recognise that stranded Odysseus on a western shore,
that perplexed Sinbad with sunken shoulders who has long lost his
bearings?

Scheherazade, which tale will you charm us with tonight?

The sand hit hard, just a thud on the water's edge.

Kahina, protect us from the next blow.

The path narrows with each beat.
Most of the ripples which arise when the water is hit, simply die out,
only a few ever bounce back. If it weren't for these returning
ripples,
what would be remembered?

We delay surfacing for a time.
Our memory continues to unfold
as crossroads multiply and unforeseen rhythms arise.

---

* *Although rooted in the Straits of Gibraltar, Gharb is a free-flowing open space.*

INTERVIEW

The Maktoob Project:
Bi-National Translation of Arabic Literature into Hebrew

> The translation of Arabic literature into Hebrew has always been a very sensitive topic for Arab writers, who become divided between supporters and opponents. Supporters see the translation process as a form of support for the Palestinians against the Israeli occupation. As for the opponents, they consider agreeing that their works be published in Hebrew is a form of normalization with the Israeli occupation.
>
> Banipal conducted the following interview with the editors in charge of Maktoob, the most recent and important project for translating and publishing Arabic literature in Hebrew.

Q: To start with, we'd like you to give us a general idea of the Maktoob project and tell us why Arabic literature should be translated into Hebrew.

A: Maktoob is an independent cultural and political project devoted to translating Arabic literature into Hebrew and making it available to the public. It was set up in 2016 as a joint initiative by Palestinians and Jews, citizens of Israel, who wanted to challenge the Israeli Orientalist approach and discourse vis-à-vis Arabic culture and people, to resist the colonial relations and oppose its cultural and political underpinning. The Maktoob people believe that making Arabic and Palestinian literature available to Hebrew readers – through bi-national teams of translators – is a form of resistance to the system of segregation and the colonial relationship between Jews and Palestinians, including the linguistic apartheid that exists where 99 percent of Israeli Jews cannot read a literary text in Arabic and Arabic books account for less than one percent of the books translated into Hebrew from foreign languages. Under this system, a colonial power structure dominates the relationship between the two languages, Orientalism prevails in the Israeli view of the Palestinians, the Israeli media practise racial

THE MAKTOOB PROJECT

Yonatan Mendel, Yehouda Shenhav-Shahrabani, Hannah Amit Kochavi, Eyad Barghouty, Rawya Burbara

incitement against the Arab world and portray it superficially, and Palestinian history and the Nakba are denied in Israeli school curricula and academic institutions.

The Maktoob project sees translation as a communal cultural and political activity, as an act that seeks to change reality and to envision a model for shared sovereignty, and not as part of a disengaged, individual aesthetic and literary activity alone. At Maktoob, the translation is done according to a special method quite distinct from the methods used in other translation projects. It is a bi-national and bilingual process, in that Palestinian editors and translators who know Hebrew well play a central role in all stages of the process. Furthermore, the Maktoob method integrates "voice" into the textual translation process and conveys the sense of the Arabic words in Hebrew in a way that is different from the prevailing methods of literal translation, which are colonialist methods adopted to suit the Western Jewish ear.

The Maktoob series project is an independent, non-commercial and non-profitmaking cultural and political project with no links to any official or government institution. It uses the revenue from translations to finance translating more books from Arabic to Hebrew and publishing them, as well as to finance local Palestinian cultural projects.

The small editing group includes: the chief editor, Professor Yehouda

Amputated Tongue:
Palestinian Prose in Hebrew

Time of White Horses
Ibrahim Nasrallah

Children of the Ghetto – My Name is Adam by Elias Khoury

Memory in the Flesh by Ahlam Mosteghanemi

Shenhav-Shahrabani, a well-known critical sociologist, an anti-colonialist and supporter of the Palestinian cause, a translator and writer, author of the book *The Arab Jews* (2006); deputy editor Eyad Barghouty, a writer and translator; deputy editor Dr Yonatan Mendel, a sociolinguist and opponent of Orientalist concepts in teaching Arabic and author of *The Creation of Israeli Arabic* (2014); translator and editor Kifah Abdul Halim; and editorial coordinator Hanan Saadi.

Q: Is Maktoob a publishing house or a series of books published by different publishers?

A: It's a book series. All the decisions are taken and all the work on the books is carried out by the small editorial board totally independently and professionally – from choosing the books, checking and editing them, acquiring the publication rights and even the book production. Several publishing houses are then asked to help, mainly with distributing the books to bookshops and to the reading public.

The Letters - Mahmoud Darwish and Samih al-Qasim

Q: Which titles have been published so far?

A: Since 2017 we have issued an average of four books a year, and altogether about twenty publications so far. They included translations of novels, short stories and poetry, Palestinian and Arab, related to the Palestinian and Arab historical narrative in the colonial context. These were *Time of White Horses* by Ibrahim Nasrallah; three novels by Elias Khoury – *My Name is Adam: Children of the Ghetto*, *Stella Maris* and *Majma' al-Asrar*; *Memory in the Flesh* by Ahlam Mosteghanemi; a children's book, *The Children Laugh*, by Zakaria Tamer; *The Letters* by Mahmoud Darwish and Samih al-Qasim; *Walking on Winds* by the late Palestinian writer Salman Natour, who was one of the founders of the Maktoob series; and *Bardakana*, a novel by the Palestinian writer Eyad Barghouty. We have also published *Bi-Lisan Mabtoura* (lit. *Amputated Tongue*), an anthology of Palestinian literature translated into Hebrew, with 73 stories by 57 Palestinian writers from Israel, the West Bank, the Gaza Strip and the diaspora. Last year we published a translation of the novel *Shlomo the Kurd, Me and the Time* by the Iraqi Jewish writer Samir Naqqash.

Shlomo the Kurd, Me and the Time by Samir Naqqash

We have also published translations of historical books and diaries, such as *'Aja'ib al-Athar fi'l-Tarajim wa'l-Akhbar* (*The Marvelous Compositions of Biographies and Events*) by the Egyptian historian Abd al-Rahman al-Jabarti and *Year of the Locust: A Soldier's Diary and the Erasure of Palestine's Ottoman Past*, edited by the well-known Palestinian scholar Salim Tamari.

In poetry we have published a translation of *Luzumiyyat* (*Luzum ma la yalzam*, or '*Unnnecessary Necessities*') by Abu al-Ala al-Ma'arri and *I Own Nothing Save My Dreams: An Anthology of Ezidi Poetry in the Wake of a Genocide, 2014–2016*. We also have our Notebooks project for Palestinian poets and writers, which has published *A Refugee and a Washing Line* by the poet Raja Ghanim Danaf; *Routine*, a collection of microfiction by Mahmoud Shukair, and *The Days of Tanzim*, a play by Ayman Kamel Agbaria.

Q: According to our information, some publishers in Israel have published works of literature without the consent of the authors. Has Maktoob obtained the consent of the authors whose works it has published?

A: In the Maktoob project we have a clear policy. Nothing will be translated without the approval of the writers or their heirs. We think that translating without permission is literary theft and especially in light

The Children Laugh by Zakaria Tamer

of power-relations also a cultural-political crime. We have made our position on this public in several cases where it turned out that Israeli publishers had allowed themselves to translate and publish texts by Arab writers without their permission. We strongly objected to those publications. We are aware of the circumstances, the problems and the debates about translation into Hebrew, and we respect the political views and positions of the writers when they reject translation, but we are most pleased when writers agree to have their works translated after understanding the special nature, the identity, the aims, and the political and cultural importance of our project.

Q: Might we know how the literary press in Israel has reacted to these published works? Have they been reviewed in Hebrew newspapers?

A: Yes, most of our books have been reviewed in Hebrew newspapers and have attracted attention in the most important cultural and literary supplements. Of course some books have received more attention than others and have had many reviews, especially Elias Khoury's *Children of the Ghetto*, *Bi-Lisan Mabtoura* which is an anthology of Palestinian stories, and *The Children Laugh* by Zakaria Tamer.

Q: And have Israeli readers shown much interest in the books?

A: Here too it varies from book to book. There are books that have reached thousands of readers and have been surprisingly successful. Other books have received less attention from general readers, but rather from the academic and literary elite and from people with an interest in historical studies. At this stage the Maktoob project is trying to reach a wider audience and strengthen the political-cultural challenge that these books pose. We also want to harness the outcomes of the project – and not less important, the process of bi-national work and translation – in order to push forward a different relation between Jews and Palestinians, as well as a notion of a shared sovereignty.

BOOK REVIEWS

Joselyn Michelle Almeida reviews
**Fugitive Atlas: Poems
by Khaled Mattawa**
Graywolf Press, USA, 2020
ISBN: 9781644450376,
paperback, 126 pp., $18.00

Personal and collective lives of peoples in West and East

Khaled Mattawa effortlessly navigates between Middle Eastern, American, and World literary traditions in *Fugitive Atlas* (2020), his most recent poetic tour de force. Readers of *Banipal* will be familiar with his ability to harmonize the polyphonous intertextuality in these archives as a poet, translator, and scholar– whether in poetry collections such as *Amorisco* (2008), *Tocqueville* (2010), for which Mattawa won the Arab American Book Award (2011), and *Mare Nostrum* (2019); his translations of Adonis, Fadhil Al-Azzawi and other significant contemporary Arab poets; and several anthologies of Arab American poetry and fiction. His prolific and award-winning work in the field of Arabic literature in English, recognized by awards like the MacArthur Fellowship (2014), make him a leading voice in the current Renaissance of Arab American letters and one of the most significant American poets writing today.

The manifold poetic routes that Mattawa sets in motion across the five sections which comprise *Fugitive Atlas* interconnect the personal and collective lives of peoples in West and East, and render a deeply elegiac map of humanity's shared planetary experience in the beginning decades of the 21st Century. Through original and masterful experiments with poetic form, Mattawa constructs a sen-

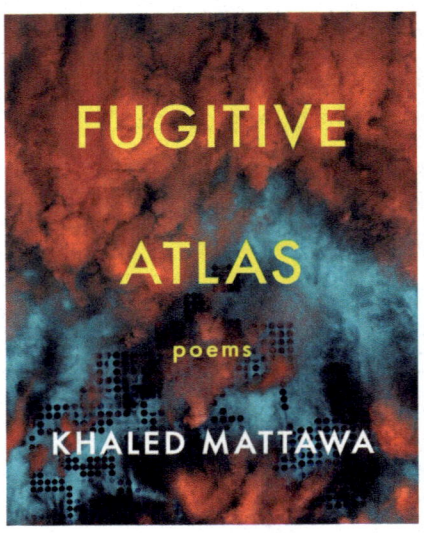

sibility that inhabits both transnational and translocal imaginaries, engaging the themes of loss, war, displacement, and the longing for return, justice, and restitution. One of the central preoccupations of *Fugitive Atlas* is the figure of the refugee as both victim and survivor of conflict and displacement, which has personal dimensions. Mattawa's family fled from Libya in 1923 after the Italian army invaded Misrata, where they lived, and undertook the arduous land journey of 1,000 miles to safety in Egypt before the family's eventual return to Libya after World War II.

Through religious forms such as the psalm and the hymn, and more classical ones such as the ode, the qassida, and the 'alam, the acrostic form of the Bedouin elegy, Mattawa brings to life the intersection of mythical, personal, national, and global histories. His virtuosity extends to other Eastern forms, such as the Japanese haibun, a prose meditation that concludes with the more familiar renga. Critic Phillip Metres traces the haibun to Basho, yet the combination of a prose reflection that ends in a poem also shares a Western Counterpart in Dante's *Vita Nuova*. Like Coleridge and Borges, Mattawa also experiments with marginalia and bibliographic elements, such as the index form to move poetry beyond the page. The plurality of poetic forms in *Fugitive Atlas* finds an echo in the diverse sources that inform it. As Mattawa's notes indicate, these range from the Egyptian Book the Dead (circa 1550 BCE), to Shakespeare's Sonnets, Percy Shelley's "Ozymandias", Walt Whitman's *Song of Myself*, T.S. Eliot's *The Wasteland*, and Octavio Paz's "I Speak of the City, as well as Arabic writers such as Amal Dunqul and Abu Bakr Kahal.

This wealth of named and unnamed allusions resonate throughout a work that engages the problem of being human since the creation according to Abrahamic and other world religions in poems such as

BOOK REVIEWS

Khaled Mattawa

"A Dream of Adam" and "An Idea for a Short Film". The long durée of Mattawa's gaze, however, offers no comfort in this unflinching elegiac meditation on humanity's shared tragic fate, one that in the present feels unmoored from the stability of the past and traditional understandings of divinity. For Mattawa, man – here a representative of humanity– is "God's last choice" (p7) after creating the natural world, and nevertheless, a choice that the divine being needs in order to exist. In "Shikwah," the poet provocatively uses apostrophe to ask the divinity "How / will you fare, alone again in the empty vast" (p9). Can the sublime exist without the human to perceive it? As in Percy Shelley's "Mont Blanc," the question remains unanswered.

The indeterminacy that surrounds unanswered questions is one of the few saving graces in Mattawa's universe, since the answers that human history does yield involve conflict, extinction, and dispossession, "A history enfolding words nourished on blood," like the poet declares in "Anthropocene Hymns" (p11). The stark truth of power and corruption cuts through any objection that might be posed, as the poetic voice demands indignantly "Don't tell me we are not who we are" (p13) in a line that both in sense and sound invokes Baudelaire's acerbic "Hypocrite lecteur / mon semblable, mon frère." The challenge for humanity is "How to stop thinking of bodies / as worth extinction, worth eating or enslaving – / brought to whip or firing squad" (p13).

Throughout *Fugitive Atlas*, the poet suggests a continuum of systems of violence that encompass nature and humanity alike. These systems imbricate every aspect of life, as revealed in "Plume" and "Our Neighbors: Poisoned City," the haibuns on the poisoned water in Detroit and Flint, Michigan, or as catalogued in "Occupation: An Index". While alluding to the Israeli / Palestinian conflict, the poem also speaks to the experience of those who have been colonized by a foreign power. The narrative voices within the poem alternate between those of colonizer and colonized, and an unnamed historical observer; the poems challenge the reader to examine the terrain between observer and witness. The transnational becomes the translocal in the haibun "Our Cities", in which the cities of the

Middle East "All have their counterpart here in America" (p118).

The landscape of war overshadows the second half of the book, including section IV, the titular section. The poems move between Mattawa's experience of return to Libya after the death of dictator Muammar Al-Gaddafi, and the plight and extraordinary courage of people trying to flee from the devastation of conflict in the Mediterranean. The poet offers contrasting portraits of return in "After 42 Years" and the more formal "42 Years Revisited," an 'alam. The impossibility of returning to a time before the violence of the regime, and recovering the lives and time lost requires a different kind of redemption, "There is no 'after' until we pray for all the dead" (p52). Paradoxically, the containment of the 'alam points towards "more slaughter" and the repetition of the cycle of violence (p55). The tension between form and content in this 'alam indexes the depth of the wound in the collective and individual national psyche resulting from civil war.

In the context of conflict and its aftermath, the psalm becomes an almost talismanic form in poems like "Psalm for the Medics," "Psalm on the Road to Agadez", "Psalm for Crossing Nimroz," and "Constance Psalm," where the word becomes a sign of life in the face of extreme danger and terror. His composite poem "With Lines Taken from Walt Whitman" yokes Whitmanian exuberance to the brutal reality facing those who make the terrifying Mediterranean crossing to Europe from North Africa, amplifying the urgency of their plight and the dehumanization they encounter from traffickers, European states, and even well-meaning organizations.

Notwithstanding the wastelands of past and present history that the reader crosses with the poet in *Fugitive Atlas*, the collection contains flashes that signal other, perhaps more hopeful, potential histories. The invocation of the figure of the mother at the beginning of the book and the poet's daughter at its closing suggest another world unseen with something like wonder and the possibility of love. In one of the versions of the myth of Atlas, the titan reveals the spheric shape of the world and the constellations to humanity. Mattawa's *Fugitive Atlas* similarly gives us the shape of what we are with the consciousness that there is "No place else to go / Nowhere but this earth" (p13) as an urgent challenge to make our world as habitable as humanly possible.

Stephanie Petit reviews
**De Weekendmiljonair
(The Weekend Millionaire)
by Abdelkader Benali**
Published by De Arbeiderspers,
The Netherlands, 2019
Hardcover, 232 pages
ISBN: 9789029529105

Between Rotterdam and the Land of Atlas

Abdelkader Benali (b. 1975, Ighzazene, Morocco) rose to fame in the Netherlands, the country to which he emigrated with his family as a child, with his 1996 debut novel *Bruiloft aan Zee* (*Wedding by the Sea*). The book was awarded the prestigious Geertjan Lubberhuizen Prize, was translated into several languages, including English, and made the author, then aged just 21, into a national literary star. Since then, Benali has written multiple novels, plays, essays, and, with his wife Saida Nadi-Benali, a cookery book. He is also a popular media personality with a large following on social media.

In the English-speaking world, however, Benali's writing is relatively little-known. The English translation of *Wedding by the Sea* did not receive the attention it deserved, and his subsequent fiction remains largely untranslated. Attentive English-language readers are more likely to be familiar with Benali through his opinion pieces (he wrote an open letter denouncing the introduction of the so-called 'Burqa ban' in the Netherlands in *The Observer* in 2010). Indeed, throughout his literary career Benali has actively positioned himself as a Moroccan-Dutch writer – a kind of cultural mediator, if you will – who speaks about the myriad complexities around immigration and multiculturalism. This commitment also underpins his latest novel, *De Weekendmiljonair*, published in the Netherlands in 2019.

The novel is told from the perspective of Osama, a twelve-year old boy, born and growing up in Rotterdam. In most respects, Osama is an ordinary teen (he idolises Maradona and a glimpse of the bra department in a department store sends his hormones through the roof). But he is also growing at an abnormally fast rate – aged twelve he is already a full head-and-shoulders taller than everyone else, and his rapid growth leaves him in near-constant physical pain. His doctor recommends him for specialist treatment at a clinic in Switzerland, but this is no easy ask, especially as his family are expected to stump up half of the medical costs themselves.

Osama is the only child of Ahmed and Laila, Moroccan immigrants struggling to make ends meet. Ahmed is a precariously-employed labourer. Laila is a housewife. At the opening of the novel, the family have just been rehoused for the umpteenth time, and are living in a dark, damp flat that is making them miserable. Ahmed obsesses incessantly over the ridiculous points system that might enable them to move to better accommodation. He spends his time calculating points: points for leaking taps, points for mould, points for noise. But despite their pleas for sympathy from the local authorities (during an inspector's visit Ahmed makes Osama pretend he is as sick as a Dickensian urchin) they appear utterly stuck there.

Luckily then, the family are provided with some much-needed distraction in the form of their neighbour Loes, a likeable, chain-smoking loudmouth. Everything she knows about Arabs and Muslims Loes has learnt from the television and, intrigued by the exotic new family in the neighbourhood, she approaches them by offering them her old sewing machine. At the end of their first meeting she insists on hugging Ahmed, then his wife, and lastly Osama. "Neighbour, don't worry. For us here a hug is just a hug. It's okay. Hugging is fine. Men and women," she assures Ahmed. But her warmth and openness are disarming, and even Laila, initially alarmed by her husband-embracing neighbour, grows rather fond of Loes.

When Ahmed loses his job he decides to take money-making matters into his own hands, and 'buys' (read: acquires in circumstances that aren't quite proper) a Transit van from which he starts removing and selling on unwanted household goods around Rotterdam. Osama is quickly roped into his father's business and, on weekends and after school, he accompanies him in the van, reading out directions from their A-Z and helping with loading and unloading furniture. On good days, they call the work "Operation Weekend Millionaire", and ride high on the feeling that "through hard work and with a little bit of luck we could be millionaires one day". But the work is physically taxing, especially for Osama. Their everyday transactions with Dutch people are also wrought with prejudice and racism: When arriving at a house in one of Rotterdam's wealthiest neighbourhoods to pick up an unwanted bench, its owner derides his wife for allowing "the darkies" to have it. As a life-lesson, Ahmed warns his young son to keep his head down, speak as little as possible, and leave as quickly as possible, so people remain comfortable around "a foreign man with a strange accent who came to collect their furniture".

Insightful, charming and bittersweet, *De Weekendmiljonair* is an immensely readable novel that, despite its breezy style, brims with astute observations about life in a multicultural community. Its depiction of the experience of cultural uprooting is also intelligent and well-drawn. In many ways Ahmed and Laila's story is that of every migrant searching for a better life, and, as so often happens, there is an enormous gap between the opportunity and prosperity they imagined and life as it has turned out, which tinges the novel with a profound sadness.

Ahmed in particular appears rather lost in his host environment,

Abdelkader Benali

navigating the margins of the bureaucratic state, and mumbling his way through interactions with native Dutch people. "I couldn't believe that my father had made himself so small," Osama observes. Ahmed longs to return home, back to "the Land of Atlas", where, despite political and economic hardship, he lived with dignity in a cultural framework that was his own. His homeland remains his central space of reference – for him, it is the place in which his family ultimately belong. But while this engenders a sense of emotional estrangement from his life in the Netherlands, this is not so for the Dutch-born Osama, who secretly hopes that they will stay in Rotterdam, close to Loes.

Some readers may find the simplicity of the narration in *De Weekendmiljonair* too simple, and its happy ending (a sudden availability of affordable medical treatment for Osama, a new home in Rotterdam for the family) a little too predictably feel-good. Despite this, *De Weekendmiljonair* is as lucid a story about the cross-generational experience of migration as one could wish for. For this reason, I hope it will make it into an English translation, bringing it to new audiences.

BOOK REVIEWS

Becki Maddock reviews
Agadir by Mohammed Khaïr-Eddine
Translated by Pierre Joris and Jake Syersak
Publisher: Dialogos / Lavender Ink
Pub Date: 20/8/2020
Pbk Pages 134
ISBN: 978-1-944884-85-7

A Guérilla Linguistique

Agadir is not your average novel. I guarantee you will not read anything else like it this year, or perhaps ever. Sometimes described as a hybrid novel, it is not a novel in any conventional sense. Mohammed Khaïr-Eddine's intense writing intentionally subverts traditional literary models. There is no plot or character development in *Agadir*. The work begins with a two-page paragraph, consisting of a single sentence containing no punctuation but for an initial capital letter and a final full stop. But do not be deterred, it is worth persevering. The punctuation kicks in on the third page. The experimental work incorporates many different styles of writing. There are passages of prose, some with punctuation, some without; there is poetry and there is dialogue, often written in the style of a script for a play, and incorporating many poetic speeches. There is a letter from the narrator's "future assassin", a man trying to locate his house, destroyed by the earthquake. Some parts of the text are all in upper case. Some are merely a list of words: "milestones pedestrians motorists cyclists kings chestnuts writers logistics…" But each word is important.

The English edition of *Agadir* includes a useful introduction by Khalid Lyamlahy, a Moroccan academic whose PhD focused on the work of three contemporary Moroccan writers, including Khaïr-Eddine. The introduction provides some background on the author's

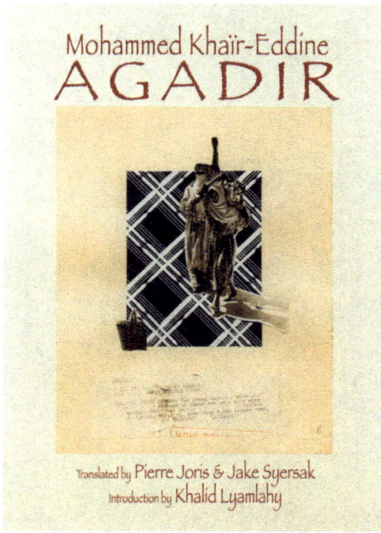

life and work, helpfully setting *Agadir* in context and explaining some of the characteristics of Khaïr-Eddine's unique writing style.

Readers who wish to learn more about Khaïr-Eddine's work would also be well advised to refer to Banipal 10/11 (2001), which contains a special feature on the author, featuring translations of his work and tributes to Khaïr-Eddine from writers who knew him, including Pierre Joris, Jean-Paul Michel and Samuel Shimon.

Poet and writer Mohammed Khaïr-Eddine was one of the most innovative North African writers of his generation. He was born in 1941 in Tafraout in the Anti-Atlas mountains of southern Morocco. He was part of a group of Moroccan poets and artists who founded the avant-garde journal *Souffles* (Breaths) in 1966. It was banned in 1972. Khaïr-Eddine wrote in French, publishing both poetry and prose works. He lived in Paris from 1965 to 1979, and then between Morocco and France until his death in 1995. In 1968, he won the Jean Cocteau Prix des Enfants Terribles, which had been created to recognize original and provocative writers. Mohammed Khaïr-Eddine is one of the writers who can be credited with introducing new and original literary techniques to the Maghreb, techniques that are much in evidence in *Agadir*.

Agadir, Khaïr-Eddine's debut prose work, was originally published in French in 1967. It is loosely based on the 1960 earthquake, which devastated the city of the title. Khaïr-Eddine worked for the Social Security Department, between 1961 and 1963, conducting surveys among survivors of the earthquake. Likewise, the narrator of the novel is a civil servant, sent to the city "in order to sort out a particularly precarious situation". But the earthquake is a metaphor for much more. As Lyamlahy's introduction to the novel tells us, Khaïr-Eddine's aim was "to symbolise the political and social earthquake

Mohammed Khaïr-Eddine

which has been devastating the Third-World for years".

Through his text Khaïr-Eddine voices a violent criticism of patriarchy and power, both religious and political. The author's friend, poet Jean-Paul Michel, has suggested that the author's childhood experience of his father's abandonment of him and his mother helps us to understand his revolt against patriarchy, many examples of which can be found in *Agadir*, which features multiple patriarchal figures (kings, imams and government ministers, some human, some, such as President Marmoset, in animal form) and ends in a dialogue with "His Father". Historical, contemporary and legendary figures interact across time and space in Khaïr-Eddine's text. The monarch, described as the "hydra of the era" by "Yusuf, the First King", comes in for particularly harsh criticism: "His Majesty whose gift to me is terror"; "the king feeds off the blood of the people". Indeed Khaïr-Eddine's criticism of the monarchy led to his arrest on his return to Morocco in 1979.

Khaïr-Eddine intends to shock. He described his writing as a "guérilla linguistique", which can be understood as a kind of "linguistic guerrilla warfare", in which his poetics of violence is directed as much against the text itself as at the society it criticises.

Although fighting against many things, Khaïr-Eddine's surreal text also advocates for change, for example in his consideration of how and where and whether the city be reconstructed: "MAYBE TO START WITH BUILD WELL-ALIGNED HOUSES ON ONE SIDE AND ON THE OTHER thus leaving a wide enough space between them" he suggests. But the debate rages on:

"I want to assist in the construction of this city
There won't be any construction Listen to me The city has never existed There was a lot of propaganda about it but there never was a city here"

The question of "if it is permitted to build on the ruins of a dead city" encompasses many of the issues that *Agadir* addresses in its unique way; questions of justice and authority, and of identity, memory, home and belonging. The narrator discusses ancestry with "The Stranger", who describes himself as "the special envoi of Her Majesty, the Kahina" (a 7th century Amazigh queen who appears several times in *Agadir*):

"THE STRANGER
You certainly don't lack disrespect for your ancestors.
I
So you are my ancestor. And that stone, it wouldn't be my grandmother by any chance?
THE STRANGER
You are insulting yourself. That's regrettable."

Later, the statement "I am a writer", precedes an imagined passport, where the name and nationality are blank (merely a question mark) but the holder's profession is given as "Rebel". This is followed by a pages-long poetic diatribe in the stream-of-consciousness style on blood and identity: "my blood I'll have to croak some day, I slam shut the doors of my blood, in its quagmires I lose the Ruby of rubies, the Blood of bloods and the Worst of the worse, my publisher blood, my blood I exile myself with tons of turtle doves…"

BOOK REVIEWS

On the cover of the English edition of *Agadir* is a collage by Moroccan-French artist, Yto Barrada, inspired by *Agadir*. A collage is appropriate. *Agadir* is a literary collage, a work of art. A carefully constructed text that reads like a stream of consciousness, perhaps a reflection of the author's belief that it is the writer who is possessed by the language, rather than vice versa*. Khaïr-Eddine's word choice is very specific, often employing rare, exotic words; not mere rock but "schist", not a generic wasp but a "sphex", not just any old mosquito but "stegomyia". The novel is bursting with interesting and thoughtful images. Sounds, smells and images are skilfully woven into the narrative: the "hyper-odor" of the "exhalations of croaked rats" in a city that "oozes a red and white-veined drop onto the misty terrain's folds".

The passages of dramatic dialogue are populated by a panoply of characters. Political debate and the problems of society are expressed in the voices of the narrator's cook and servant, the townspeople, leaders past and present, real and legendary, and even animals. At one point the narrator finds himself in a surreal city populated by animals, somewhat reminiscent of *Animal Farm*.

In some passages, the stream of consciousness combined with a lack of punctuation evokes the disjointed, surreal nature of a dreamscape. And as in a dream, the scene suddenly changes. "We came at dawn. I don't know why we're here...We're not in a street. In fact,

Letters to Denis Johnson-Davies from Palestinian poet Tawfiq Sayegh and from Jordanian writer Ghaleb Halasa will be published in the next issue

I'm finding it impossible to make the place out." In fact, the author has admitted to writing down his dreams and incorporating them into the narrative.

The aforementioned features of Khaïr-Eddine's text must have made *Agadir* an interesting challenge for its translators. Khaïr-Eddine's masterful and original manipulation of language has been cleverly translated into English by Pierre Joris, a Luxembourg-American writer who has published more than 50 books of poetry, essays, anthologies, plays and translations; and poet, translator and editor Jake Syersak, whose translation of another innovative Amazigh poet, Hawad, appears in *Banipal 67*.

The question of language is multi-faceted and interconnects with that of identity in Khaïr-Eddine's work. An Amazigh, raised in a country whose official language was Arabic, he made a deliberate choice to write in French, delighting in subverting and reinventing it, playing with the language. Translation of *Agadir* is not a linear one-to-one practice. The text is Moroccan, incorporating Arabic and Amazigh words. The translation tends to keep these, reflecting the way they appear in the French text, and words for local Moroccan garments and concepts, such as gandoura, gimbri, choukkara, souk, raïs and caïd, appear in the text with no explanations. The translators have succeeded in bringing the text to the anglophone reader, without losing the essence of the original language. Indeed, Joris has written in his foreword to *Scorpionic Sun*, a collection of Khaïr-Eddine's poetry, translated by Conor Bracken (Cleveland State University Poetry Center in 2019), that the reader wondering what the original French was is to be considered a good thing.

In addition to its innovative style, Francophone Moroccan literature of this era offers an insight into an important stage in Morocco's cultural and political history. This translation helps to bring that literature to an anglophone audience. Disturbing, disquieting, but never boring, *Agadir* is a book that makes the reader work, think and question. It is not a book to read once but rather it is a work of art to return to again and again, each time discovering something new.

LITERARY AWARD

The American translator Kay Heikkinen wins Saif Ghobash Banipal Prize for Arabic Literary Translation

The 2020 Saif Ghobash Banipal Prize for Arabic Literary Translation was awarded in February this year to Kay Heikkinen for her translation of the novel *Velvet* by Huzama Habayeb, published by Hoopoe Fiction. Following the shortlist of five titles that was announced on 24 November 2020, the judges were unanimous in naming Kay Heikkinen as the winner of the £3,000 prize, which was awarded by the Society of Authors at an online ceremony on 11 February 2021.

The judges in this 15th year of the Prize comprised Emeritus Professor of Arabic, University of Durham Paul Starkey (Chair), fiction editor at *The Guardian* Justine Jordan, writer, publisher & broadcaster Nii Ayikwei Parkes, and film director & philanthropist Omar Al-Qattan.

THE JUDGES' REPORT

"Kay Heikkinen deserves the highest commendation for her sensitive translation of Huzama Habayeb's award-winning Arabic novel *Mukhmal*, published in 2016. The novel is an intense and vivid story of one woman's life in a Palestinian refugee camp, told with sensitivity to the sensuous but tragic world of its heroine but above all to her disturbing and almost heroic defiance of reality. The coarseness of Hawwa's everyday life stands in stark contrast to the softness of the material around which much of her world revolves. On one level, the novel is a study of the claustrophobia of poverty and oppression, of daily lives shorn of all tenderness and of the stranglehold of family and patriarchy. Throughout it all, however, there

Kay Heikkinen

remain dreams of individual fulfilment and the possibility of love and escape, turning the novel into a celebration of the triumph of the imagination over the mundane.

"Hawwa's story is told in a rich, carefully crafted Arabic that represents a significant challenge for any translator, requiring stamina and resilience as well as accuracy and precision. The judges were impressed by the way in which Kay Heikkinen's translation has succeeded in conveying not only the sense but also the mood and emotion of the original, bringing to life a narrative that vividly portrays the repressive life of ordinary Palestinian women while scrupulously avoiding any hint of political platitude. Her translation faithfully adheres to the elegance of the original without losing the deeply tragic tenor of its events.

"The judges were impressed by the quality of several other shortlisted translations, including two shorter works, but after extensive discussion reached the decision to award the prize to Kay Heikkinen for a translation that they considered to be of outstanding quality and which deserves to enjoy the same success in English as it has already done in Arabic, through the award of the Naguib Mahfouz Medal for Literature in 2017."

WINNER Kay Heikkinen reactS to the news:

"I am overwhelmed! I cannot begin to thank you as I would like to. Nor can I begin to thank Huzama Habayeb as she deserves, both for writing this beautiful book and for her unfailing and unstinting support throughout the translation process. I am delighted at the recognition of her accomplishment in writing such a beautiful human story of a courageous woman, who retains a capacity to be lighthearted in the face of crushing circumstances, and of her accomplishment in writing a new kind of Palestinian story, one that engages with politics only very indirectly. I'm grateful also to all those at Hoopoe who championed this project, as well as to the Banipal committee—more grateful than I can say. Thank you all."

ABOUT THE TRANSLATOR

Kay Heikkinen is a translator and academic who holds a PhD from Harvard University and is currently Ibn Rushd Lecturer of Arabic at the University of Chicago. Among other books, she has translated Naguib Mahfouz's *In the Time of Love* and Radwa Ashour's *The Woman From Tantoura*.

ABOUT THE AUTHOR

Huzama Habayeb is a Palestinian writer who was born and raised in Kuwait, where she started writing and publishing short stories, poetry, and journalistic pieces as a student of English language and literature, and her journalistic writings were published in several newspapers and magazines. When the Gulf War erupted in 1990, she fled to Jordan and established her reputation as a short-story writer.

Huzama Habayeb

Habayeb's first novel, *Asl al-Hawa* (Root of Passion), was published in 2007, gaining wide critical acclaim, and her second novel, *Qabla an Tanama al-Malika* (Before the Queen Falls Asleep, 2011), was described by critics as an epic novel of the Palestinian diaspora.

Her third novel, *Mukhmal* (*Velvet*), for which in December 2017 she was awarded the Naguib Mahfouz Medal for Literature, was first published in Arabic in Beirut in 2016 by the Arab Institute for Research and Publishing.

ABOUT THE BOOK

Velvet by Huzama Habayeb (Palestine)
Published by Hoopoe Fiction (an imprint of AUC Press),
Cairo, 2019
ISBN: 9789774169304. Pbk,
272 pages, £10.99 / USD17.95.
Kindle £9.41 / USD12.42

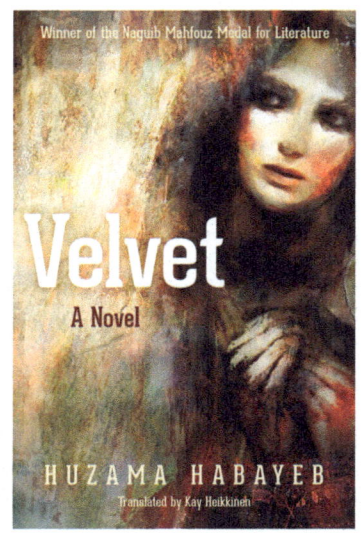

Hawwa is a child of the grinding hardship of a Palestinian refugee camp. She has had to survive the camp itself, as well as the humiliation and destruction of an abusive family life. But now, later in life, something most unexpected has happened: she has fallen in love. *Velvet* unfolds over a day in Hawwa's life, as she makes plans for a new beginning that may take her out of the camp. She sifts back through her memories of the past: the stories of her family, her childhood, and her beloved mentor, who invited her into the glamorous world of the rich women of Amman. This is a novel of enormous power and great beauty. Rich in detail, it tells of the women of the camp, and the joy and relief that can be captured amid repression and sorrow.

"This is Huzama Habayeb's third novel and marks a high point in her writing career, with the Arabic original, *Mukhmal*, awarded the Naguib Mahfouz Medal for Literature in 2017. It was hailed by the judges as "a new kind of Palestinian novel" that wrote about the "everyday lives of Palestinians", and about the "human condition" through its portrayal of woman [...] *Velvet* is a heady, emotional read." *From the review of Velvet by Margaret Obank, Banipal 68 (Summer 2020).*

CONTRIBUTORS

Hassan Abdel Mawgoud (b. 1976) is an Egyptian writer and journalist, who has published three short story collections and two novels. His first novel, *Cat's Eye*, won a Sawiris Cultural Prize in 2005 and has been published in German translation. His collection *Huroub Fatina* (Ravishing Wars), published by Al-Kotob Khan, Cairo, 2018, won the 2020 Yusuf Idris Prize. In 2003 Abdel Mawgoud won the Dubai Journalism Award for his reportage entitled T*ales of the Monks of Natron Valley*. He lives in Cairo and is deputy editor of the literary weekly Akhbar Al-Adab.

Ammar Almamoun is a Syrian journalist and literary critic, living in Paris.

Joselyn Michelle Almeida is a poet, editor and scholar, specializing in the transoceanic Anglo-Hispanic archive during the Age of Revolutions. Her poetry collection *Condiciones para el vuelo* (Conditions of Flight) was published in 2019. She has a PhD from Boston College. Before her current appointment at La Salle Centro Universitario Madrid, she taught at the University of Massachusetts, Amherst, USA.

Raphael Cohen is a professional translator and lexicographer who studied Arabic and Hebrew at Oxford and the University of Chicago. He is based in Cairo and is a *Banipal* contributing editor. He has translated novels by Mona Prince, Ahlam Mosteghanemi, Eslam Mosbah, George Yarak and Mohamed Salmawy. He has introduced and translated the forthcoming *Poems of Alexandria and New York* by Ahmed Morsi (Banipal Books, 2021).

Trino Cruz – See page 182.

Miled Faiza is a Tunisian-American poet and translator. *Remains of a House We Once Entered* (2004) was his first collection. He translated into Arabic the 2017 Man Booker Prize-shortlisted novel *Autumn*, as well as *Winter*, both by Ali Smith. He also translated Shukri Mabkhout's *The Italian* (with Karen McNeil). He teaches Arabic at Brown University, USA.

Fayez Ghazi is a Lebanese writer whose first novel *Munay* (My Wish) was published by Dar Abbad in 2013, and his second *Azhar al-Mawt* (Flowers of Death) in 2020 by Dar al-Farabi, Beirut. He writes for several Arab newspapers and websites.

Mayada Ibrahim is an editor, translator and writer from Sudan, who works in Arabic and English. She has worked for international publishing companies editing fiction, nonfiction, poetry and children's literature, including books such as *Beirut, Beirut* by Sonallah Ibrahim, *The Bamboo Stalk* by Saud Alsanousi, and *The Hidden Light of Objects* by Mai a-Nakib.

Azher Jirjees is an Iraqi writer and novelist, born in Baghdad in 1973. From 2003 onwards, he worked as a journalist in Iraq, publishing articles and stories in Arab newspapers and periodicals. In 2005, his satirical book about terrorist militias, *Terrorism . . . Earthly Hell* was published, resulting in an assassination attempt on him and he was forced to flee from Iraq, going to Syria, then Morocco and finally to Norway, where he now lives permanently. He has two short story collections, *Above the Country of Blackness* (2015) and *The Sweetmaker* (2017). His first novel, *At Rest in the Cherry Orchard* (2019) was longlisted for the 2020 International Prize for Arabic Fiction (IPAF.) He is a cultural editor for the Norwegian *Telemark* newspaper, and a simultaneous interpreter between Arabic and Norwegian.

Samira Kawar is an experienced energy journalist and literary translator. She has contributed translations to Banipal since it started, and is a founding trustee of the Banipal Trust for Arab Literature. Her translations include *The Eye of the Mirror* by

CONTRIBUTORS

Liana Badr (2008) and Abdul Rahman Munif's *Story of a City: A Childhood in Amman* (1996).

Khaled Khalifa was born in Aleppo, Syria, in 1964 and holds a BA in Law from Aleppo University. His first novel in 2000, *The Notebooks of the Bohemians*, has been followed by many highly successful works: *In Praise of Hatred* (2006), shortlisted for inaugural 2008 IPAF; *No Knives in the Kitchens of this City* (awarded the 2013 Naguib Mahfouz Medal for Literature and shortlisted for the 2014 IPAF; *Death is Hard Work* (2015); and his latest *No One Prayed Over Their Graves,* longlisted for the 2020 IPAF. He has also written many successful screenplays for TV series and for cinema, and writes regularly for different Arab newspapers, continuing to live in Damascus.

Becki Maddock is a translator and researcher. She translates from Arabic, Persian and Spanish into English. She has a first class BA in Arabic and Spanish (Exeter University) and an MA in Near and Middle Eastern Studies from SOAS, University of London.

Rosie Maxton has an MA in Arabic and Medieval History from St. Andrews University and an MPhil in Arabic Studies from Cambridge University. She is pursuing a PhD at Somerville College, University of Oxford.

Karen McNeil is an Arabic-to-English translator. She has translated the 2016 IPAF winner *The Italian* by Shukri Mabkhout (with Miled Faiza), as well as poems and short stories for *Banipal* and *World Literature Today*. She was a revising editor of the Oxford Arabic Dictionary (2014) and is currently completing a Ph.D. in Arabic linguistics at Georgetown University, with a focus on the sociolinguistics of Tunisia.

Ibrahim Nasrallah was born in Amman, Jordan, in 1954, and raised in Alwehdat Palestinian refugee camp there. He worked in journalism from 1978 to 1996. Since 2006 he turned to writing full time. He has published 14 poetry collections and 16 novels, with four published in English translation, the first *Prairies of Fever* in 1996, and, more recently, *Gaza Weddings* (2004, English edition 2017). His novel *The Second Dog War* won the 2018 IPAF, while *Time of White Horses* was shortlisted for the 2019 prize, and *Lanterns of the King of Galilee* longlisted for the 2013 IPAF. His novel *The Spirits of Kilimanjaro* (2015) won the 2016 Katara Prize for the Arabic Novel, and in 2020 he won the prize again for *A Tank Under the Christmas Tree*.

Stephanie Petit studied Linguistics at SOAS University of London. Since 2017, she has worked as a Digital Archivist in the Endangered Languages Archive, SOAS.

Leri Price graduated from the University of Edinburgh with First Class Honours in Arabic. She has translated three novels of the Syrian author Khaled Khalifa, *In Praise of Hatred* and *No Knives in the Kitchens of this City (*her translation was shortlisted for the US 2017 National Translation Awards and the 2017 Saif Ghobash Banipal Prize for Arabic Literary Translation, and also listed in "Best Books of 2016: Fiction in Translation" by the Financial Times). Her translation of *Death is Hard Work* (Faber & Faber 2019), won the 2019 Saif Ghobash Banipal Prize and was longlisted for the 2019 US National Book Award for Translated Literature.

Nancy Roberts has translated many novels by Arab authors, including Naguib Mahfouz, Salwa Bakr, Mohamed el-Bisatie, Ezzat el Kamhawi and Hala El-Badry, also Ghada Samman, Laila Aljohani, Ahlem Mosteghanemi, and Ibrahim Nasrallah. Her most re-

---

For more information on all the authors in *Banipal 70* and all the translators, writers and reviewers, please go to: **www.banipal.co.uk/contributors/**

CONTRIBUTORS

cent is *The Slave Yards* by Najwa Bin Shatwan, Syracuse University Press, 2020, with its original Arabic shortlisted for the 2017 IPAF.

Fakhri Saleh was born in Jenin, on the West Bank, in 1957. He is a well-known writer and literary critic and has published many books on Palestinian literature, the Arabic novel, poetry, and literary criticism. He has translated into Arabic Terry Eagleton's *Criticism and Ideology* and Tzvetan Todorov's *Mikhail Bakhtin: The Dialogical Principle*. He studied English literature and philosophy at the University of Jordan. , His new book, *Karahiyat Al-Islam*, discusses the encounter of Islam in intellectual circles in America and Britain, focusing on Bernard Lewis, Samuel Huntington and V. S. Naipaul.

Mahmoud Shukair – see page 100.

Alawiya Sobh was born in Beirut in 1955. By the early eighties, she was publishing her fiction, poetry, and literary reviews in the leading Beirut daily *An-Nahar* and in 1986 became editor-in-chief of *Al-Hasnaa'* women's magazine. In the early 1990s she founded *Snob Al-Hasnaa'*, the best-selling women's cultural magazine in the Arab world today, and remains its editor-in-chief. Her novel *Maryam al-Hakaya* (*Maryam: Keeper of Stories*), acclaimed as a novel of epic dimensions, won her the 2006 Sultan Qaboos Award. Her novel *Ismahul Gharam* (*It's Called Love*) was longlisted for the 2010 IPAF, and her latest *Aan Ta'ashaq Al Hayat* (*To Love Life*) shortlisted for the 2021 Sheikh Zayed Book Award.

Hannah Somerville is a London-based investigative journalist and former health reporter. She has a BA in Arabic and Spanish from the University of Leeds and an MA in Arabic Literature from SOAS, University of London. Her dissertation focused on body politics in new Egyptian 'dystopian' fiction.

Paul Starkey is an award-winning translator and Emeritus Professor of Arabic at Durham University. He is Chair of the Banipal Trust for Arab Literature and a contributing editor of *Banipal*. Recent translations include *Praise for the Women of the Family* by Mahmoud Shukair (2016 IPAF shortlist), and *The Shell* by Mustafa Khalifa, for which he was awarded the 2017 Hamad Translation Award.

Susannah Tarbush is a freelance journalist specialising in cultural affairs in the Middle East. She writes the Tanjara blog, and is a consulting editor of *Banipal* and regular reviewer.

Katia al-Tawil is a Lebanese novelist, critic and a university lecturer. She wrote on literary criticism for *Al-Hayat* and *An-Nahar* newspapers and now for *Independent Arabia* online. Her second novel, *Al-Jannah Ajmal min Ba'aid* (*Paradise is more Beautiful from Afar*) is just out with Naufal Books.

Aida Fahmawi Watad graduated from Haifa University in 2009. She is currently a senior lecturer in Arabic Language and Literature at Al-Qasemi Academy, Haifa, and researches modern Arabic literature. In 2017 she founded the "Akthar min Hayat" (More Than One Life) readers' club, in which she hosted numerous Arab and Palestinian scholars and writers (in person and over Skype).

Jonathan Wright studied Arabic, Turkish and Islamic History at St. John's College, Oxford University. He an award-winning translator of fiction by Arab authors, including Mazen Maarouf, Amjad Nasser, Ahmed Saadawi, Hassan Blasim, Saud Alsanousi, Youssef Ziedan, Hamour Ziada and Khaled el-Khamissi. His latest work is *God 99* by Hassan Blasim (Comma Press, 2020).